THE PRESIDENT'S SHADOW

Books by James Patterson featuring the Shadow

Circle of Death (with Brian Sitts)
The Shadow (with Brian Sitts)

For a preview of upcoming books and information about the author, visit JamesPatterson.com or find him on Facebook, X, or Instagram.

THE PRESIDENT'S SHADOW

A SHADOW THRILLER

JAMES PATTERSON
& RICHARD DILALLO

Little, Brown and Company
New York Boston London

The characters and events in this book are fictitious. Any similarity to real persons, living or dead, is coincidental and not intended by the author.

Little, Brown and Company
Hachette Book Group
1290 Avenue of the Americas, New York, NY 10104
littlebrown.com

First Edition: June 2025

Little, Brown and Company is a division of Hachette Book Group, Inc. The Little, Brown name and logo are trademarks of Hachette Book Group, Inc.

ISBN 978-1-538-72194-0 (pb) / 978-0-316-58464-7 (large print)

LCCN is available at the Library of Congress

10 9 8 7 6 5 4 3 2 1

CCR

Printed in the United States of America

THE PRESIDENT'S SHADOW

PROLOGUE

I CANNOT STOP thinking about college.

This afternoon is Maddy's graduation from City College of New York, and the only person more excited than me and my wife, Margo, is Grandma Jessica. Unfortunately, the day and time of the graduation conflicted precisely with a vitally important meeting I was scheduled to attend at Kyoto University, and I'd found myself split between the campuses. When I mentioned this to my family, Jessica had the no-nonsense solution.

"Well, you can handle this conflict in one of two ways, Lamont," she said, as she prepared to take our family dog, Bando, on his morning walk. "You can do the right thing *or* you can go to Kyoto University. I know you'll do the right thing."

And so I did the right thing. But... instead of going to Japan myself, I sent Jericho Druke, one of the best and the brightest members of my team. I planned to attend the Kyoto meeting via Ultima-Vid, the newest incarnation of

Zoom. The fact that Jericho Druke would actually be sitting next to the chairperson of the Kyoto Nuclear Control Department at Kyoto U in the mountainous and beautiful Tamba Highlands of Southern Japan makes me feel like I'm missing out, but like Jessica said—I can miss out on work, or I can do the right thing.

The video meeting begins. The images are so crisp and clear I can even enjoy the beauty of the huge green mountains outside the building where Jericho and the Kyoto professor sit. The rolling hills seem to teem with life. The wind blows the leaves, and I think I can even spot some small creatures moving about in the treetops.

But an unnatural movement catches my eye, right before the unthinkable happens. Incredible. The mountains begin to explode and crumble. Great piles of rocks and trees and soil come racing down, the green colors of life overwhelmed by the brown of the earth and the gray of smoke. Jericho and the professor jump up and rush toward the door. But there is no time. No time to escape. It all happens too fast. Tons and tons of debris crash through the windows. Within seconds the building walls collapse. Screaming. Sirens. The Ultima-Vid feed shows only a massive amount of rubble and dust and dirt. It refuses to lose connection, forcing me to watch it all play out in real time.

I jump to my feet, screaming. Margo and Maddy come running into the room, only to stand in shock as they watch the destruction on the screen, the audio feed still filling the room with endless wails of both sirens and people.

I am beyond horrified. I stand helpless, wishing I could crash through the screen and do something, anything. Anything to help the thousands of people at the university who have been annihilated. And most of all, most of all... my friend, my colleague, the best and the brightest, Jericho.

CHAPTER 1

THE ENTIRE CRANSTON family household is suddenly plunged into a state of shock and sadness. All of us loved and respected Jericho so much.

"Forget my graduation," Maddy tells me, knowing how bad I feel that I wasn't there to help. "You've got something more important to—"

"No," I say firmly. "We may have lost Jericho in this nightmare. But we're not going to lose one of the most important days in your life."

"But—" Maddy begins to say something. I cut her off.

"No arguing, Maddy. I'm coming to your graduation."

Maddy's graduation is a day for her to shine, and her brightness is a beacon through all the haze that surrounds me now. I also want to show Maddy that I am completely in her corner, which I haven't done a great job of lately. We've been arguing about her decision to take a summer internship in the New York City public defender's office, even though she knows I have very little use for anything remotely related to government work. Her next move after the internship bothers me equally. In the fall, Maddy plans on going to law school. I would much prefer that she finish training in Tibet with Dache and then get out into the real world and do something to help.

But now is not the right time to continue this argument, and she knows it.

"Okay," Maddy says. "But don't forget that you'll have to sit through the guest speaker's commencement address."

"Oh, damn," I say. The *Right Reverend* Lanata Hooper. The warmongering scum-bucket capitalist who's made billions of dollars off the poor. How could I possibly forget?

"That woman has no more right to use the title 'reverend' than..." I don't finish the sentence.

A deadly silence overwhelms the room. Maddy, Jessica, and Margo all exchange worried glances.

After waiting for the world's longest minute, Margo finally speaks. "What's wrong, Lamont? You look like you're in another world."

I open my eyes and speak softly.

"I am in another world," I say. "A world without Jericho."

CHAPTER 2

THE CCNY GRADUATION is being held at the huge open-air Corpus Field, where the grand old Yankee Stadium once stood many, many decades ago.

The graduation sky this afternoon is dark, depressing, not quite raining, but ready to start at any minute. The gloomy weather matches the family's mood. Rain would only make it worse, but it might be more fitting.

I watch the happy, excited people surrounding me and try to force myself to join them emotionally. But even for someone with the powers of mind control, it's impossible, and that only makes me more angry. Maddy deserves better. She deserves to have my full attention. When the Right Reverend Lanata Hooper is introduced, the audience erupts with a loud clash of both boos and cheers. Margo and Jessica join the chorus of boos. Then Jessica turns toward me. "Don't even consider it," she warns me.

I smile, some positive emotion welling at the thought of how wise she is, how well she knows me.

"You want to do one of your mind-control interferences," she says. "But this is Maddy's day. We can't go spoiling it."

"I wouldn't dream of it," I say. Still...I need to do something. After doing nothing as I watched Jericho die, I need to take action.

A few misty drops fall from the sky as Lanata Hooper rattles on and on about the "bright future ahead, in a land where wise people take control over the weak and foolish, a future of fine worldly goods..."

I can't stand the vile philosophy any longer.

I call upon my powers, and suddenly the graduation speaker stops speaking.

Both Margo and Jessica turn their heads toward me. They know something's up.

Jessica is angry. "Lamont, you *promised*..."

I nod, and the speaker resumes her speech. But suddenly it takes a completely unexpected turn.

"Now I would like to ask for a minute of silence," Hooper says. Her voice is gentle, serious, and calm. "I would like us all to dedicate this time to remember and honor our academic friends who perished so tragically earlier today in Kyoto, Japan."

The huge crowd falls silent. We all bow our heads. Then the rain begins to fall.

CHAPTER 3

I CANNOT SHAKE the images of Jericho from my mind. Still, when Margo suggests that we all go to dinner to celebrate Maddy's big day, I agree.

"What'll it be, Maddy? High-class French food or down-home barbecue?" I ask.

To everyone's surprise, Maddy says, "I could go for a big honkin' chunk of porterhouse steak."

"You're on. But before we go eat, I have a question for you."

"I smell one of Lamont's dad jokes coming," says Margo.

"What do you get when a waiter drops your steak on the floor?" I ask.

Maddy doesn't miss a beat. "Ground meat." Groans. Fifteen minutes later, we're seated at the last great steak house in New York City, the Strip House.

Margo, who really knows her way around a wine list, orders her favorite Burgundy, a Chambertin, vintage 2032. I order four sixteen-ounce steaks. "One *medium*, one *rare*, one *very* rare, and one that's *blue.*" Margo and Jessica seem confused.

Maddy says, "Blue means that the steak is as close as possible to being raw."

"This girl is unbelievable," I say. "First she knows my dad joke. Then she knows my secret food info. I've got nothing left to teach her. I guess CCNY was good for something." I bite down on how I'd like to finish the sentence, something about wasting her talents on the government.

We all toast Maddy. Then, at her suggestion, we raise a glass to the memory of Jericho.

Everything is turning out okay...except for the five obnoxious young professionals at the next table. Margo glances over and identifies them as "a bunch of jerks, finance guys."

Maddy says, "Yeah, but two of them are women."

"Okay," I say. "A bunch of finance jerks, men *and* women. Does that make it better?"

Maddy says not at all. But the tables are so close that it's hard to ignore this offensive group, and the mood that was just beginning to lift evaporates.

"So," one of the men at the other table goes on, "I said, 'Don't waste my time if you don't have a minimum of four hundred million to drop on this deal.'"

Another man chimes in. "The big question is, did you get the babe to come back to your place?" Everyone laughs. Even the women. Disgusting.

They all roar at comments like "That IG guy didn't know

a Treasury bond from his ass or his partner's ass or his boss's ass."

"Hey," Maddy says, working hard to stop contempt from entering her voice. "Do you guys think you could keep your voices down?"

The people at the other table look at one another and laugh. One of the two women even parodies Maddy's question with old-fashioned sarcasm. "Weeeelllll, excuse me!" the woman says. And, of course, all her colleagues laugh.

"You're a bunch of spoiled goons," Maddy says.

One of the men fakes a combination of sincerity and seduction, saying, "Oh, maybe if that grumpy little girl joined our table she might have a little fun. How about it, babe?"

I have a front-row seat to this clown show, and I've just about had enough.

Only Margo notices the glint in my eyes, and a smile pulls at the side of her mouth.

Then we hear Finance Guy One gesture to Finance Guy Two and say, "Hey, Andrew, pass some of that Strip House special steak sauce this way, bro."

Andrew does what he's asked to do. But not exactly. He turns the pitcher of hot brown sauce over the head of Finance Guy One.

"What the f...?" The man jumps to his feet, brushing sauce off his clearly expensive suit coat. "That's not funny, dude."

Maybe not to him, but Margo and I laugh hard. Jessica and Maddy turn to see what's happening.

Finance Guy Three is on his cell phone. He gestures to his pals and says, "Keep it down, guys. I'm on an important…" But he's not being important for long. His super-duper, newer-than-new cell phone bursts into flames, and Number Three has no choice but to drop the flaming phone into his drink special: a ninety-dollar-a-glass tumbler of Macallan Scotch. The smell of melting plastic mixed with high-end liquor fills the room as other patrons leap to their feet.

But their gaze isn't being drawn to the action inside the restaurant; they're all looking at the sidewalk outside, where three teenagers are arguing.

I can sense that the sidewalk confrontation is about to become dangerous, very dangerous. Sure enough, one of the teens pulls out a switchblade and plunges it into the throat of another. The young victim falls to his knees, bleeding, hands clutching at the blade.

I'm on my feet and through the door, jumping over the body oozing blood onto the sidewalk. Meanwhile the two perps are running like crazy down Sixth Avenue.

CHAPTER 4

TWO OTHER MEN—older, dressed in jeans and black windbreakers—appear next to me on the scene.

"Get help fast," I yell at them, motioning toward the bleeding body on the sidewalk. One guy presses a button on his handheld. The other turns to me, extending a hand.

"I'm Daniel Goyette, NYPD Narc and Drug Investigation. This is my partner, Ron. We were hoping to catch these young dealers in the act, but it looks like their little exchange went wrong somehow."

"Great work you guys are doing!" I say angrily. "Mind if I step in and actually do something?"

I use my powers to subdue the escaping perps. I grab one and am about to get a stranglehold on the other, the one with the knife, when I hear a woman's voice. Loud. Clear. It's Maddy.

"I got him," she yells as she forces the killer to the ground. I watch her twist the killer's arms behind his back. The guy is struggling. He's strong. Maddy is working hard.

"I can take over," I say, jogging to join Maddy while maintaining a mental hold on the dealer I've already subdued, planning to put a heavy mental foot on her catch.

But suddenly the guy breaks free.

"I'll get him," I yell, but Maddy doesn't hear me or she doesn't *want* to hear me. She's determined to use her developing mind-control powers to smash the killer against a double-parked car on Fifth Avenue and 12th Street.

But she makes a terrible miscalculation. Instead of smashing the runner against the car, she smashes the vehicle against two nearby parked cars. The impact is so great that all three cars collapse into one another like an accordion. Even worse, an innocent young woman who'd been crossing the street is now caught between the cars.

I release the perps I'm holding, then kneel down to help the innocent bystander. But it's a feat even the Shadow can't execute. The woman is dead, a mass of blood and skin and bones.

Maddy is horrified, hands covering her face. I'm angry and sad; angry that Maddy took such a huge leap before she was ready, and sad for this young woman whose life was just beginning.

"I was hoping that I could help, Lamont," Maddy says. She's in tears. "I wanted you to see that I was learning."

"Damnit, Maddy. You're ready to work with me when Dache and I say you're ready. That's clearly not now." I know that Maddy is heartbroken, but an innocent person is dead, and a terrible killer escaped. Crime and death and horror and sorrow. They're everything the Shadow fights against.

CHAPTER 5

BACK AT HOME we try to relax, but it's impossible. After the tragedy of Jericho's destruction, the wild, unusual graduation speech, and the terrible catastrophe of the drug bust gone wrong, it feels as if nothing will ever be the same. Peace and comfort will never show up.

Maddy and Jessica go to their bedrooms. Margo is brewing tea.

I sit alone in my office. No screens, no gadgets, nothing. I stare straight ahead, searching for clarity.

Then the door opens and Margo walks in, a steaming mug in her hand. "Am I disturbing you?" she asks.

"How can I be any more disturbed than I already am?" I retort, then regret my tone when I see her searching for the hint of a smile on my face.

She doesn't find it. There'll be no joy in this house tonight. She lets a few seconds pass and then speaks.

"Listen," Margo says. "I overheard what you said to

Maddy. I just wanted you to know that I think you handled it really well."

"Thanks, I guess," I say.

"That was a tough conversation," Margo says.

"And a worse situation," I tell her. "Maddy's got to learn... she's got to learn so many things if she is going to help me straighten things out in this tough world. The powers she's being trained in are both a blessing and a curse. She's got to proceed with speed and caution."

"Speed and caution are not always the best partners," Margo says.

"I appreciate your concern," I say. "Maddy has so much potential. I just want it all to develop properly. Today was clear proof that she's not ready."

There is silence. Margo reaches out and holds my hand. My fingers wrap around hers, and I finally find a small amount of comfort, but I don't want to mislead her into believing that everything is better now.

"I need to tell you something," I say.

Need. To Margo, that's a frightening word coming from me. Someone who presents himself, even to those I love most, as private. Thoughtful and strong.

"What is it?" she asks.

"I will never get over Jericho's death."

Another silence. All she can do is hold my hand even tighter.

CHAPTER 6

MADDY'S FIRST DAY in the public defender's office is not going well. She dreads the moment when she gets home and Margo and Lamont ask her the inevitable questions, "So, how'd it go? How was your first day?"

Her half-a-lie response will be, "It was interesting."

She knows Lamont thinks her summer would be better spent working in Tibet developing her mental and physical powers. So she will adjust her answer quite a bit. The truthful response would be, "It sucked big-time."

Her day consists of taking orders from anyone in the office. She makes the coffee in the big coffee machine and then makes more when people complain that the pot's empty. She fetches sandwiches for lunch and takes the blame when the deli screws up one of the orders. She formats hundreds of PowerPoint presentations. When one particularly snotty young paralegal asks her to pick up his copies, Maddy says, "You must be kidding. The printer is ten feet from your desk." He doesn't even look at her when he replies, "Yeah, but you're the one standing up already."

Finally she's had enough and decides to speak up. A risky move. Her immediate supervisor, R.J. Werner, is a whip-smart Yale Law School graduate only a few years older than she is. During her interview—serious, quick, and very annoying—he told her, "My work philosophy is very simple. Do it by the book or don't bother doing it."

She doesn't know if "by the book" means getting walked all over, but if that's the case, she'd like to throw that particular book at his head. Summoning up all her nerve, she knocks on his door.

"Something wrong?" he asks. Then adds, "Already?"

"I thought this job would be a chance to learn social work and criminal law," she says, holding her hands behind her back so R.J. can't see how much they are shaking.

"So far, all I've been doing is household chores and delivering packages," she says. "I'm not learning anything, except everyone's coffee order."

"I getcha," R.J. says. And Maddy thinks for a moment that he does indeed "get her."

Maybe R.J. is a reasonable, decent person under that ridiculously businesslike exterior.

"That's good to hear," says Maddy.

Then R.J. says, "Don't get too excited. I'm going to give you an actual assignment. But it entails taking the subway, going to a really miserable place, and, most likely, dealing with a rude, unpleasant person."

"Lay it on me," Maddy tells him, thinking it didn't sound terribly different from what she was already doing.

"Here's what you need to do," he says. "Download the Justice Systems General Form app on your cell phone and get yourself over to the 19th Precinct. There's a young woman over there who's coming up for a pre-bail evaluation. Try to get some info out of her. And don't let her bullshit you. Happy now?" he asks, no smile, no charm.

"I'm all over it," Maddy says, and she can't believe she's given such a corny response.

"Yeah, sure," R.J. says. "And, oh, by the way, on your way back could you pick up my clean shirts at Valley Cleaners downstairs?"

Maddy is about to say something, but R.J. speaks, still serious. "Just kidding," he says.

But Maddy's not sure that he is.

CHAPTER 7

ACCORDING TO MADDY'S police-assigned handheld screen, the young woman's name is Belinda Miller. Maddy buys that.

Maddy's screen also says that Belinda Miller's age is eighteen. Maddy is not buying that. This woman... girl... could easily be thirteen or fourteen. Certainly not much older than fifteen.

They sit across from each other on junky folding chairs.

"My name is Maddy. I'm with the New York City public defender's office, and I'm here to help you fill out some forms for your hearing."

Maddy waits for a response from this snarly girl with the bloodshot eyes and long, greasy blond hair. But Belinda doesn't even bother to look at Maddy. Instead she twists around in the folding chair and focuses on the cement wall behind her. Belinda is silent, and it's fairly obvious to Maddy that she doesn't plan to participate in this meeting.

Maddy is a combination of nervous and angry and anxious,

but she stays determined. She waits exactly thirty seconds, and then she tries all over again.

"Look, Belinda, we're going to get this thing filled out one way or another," Maddy says, and she's surprised at her own tough voice. Still no response from Belinda. Maddy tries again. Then Maddy decides to yell.

"I'm the only person in this building who is actually here to help you," Maddy shouts. "So turn around in your damn chair and look at me."

Belinda doesn't turn around, but she does twist her neck and she takes a good look at Maddy, as if the only type of language she responds to is yelling. Finally she speaks.

"Wanna help? Get me the hell out of this place."

"That's exactly what I want to do."

"Yeah, that's what everyone wants to do. That's why the cops arrest us low-level dealers trying to pick up some cash, but nobody does shit about the big-shot scum doing the worst things."

Maddy tries to show how tuned-in she is.

"You mean your bosses are dealing drugs? Sorry, but you don't exactly look like a drug dealer."

"Lady, that's the point," Belinda says, rolling her eyes. "The smart ones figured out a long time ago having a bunch of shady-looking men standing on the street was like waving a red flag. But some young girls wandering around with ice-cream cones—who questions them? Anyways, if I told you anything, they'd kill me, and you might not make it out in great shape neither."

Maddy feels some random power building up inside her. She's going to help this girl. At the very least she's going to get information that might clue her in to what Belinda's talking about.

"C'mon. I can help you if you level with me," Maddy says, and she means it.

Belinda turns her face toward the wall again.

"Give yourself a break," Maddy says.

Belinda says nothing.

"My department can help," Maddy says, remembering the young woman she'd accidentally killed using her mind power. If she saves a different one, does it cancel that out?

But Belinda has totally stopped talking.

"I have friends, good friends who aren't cops who really can help you," Maddy says. She can't even imagine Lamont stepping into this rat's nest. But she'll figure out how to deal with that later.

Still nothing from Belinda. Then Maddy softly says, "Please."

Belinda turns around. She's crying. Suddenly she stands up and approaches Maddy. Maddy moves her finger very near the Panic button on the side of the small card table. She's ready to push.

"You wanna learn something about me and my life, lady? Mom's new boyfriend took a liking to me, you get it? It was pretty clear I had to put out or get out, and I went with the last one. Now I'm trying to make a decent kind of living—"

Her face colors in anger when she sees Maddy's reaction. "No, not like *that*! That's exactly what I'm trying *not* to do... even though sometimes the customers get a different kind of idea about what services the girls have on offer."

Belinda pulls at the neckline of her police-issued brown jumpsuit and points.

Her neck is covered in bruises in the shape of handprints. The skin on her chest and shoulders is riddled with open cuts and scratches.

"Sometimes I gotta make it real clear to them that the only thing I've got for sale is in my pockets, not my pants."

Maddy is appalled, shocked into silence.

But before she can ask any more questions, her police cell phone rings.

Maddy looks at the caller name.

It's her boss. R.J.

CHAPTER 8

"WHERE THE HELL are you?" R.J. shouts.

Maddy is still reeling from Belinda's injuries, so she shouts right back at her boss.

"Where am I? Do you understand how time works? I'm with Belinda at the 19th Precinct. You sent me here, if you remember."

"Listen. This assignment should take about five minutes. Just get some basic info. Name. Home address. The other stuff you can get online. Previous arrests. ER visits. Then get her version of the arrest. Keep it all brief."

The lack of cooperation is coming at Maddy from two people now. Belinda and R.J.

"I'm doing my best here, R.J. Maybe if you listened..."

To Maddy's surprise, Belinda is holding up her hands in the traditional "calm down" gesture. Is this a kind of breakthrough? Is Belinda suddenly cooperating?

But Maddy takes the advice. She tries to play nice with R.J.

"Listen, sir. This young woman needs medical attention. It looks pretty serious to me."

"Yeah. They all need medical attention. Get what you came for and then get the hell out."

Staying calm, Maddy says, "She has to see a doctor."

R.J. doesn't even ask what the medical problem us. The young woman could be bleeding out. Broken legs. Heart attack. OD. Whatever.

"Download the Medical Condition app. Fill out a request form. Send it to Police Health and be sure to cc me on it. They'll see if it requires a PA exam."

Maddy is back to full speed.

"But she needs to be seen now."

"Damnit. Do what I tell you to do. Just do it. And do it fast. We need you back here."

For what? Maddy thinks. *Does someone's dog need to be walked?*

But she doesn't get a chance to ask.

R.J. hangs up.

CHAPTER 9

MADDY IS ABSOLUTELY certain of one thing: R.J. is not going to break her. She'll prove that she's the best thing that ever happened to the New York City public defender's office.

She downloads a Temporary Release form on her handheld, forwards it to the NYC Judicial Procedure Office, and, within a few minutes, receives approval to accompany Belinda on a "necessary departure and absence" release for two hours.

When Belinda changes out of her prison uniform and into her "work" clothes, Maddy is surprised to see someone who actually looks like... well, not a woman but a middle school student who's late for geometry class—backpack, blue polo shirt with the alligator insignia, black skinny jeans.

Maddy can't help but say, "Wow. Not what I was expecting."

Mistake. Belinda snarls a tiny bit and speaks.

"What were you expecting? A T-shirt that says, I DEAL DRUGS, BOGO TODAY?"

Maddy says, "My mistake, sorry. Just tell me where we're going."

Where they quickly end up is a badly lit parking area beneath Second Avenue and the 59th Street Bridge.

What Maddy sees are three other girls, all of them dressed and groomed like Belinda. As a group they could be waiting for the school bus.

"You understand this yet?" Belinda asks.

"I'm beginning to," Maddy answers.

Then she sees one of Belinda's friends, a girl who is actually dressed in a navy-blue jumper over a white blouse with a Peter Pan collar, looking like the Catholic school girls she'd see in books and movies from a hundred years ago. The girl is talking to a very ordinary middle-aged guy. The guy is chubby. A significant glob of belly hangs over his belt. They talk for a few minutes. The guy nods. Then they disappear behind a filthy NYC Sanitation truck, the girl glancing over her shoulder as they go.

A black Lexus pulls up and stops. Another "coworker" of Belinda's approaches the driver's side and begins talking to the driver. Maddy steps a little closer. What surprises her is the driver's good looks—college type, early twenties, not unlike the finance guys from dinner the other day.

"I just don't get it," Maddy says. "That guy looks like his dealer should be wearing a three-piece suit and delivering to his door. He's not the kind I expect to see on the street, buying drugs."

"It's real simple, lady. He wants to feel like a badass, he wants to take the risk of getting caught. For some people, the drugs aren't even the point. They like the *feeling* of doing something bad. Others, they like to come down here and see how the other half lives, then go back to their high-rise, taking what they bought with them."

"Poverty tourism," Maddy says, shivering.

"Yep," Belinda agrees. "And some of them get it in their heads that they're actually helping us, you know? Like I had one of my regulars apologize to me because he bought off someone else, in a nicer part of town. And I'm like, bitch, you think I didn't sell that shit to someone else?"

"Wow," Maddy says, watching as the girl and her customer emerge from behind the sanitation truck. He pulls on her elbow, stopping her from walking out onto the street until a car passes. "They really do think they're helping you, don't they?"

Belinda snorts. "What they don't know is, nobody can help girls like us."

CHAPTER 10

JESSICA, MARGO, MADDY, and I are seated in front of our Communication Vector, a massive screen dedicated solely to watching events outside the United States.

Today we are watching the Oberon Awards for Literacy and Peace. The ceremony takes place in Copenhagen, Denmark. I was on the voting committee. Actually, I was chairperson of the committee, but I've been sworn not to blab. It's hard not to spoil the winner for the others, but we've had so little clean, good fun recently that I'm sitting on it—not that everyone appreciates that.

"In five minutes we're going to know who the winner is anyway," Margo says. "So why don't you just tell us now?"

I shake my head no and stay focused on the lavish ceremony on the screen. The only thing I say is, "Maddy, you can stop trying to intercept my brain patterns. I've enforced a mental barrier that prohibits you from entering. Maybe with another year of training you'll be able to connect to me. But you've got a long way to go."

Then Jessica says, "Everybody quiet down. The guy who runs Denmark..."

"Sometimes called 'the king,'" Margo says with a wry smile.

"Is about to announce the winner," Jessica goes on, ignoring the interruption.

The translation at the bottom of the screen tells us what the king is saying:

> **This citation is especially meaningful in these times of world turmoil. Therefore, it gives me great pleasure...**

Then suddenly everything changes. The picture on the Communication Vector starts to shake. I can barely make out people in the audience running, but I can clearly hear their screams and cries. Dignitaries and celebrities are rushing to leave the scene.

It seems like the earth under Copenhagen is shaking. Is this Copenhagen's version of the catastrophe that destroyed Kyoto? Then I watch as the king himself falls to the ground. Jessica and Margo gasp. "It could be an assassination attempt," I tell them, keeping my voice calm. Then a Danish word appears over the images of chaos:

> **NYHEDSOPDATERING**

Margo says, "What the hell does that mean?" And almost as if the screen heard her and decided to help, the English translation of the word pops up:

NEWS UPDATE

I stand in a kind of suspended panic and watch. Margo, Maddy, and Jessica move to the edge of their seats. We are not merely wide-eyed and overcome with fear. We are terrified. We are a quartet of people who are used to taking action, being in control. Our bodies are practically humming with the need to do something, but what?

The voice of a Danish news announcer comes on. It is shaky, loud.

An English translation begins scrolling across the screen.

The news is horrifying. Far worse than an assassination attempt...or anything else I could imagine.

CHAPTER 11

I DON'T KNOW a word of Danish, but I don't need to understand it to realize the seriousness of whatever is happening. There is sheer panic in the newscasters' voices. They seem to be talking over one another, interrupting one another, yelling at one another. The English translation can't seem to keep up with the words being spoken.

We see the English words:

A DEVASTATION IS ABOUT TO APPEAR.

"A devastation is about to appear?" I ask aloud. What does that even mean? I think of Kyoto. Is this a replay of that madness? Will mountains fall? Will the Earth crack open?

Then we hear more of the mishmash of foreign words.

"Baltic!" shouts Margo. "They're saying something about the Baltic."

"The sea," Jessica says. "The Baltic *Sea* is where Denmark is."

Now, finally, English words come swirling by on the screen:

A TIDAL WAVE, UNLIKE ANY TIDAL WAVE EVER RECORDED, IS ESTIMATED TO BE ONLY MINUTES AWAY FROM THE ISLAND THAT HOLDS COPENHAGEN.

I recall that most of Denmark is a peninsula, but the capital city of Copenhagen is located on a nearby island.

The newscasters sound terrified. Their words are translated for those of us watching from thousands of miles away. Panic. Nothing but panic. How could it not be? The newscasters are as frightened as anyone, but many of them are staying at their posts, boldly reporting, doing their jobs.

On the screen comes another flurry of English words.

WE ARE TOLD TO FIND SHELTER. BUT WHERE? WHERE IN GOD'S WORLD IS THERE A SAFE PLACE? WHAT IS HAPPENING? PLEASE, GOD.

Some brave fool is broadcasting now from the center of the city. Small amounts of water—nothing terrifying yet, I think—are beginning to splash onto the camera lens.

"In the back, the cathedral," I yell, as if he can hear me. "Climb to the top of the cathedral!"

"No," says Margo, her voice calm and flat. "I don't think it's tall enough."

"Of course it's tall enough," I argue, turning to her. But when I see her expression—blank and staring—I turn back to the screen. The cameraman must have dropped the camera and run away, because the only thing I can see is sky. Then I realize it's not the sky—this is the tidal wave! It reaches so high, nothing else can be seen.

I think of the people who are about to disappear—all the extraordinary, notable people gathered for the awards ceremony. The scholars, artists, scientists, doctors, writers, the international array of presidents, kings, and queens. Not to mention everyone else; the sound engineers, the chefs who make the sandwiches, the parents who have taken their children to witness this great and glorious event. I cannot control my beating heart and my fear.

And then the screen goes black.

CHAPTER 12

LIKE A CRAZED pianist at his keyboard, I begin pushing buttons and twirling knobs. With no communication system, we are lost.

The black screen takes on a gray-blue color. It is one of those sickening, creepy shades that tells you there's something wrong with your video systems. But in this case it is telling us that there is something wrong, terribly wrong, with the entire world.

Then the grayish color on the screen becomes haphazardly streaked with white lines.

"Look. You see those white lines?" Margo yells. "I think it's water. Waves. Yes! It's water!"

"How are they filming this?" Jessica asks.

I tell them that I can only assume that a dedicated newscaster, pilot, and cameraperson have taken to the sky in a helicopter. They may become the only survivors in all of Denmark.

The great blur of white lines and gray seems to wither away, then becomes smaller. The helicopter is flying higher and higher, trying to escape the tidal wave.

We watch, hypnotized, as the screen reveals what looks like a toy city about to drown.

The long view of the city of Copenhagen is nauseating and mesmerizing at the same time. We watch as the waves move closer, become bigger. There is no sound now, but the pictures are so compelling that we can imagine the roar. How big are the waves that have begun erasing the coast of Denmark? Are there actual words beyond *billions*? Zillions? Mega-zillions? Infinite millions? Whatever the word is, the wave is ready to overwhelm the entire country.

I rub my eyes and bow my head. I think as hard as I possibly can. One thing I know for sure—this was planned. This is no simple freak of nature. This is, at the very least, a phenomenon viciously aided by a member of humankind.

Maddy jumps in, voicing my thoughts.

"Is it connected to the thing in Kyoto?"

"Yes. It's a different kind of *thing,* but it is an equally horrifying *thing,*" I say.

Cataclysmic events like these are not coincidences. I know I'm right about this. This tidal wave was carefully calculated to annihilate the great intellects and scholars gathered for the awards ceremony in Europe. Just as the earthquakes of Kyoto were designed to do the same at one of the greatest brain centers in Asia.

The obvious question is: will this devastation today satisfy the evil goals of the person who designed it, or is this merely the beginning?

I will find out.

CHAPTER 13

EVERY CITY IN the world is on alert. But what can they do against mile-high tidal waves and disintegrating mountain ranges?

The news sources argue with one another. Each side blames the other. Politics, as always, overwhelms common sense. We all know there are no obvious solutions, but people are still scrambling for answers.

Many people blame the disasters on a mysterious force of nature. Some say we have always abused the environment. Now the environment is taking its revenge. Others believe it is the work of the god who made us. But what does that mean for those who don't believe in God? The devil's work? But who the hell is the devil?

I have meditated. I have turned the matter over and over in my brain. Yes, there is some terrible force at work. But I do not think it is mystical or magical. I do not think it is supernatural or paranormal. What we are witnessing is the triumph of a person of genius and passion, madness and hatred.

I sit in my communications room and brood. So far there have been no reports of destruction anywhere else. But I'm sure it's just a matter of time.

A *buzz* and a *click* come from my screen. I look up and see that Maddy is outside. I use a touch of my powers to allow her in.

"Have you looked at the sky?" she asks.

No, I have not. But my reflexive guess is that horror is soon to descend—clouds that rain chemicals, stars that hail firebombs.

"Look. Just look," she says.

I snap on the sky-screen and see a small streak of black flashes. The image becomes bigger and bigger. The small streak is some sort of space unit composed of six or seven travel units. Not quite rocket ships, not quite satellites. For a nanosecond I imagine some sort of crazy Santa's sleigh.

It comes closer. Then closer. I feel it might actually come crashing through my screen. Then it comes to a sudden stop. It hovers motionless over our backyard landing pad.

"What's going on?" Maddy asks.

"That airborne motorcade could only belong to one person."

"Who?"

"Maddy, I think we are about to receive a visit from John F. Townsend, the president of the Americas."

I stand up, click off my communications equipment, and say, "I'm going to go out and meet him."

"Why?" she asks.

"Because I don't want that man coming inside our home."

CHAPTER 14

THE MOMENT TOWNSEND disembarks, I'm ready and waiting.

As soon as his feet hit the ground, I remember how everything about him sickens me—the phony smile, the extended arm waiting for a handshake, the retinue of flunkies. I do not return the smile. I do not shake his hand. I ignore the army of subordinates.

I recall all too well the betrayals past world leaders like him have foisted upon me. And now I remember the expression that has guided me in the past: *Fool me once, shame on you. Fool me twice, shame on me.*

"Lamont, my friend. I come to beg for a favor," he says, his face serious.

"You've come to the wrong place, Townsend."

"The greater good, Lamont. Let us put the past behind us. Without our combined resources, the world could conceivably end. The tragedy of Kyoto, the—"

I enjoy interrupting him.

"I don't need a current events class," I say. "And you're not on camera right now, so cut the speech." But Townsend keeps talking.

"Then let's discuss how we can help humankind by helping each other."

This is the artificial sincerity he's so good at. He continues his infuriating charade.

"Let's go inside, just you and me. Let's talk. Make a plan. Secure the future."

I am burning with anger, remembering how two other world powers once deceived me when they tried to seize a superweapon—a deception that almost led to the end of the world.

"Look," he says. "I understand your hesitation. But I need you. The destruction of Kyoto, the obliteration of Denmark. I need your advice. I need your help."

I can't take it anymore.

"No president of the Americas will ever again have my help, Townsend. Here's what I advise: turn around immediately, climb back up those steps, get back into your stupid flying machine, and get the hell out of here."

CHAPTER 15

MADDY, MARGO, AND Jessica are standing side by side when I walk in. They look like an all-girl singing group from another era. This would be funny if my encounter with Townsend hadn't been so infuriating.

I'm sure my family easily figured out that the brief presidential visit had something to do with the extraordinary chaos in Kyoto and Copenhagen.

"Things in this world must be way out of his control if Townsend came to talk to you about it," says Jessica.

"Yes," I say. "President Stupid knows how terrible things are, and I think even he realizes that they will likely get worse."

"So, he was asking for your help," Maddy says. It's a statement, not a question.

"Correct."

"So what's the plan?" she asks.

"There is no plan," says Margo.

Jessica snaps her head toward Margo and asks, "How do you know that?"

"Because they only spoke for about thirty seconds," Margo answers. "Nobody can make a plan in thirty seconds. Not even the great Shadow."

"She's right. There is no plan," I say. "He wants my help. But I know his type. I'd bet everything he wants to use these tragedies for his own profit and glory. So I told him to get the hell out."

From our windows we can see the last two units of Townsend's flying motorcade lift up and into the sky.

All three women stand still, their faces filled with shock and confusion.

Then Maddy explodes with anger.

"I can't believe it," she yells. "The world is being destroyed right before our eyes, and Lamont Cranston won't try to save it?"

Maddy's outrage and passion are understandable, but she still has a lot to learn about me and my methods.

"Listen," I say. "Townsend is evil, super-evil. I would never do anything to help him, but—"

"But what?" Maddy yells. "But *what,* Lamont?"

"I *will* do everything in my power to save the world."

CHAPTER 16

THE CITY OF New York does not call it a bail hearing. The City of New York calls it a "pre-hearing evaluation and recommendation." So Maddy and Belinda are seated in a small, dirty room on Centre Street in downtown Manhattan. There are five metal chairs and two crappy tables that appear to be identical to the crappy table and chairs in Belinda's "holding cell."

"The only thing missing is that asshole boss of yours, R.J.," says Belinda, who is fidgeting and complaining. "Oh, and that dickwad doctor who kept asking me how I got hurt."

"That doctor was doing his job," Maddy reminds her. Maddy took Belinda for her medical examination after she shared how the other half lives. Belinda let him treat her cuts and bruises but fell silent when he asked questions.

Maddy doesn't know if the girl is protecting herself or the people she works for.

"Well," Maddy says, trying very hard not to show her

own distress at R.J.'s absence. "We don't have an attorney, but we also don't have a judge yet."

"The judge. Will he be sitting up there?" Belinda asks, pointing to the one chair that rests in the front of the room behind another crappy table, only that table is made of wood.

"Yes, that's where *she* will be sitting," Maddy says. "Just so you know. The judge is a woman."

"How'd you know that?" Belinda asks.

"I'm a forensic genius... I read the nameplate on the judge's desk." Then Maddy reads the name out loud to Belinda, pointing, HONORABLE ROSALIE MARTINEZ-HERMANN.

As if she'd been waiting for an entrance cue, the Honorable Judge Martinez-Hermann—heavyset and serious-looking—heads to her "bench" and sits. Meanwhile, Belinda turns to Maddy and whispers, "This isn't going to be good."

"Let's wait and see," Maddy says. Yet the moment after Maddy speaks, the judge looks up from her desk and says, "Good morning, and let's hustle. I've got a long day ahead of me."

As if on cue, R.J. Werner walks through the side door into the room.

Belinda mutters, "My lawyer looks like crap."

Maddy tells her to be quiet but silently agrees with Belinda. R.J. is wearing a pair of unwashed baggy chinos and a dark-blue shirt open at the neck—no tie—and is sporting at least three days of stubble.

"Are you connected with this case, sir?" the judge asks, eyebrows going up.

"Yes, ma'am. I'm the appointed attorney and I want to apologize for—"

"Too late," says the judge, clearly irritated by both his lateness and his appearance. She rattles off the arresting officer's report (the words *illicit substance* show up three times) and then says, "Please submit information that will persuade the court to warrant pretrial independence without restriction. Counselor, begin."

R.J. is barely able to walk across the very small room and address the judge.

"Your Honor, the great city of New York is a . . . a . . ." He searches for a word, but the word is not appearing. Finally, he says, "This city is a great temple to freedom."

The judge is immediately pissed. "Which is it, sir, a *great* city or a *great* temple?"

R.J. looks like the startled honoree at a birthday party when the crowd has just yelled, "Surprise!"

He tries to recover by saying, "Both. Both. It's both. A great city and a great temple and . . ." He is clearly off track. "And a great client. This woman, Linda, is a great person."

"Counselor!" Judge Martinez-Hermann yells. "Stop. You are wasting this court's time. I simply want the evidence that this young woman—whose name is *Belinda,* by the way—is capable of self-care and controlled independence before her scheduled trial. I need risk info and background."

And it is now, at this crucial moment, that Maddy stands up and places her hand on Belinda's shoulder.

"Your Honor, may I speak?"

"Who might you be?" asks the judge, turning her anger toward Maddy, who barrels ahead in the hope that the hearing won't be canceled.

"I also work for the public defender's office, and I merely want to point out that the police record shows no previous evidence of conviction for our client."

"You're telling me that there is no previous arrest record?" the judge asks.

"Well, not precisely. Five arrests are listed in the file," Maddy says, as she loses her footing. Beside her, Belinda flinches.

That's when Maddy decides to call upon her newly polished powers of mind control.

Maddy continues. "We realize that five arrests for possession is a large number, but the fact that no convictions took place seems to indicate that the NYPD may have been unfairly aggressive in their pursuit of my client."

Judge Martinez-Hermann nods and says, "Very well, this court will allow the subject self-oversight. The City of New York will contact the subject to inform her of a trial date, if any. One stipulation is that the subject report in person to Social Services. That would be..."

"R.J. Werner," says R.J. Werner.

"No, not you," the judge says. "The other one. The woman with a brain."

"That's you," whispers Belinda to Maddy.

"Oh, okay. I'm Maddy," says Maddy.

"What is that? Like Cher or Beyoncé? You have a last name?"

"Cranston. My name is Cranston. Maddy Cranston."

She only hesitates for a moment; she and Grandma Jessica both changed their last names from Gomes to Cranston after Lamont and Margo were married, in celebration of their newly united family.

The judge wrinkles her brow and says, "Cranston. Cranston. Hmm. That name sounds familiar."

CHAPTER 17

I MUST CONTROL my feelings. I must deal with the ache inside me. Yes, nothing will ever be the same after Jericho's death. But we must move forward. There is work to be done.

I've called together the team, a group of my bravest and most trusted associates.

Or what's left of them.

We had only just started to make peace with the death of Moe Shrevnitz, whom we lost not long ago in our battle against the Destroyer of Worlds. Today, with Jericho gone, we're yet another man short.

But Burbank, Tapper, and Hawkeye are still a formidable trio. And they'll have to do.

"Welcome," I say, to formally begin the meeting. "The recent past has delivered a series of mighty blows, with the loss of two of our dear colleagues. But the world situation has never before been so horrifying. We must become involved. If I may invoke a cliché—that's exactly what

Moe and Jericho would want us to do. Let's get down to business."

All three of them nod.

"I'll begin with the question that still has no answer: what is the connection between the earthquake disaster in Kyoto and the tidal wave in Copenhagen?"

Hawkeye speaks. "Sir, I have, if you will, a question about the question."

I know what Hawkeye's about to ask. It's going to be smart and sensible, just like Hawkeye himself.

"And your question is?"

"How do we even know that there is a connection?" he asks.

"We don't," says Burbank, jumping in. "But we've got to start somewhere."

I nod. "Your question was a smart one, Hawkeye, and Burbank's answer is equally smart. But whatever the situation, we must start from somewhere, and I don't think it's an irrational conclusion to draw."

"May I use the screen, sir?" says Tapper.

"Of course," I say. The flat screen behind me lights up in response to the voice command in Tapper's question.

"If you will, gentlemen," Tapper says as he presses a side button on his handheld. The screen fills with words.

"This is a complete listing," he explains, "of everyone who received an invitation and actually attended the Oberon Awards. You'll see the list is impressive, lots of big deals. It includes everyone from King Victor and Princess Martha of Denmark to a large number of award-winning university professors, media celebrities, artists, and authors, not to mention international news reporters and twenty-three foreign ambassadors, including one who was appointed a special envoy by President Townsend only two days before the awards ceremony.

"Everyone on this list has been vetted by confidential computer algorithms, and even the special envoy, Karen Wallace, a sixty-year-old woman and former CEO of Allied Development Medical Supplies, comes with a clean slate—"

A new list appears. This one, he explains, is a catalog of all victims of the Kyoto quake, all injured survivors, all university personnel who were at their nearby jobs on campus that day. Of the predictably mostly Japanese names, I recognize only two: a husband-and-wife team who previously assisted me in a scientific germ warfare study.

Tapper confirms that these names have also been thoroughly vetted.

"With all due respect, Tapper...what have we got? Nothing," says Hawkeye. "A bunch of heroes, a bunch of geniuses. We're looking for evil scum and all we've got is a list of saints."

"Connections," Tapper replies. "Let's look for connections."

"Kyoto was an academic setting," volunteers Burbank. "Copenhagen was essentially an academic setting, too, with its awards for peace initiatives and medical cures and general do-good stuff, but brainy stuff. Now, that's a connection."

"Can we break this down by country of origin and full background information of every person at the events?" Hawkeye asks.

Tapper presses the other side of his handheld device, and suddenly the screen is filled with pages and pages of documents.

"I've done the work already," he says, very smug and proud of himself.

"Okay," I say. "I don't know if this is a *good* start, but at least it's a start. I want everyone to explore these documents. *Any* insight, no matter how far-fetched, may turn out to be helpful. The other thing to tuck in the back of your brain is this: what in hell will these monsters do next?"

I tell them that we will reconvene in five hours...and I hope nothing earth-shattering happens before then.

CHAPTER 18

LAMONT HAS OFTEN said—perhaps too often for her liking—that if they ever give out an award for the World's Best Sleeper, Maddy would win it hands down.

In response Maddy once told him, "I think of myself as an aggressive sleeper."

"What exactly does that mean?" he asked.

"I approach almost everything I do as a challenge. Everything. Learning a foreign language. Playing basketball. Climbing a mountain in Nepal. And, yes, even sleeping. I see a clock. I see my bed. I know I must get to sleep. I push idle thoughts out of my mind, and then I get down to the business of sleeping."

When Lamont heard that, he just shook his head, squinted, then laughed. All he said was, "Maddy, you should be glad that I'm such a huge part of your life. Because I might be the only person in the world who understands what you mean when you explain something."

Tonight Maddy is sleeping precisely as she's described it:

flat on her back, arms folded, a pulsating electronic blanket folded at her waist. She breathes heavily, rhythmically, making a sound somewhere between snoring and singing. At least that's what she's doing until she hears a noise. Is it coming from the doorway? From the window? The bathroom? The...what the hell is it? She presses the Emergency button on the electronic console on her headboard.

Nothing. No alarm sounds. No lights come on. Nothing. She is frightened.

Like many people in the world, especially her family, she is super-aware of the Kyoto and Copenhagen disasters. She knows how many people expect a follow-up disaster, perhaps a whole series of unimaginable ones.

Then a voice. A man's voice, deep, clear, calm.

"The time to be awoken is upon us," comes the voice.

Who is it and what does it mean? Is he saying the word *awoken* in the sense of "It's time to be aware" or literally, as in, "It's time to wake up from your sleep"? And for that matter, is she even sure she's awake? It feels like a dream.

The dark, rich voice comes again, but this time with one very interesting additional word.

"The time to be awoken is upon us, *Madeline*."

Now she knows!

There's just one person in the world who refuses to follow her wish to be called Maddy. He insists—without fail—on addressing her as Madeline.

He makes himself known to her. He stands by the side of her bed.

It's Dache, the master teacher, the crucible of learning.

Maddy resents that Dache refuses to call her by her preferred name. She's angry at his childish teasing, but she also knows this: Dache is the real deal. Her attitude of disagreement will only be tolerated to a degree.

"Arise, Madeline. I am here to give you a very important upgraded lesson in mind control and its power. Very few others on earth receive this training. Gratitude, Madeline. Do show some gratitude."

She knows the session will be grueling. But she also knows that it will strengthen and enhance her skills. This is what Lamont wants her to do. In fact, she suspects that it may have been Lamont who requested that Dache give her this extra jolt of tough training.

Dache holds up a series of ordinary playing cards. Like a weird magician, he shows Maddy only the backs of the cards.

She concentrates. She begins unsteadily but soon rattles off correct identifications. "Ten of hearts. Ace of spades. Jack of clubs. Six of hearts. You won't catch me."

"We'll see," says Dache.

He reaches into his pockets and comes back with a big handful of rice.

"Catch!" Dache yells. Then he tosses the rice high into the air, where it hangs, suspended. "I'm keeping the kernels afloat, and now, when I say the word *begin,* you can't let them fall! Begin! Begin! Begin!"

Maddy pushes as hard as she can to will the tiny grains not to fall, but still, some do.

"Harder, Madeline. Harder! It's up to you."

Dache does not yell at her. He is no adrenaline-fueled high school coach. He is Dache. He is the leader. He is the teacher.

And so it goes, for what feels like hours. The rice stays aloft.

"Now for the truly challenging art of levitation," Dache says.

He suddenly produces six very sharp iron sabers and tosses them into the air above Maddy's head. Maddy knows that Dache would never inflict bodily harm on her. At least that's what she wants to believe.

She keeps the knives from falling...except...except... except for one saber, which falls so close to her right shoulder that she can feel the wind as it passes her and embeds its point into the bedroom floor.

Next come chains that must be unlocked.

Then fifty-pound exercise weights that must be balanced five at a time.

Lastly, the smallest, simplest, silliest lesson of all.

"There is a button on the windowsill," Dache says. "There is a spool of thread next to the button. There is a sewing needle next to the spool. There is a shirt with a missing button next to the needle."

Maddy sees the setup a few feet away.

Dache continues. "Using only your mind power—nothing else, no movement, nothing, nothing, nothing—*sew the button on the shirt.*"

The power of the mind, as taught by Dache, as learned by a chosen few, is surely not the mere intensity of concentration. Any mere mortal can concentrate and not allow their mind to wander. But this doesn't work that way. The power of the mind is the mixture of serenity and goodness, intelligence and inner strength. It is the effort to rise above the ordinary. It is the hidden supremacy of inner control.

At some point Maddy emerges into the real world. She is exhausted and exhilarated at the same time. Dache has disappeared; the only sign that he has been there is a blue shirt with five perfectly sewn buttons on it.

CHAPTER 19

THE NEXT DAY, Maddy directs her newly enhanced mind power toward a small but very important issue.

She uses her well-honed mental abilities to find Belinda's address. As soon as she discovers it—211 East 8th Street—she heads downtown. The Lower East Side.

Maddy has a rough memory of this area. But it has changed a lot since she was a little girl. Rat-infested tenements have been remodeled into high-end modern town houses. Art galleries and local restaurants fill previously abandoned shops. An area that was once a refuge for the poor now houses billionaire masters of the universe.

As Maddy walks quickly through Tompkins Square Park to Belinda's apartment, she discovers that despite the advancements, the city has failed to make any improvements to Belinda's building, which is a graffiti-covered mess.

The front door is unlocked, so Maddy has no trouble going inside. The crumbling staircase is littered with needles and shattered liquor bottles. She gags at the smell of stale urine. For a moment Maddy thinks she might not even be able to make it to the second floor, where Belinda lives.

But she does. The front door to Belinda's apartment is also open. Maddy thinks that she needs to have a conversation with the girl about personal safety, until she realizes there *is no door.* She sees Belinda sitting on the filthy floor, wearing a T-shirt and a pair of men's boxer shorts. Next to her is a mattress where a skinny dark-haired girl is sleeping. At least Maddy hopes she's sleeping.

"So, what is this?" Belinda says without standing. "Visitors' day in the ghetto?"

"Quite a place you've got here," says Maddy.

"Don't start," says Belinda. "State your purpose. Make your case, and then get the hell back uptown."

Charming as ever, Maddy thinks. But she's not about to antagonize Belinda. She will state her purpose. She is ready to make her case.

"I want to ask you about the time we spent together under the 59th Street Bridge," says Maddy.

"Send me an email, and I'll get to it after I'm done with my stocks and bonds meeting," says Belinda. But as the girl turns her head to check on her sleeping friend, it's clear to Maddy that Belinda's tough composure has been shaken.

"Listen, Belinda, let me get right to it. I don't have the experience you have. I don't have the pain you have. But I have some experience and some pain, and damnit, I want to help you. But I can't unless you share something with me. I don't mean to throw this all in your face, but I helped you in court. All I want to do is help you some more. I want the whole story on those girls you're working with."

There is a long pause. Belinda slides her hand under the mattress and pulls out a package of cigarettes.

"Lucky Strikes!" says Maddy, looking at the crumpled pack. "I didn't know they made those anymore."

"Want one?" Belinda asks.

"No, thanks," says Maddy, but even though she refuses, somehow the classic interaction of offering a cigarette warms the room with a sort of trust.

Belinda apparently decides that she doesn't want a cigarette, either. She slowly stands up and says, "You must be the only person in New York who doesn't know what goes on under the 59th Street Bridge."

"Of course I know. I was there with you. I saw drugs changing hands."

"Oh, yeah," says Belinda, her eyes going wide with fake innocence. "*That.* For shit's sake, do you really think that's all that goes on down there?

"Some of those girls go off with some bastard, and they never come back."

Maddy worried that the girls' exposure to the seedier side might go deeper than drugs, but she didn't expect this.

Belinda speaks quietly now.

"I knew them all. Annie, DeeDee, Marla, and this one," Belinda says, once again sliding her hand under the mattress, taking out a cell phone. She taps the screen a few times, then thrusts the phone at Maddy.

"That's Chloe," Belinda says. "She was my best friend."

Maddy studies the face. It could be a photo for a middle school yearbook, an end-of-summer-camp team picture. A smiling blond girl.

As Maddy studies the picture of Chloe, Belinda explodes with anger.

"Somebody is treating that bridge like a buffet," she says.

"I can help you, Belinda. I can help."

But the girl just shakes her head, a deep sadness reflected in her eyes.

"I miss my friend so much, Maddy. Chloe just disappeared. She just stopped showing up. If nobody does anything, it'll keep happening. It's going to happen to me. It's just a matter of time."

"It's not," Maddy argues, shaking her head.

"Nobody cares about us poor girls, the ones who have to do anything to survive. We're just meat in a grinder, and some sicko figured out he can pick and choose. I can get busted for dealing because some of my stuff flows up to the rich side of town. But stuff that happens to people down here stays here, and nobody does a damn thing about it."

"Not anymore," Maddy says.

CHAPTER 20

HERE'S SOME FREE advice from the Shadow.

If you really want to keep something secret, here's how: *don't share the secret information with anyone.* That may seem like common sense, but it's amazing how quickly it can go out the window. Anyone means *anyone.* That means even your best friend, your lover, your family, your associates, your assistants, your colleagues . . . anyone.

I pretty much honor this rule above all others.

That's why I'm on a macro-line third-level-incognito computer window making my own personal arrangements to travel to Harvard University in Cambridge. Third-level incognito is a system in which all information sent to a recipient self-erases. Unlike almost everything else, online third-level transmissions can *never* be recovered.

Perfect.

I've arranged to meet Dr. Atticus Henry, the world's leading geologist on earth science and abnormal physical earth material. I've also made arrangements for team members Hawkeye and Tapper to accompany me. True to my obsession to keep secret information secret, I will only inform them half an hour before departure.

I have, of course, already spoken with Dr. Henry about the phenomena at Kyoto and Copenhagen that have stunned the rest of the world.

Dr. Henry is already entrenched in examining the horrible incidents. He's conducted analyses of earth material taken from the disaster centers. He'll be sharing his results and opinions with us when we see him.

"I cannot, and will not, transmit my algorithmic theories by internet. Everything I do is watched by potentially adversarial governments, including—I'm sorry to say—our own," Dr. Henry told me. In other words, "I don't come to you. You come to me."

He has made it clear that his work may not be completely accurate, but, he said, "We must begin somewhere, and the sooner the better."

I couldn't agree more. We're on our way.

CHAPTER 21

I'VE NEVER ACTUALLY been to Harvard, not as a student, not as a professor, not even as a guest lecturer.

Even so, I'm probably one of the few people who can say that Harvard wanted me, but I just wasn't interested. I like a life with action mixed with a heavy dash of glamour.

So while other guys my age were up in Cambridge studying nuclear physics and reading Homer's poetry in the original Latin, I was in NYC drinking rare Bordeaux with Margo at the 21 Club or dancing with her at the Stork Club.

Anyway, I'm here now, strolling with Tapper and Hawkeye, on Mount Auburn Street, Harvard Yard to our right, the Charles River a few blocks to our left. In a few minutes we'll meet with Dr. Atticus Henry and start solving the horror of the recent—and literally earth-shattering—problems devastating the world.

"You know what I've noticed?" says Hawkeye. "Everyone in this city is incredibly young."

"Or are we just getting older?" I ask, grinning.

But more than that, there is real worry about these young people's future. Whatever Tapper and Hawkeye and I might learn up here in Cambridge will be used to help them.

We turn to enter the central square, the famed Yard, and a very cordial uniformed security guard stops us.

"University IDs or security passes," he says.

"We have an appointment to see Dr. Atticus Henry," I say.

"Certainly," the guard says. "I just need to see your IDs or passes."

Tapper to the rescue. Cool and confident, he begins. "Well, Dr. Henry didn't tell us we needed..."

But I don't want a delay. I can't wait for Tapper to win his verbal debate with the guard. I'd better take care of this. I enter a mind-control manipulation. Tapper hasn't even finished his sentence when the guard says, "Very well, Mr. Cranston. Dr. Henry is expecting you. If you like, I can call a Harvard guest leader to accompany you. That way, if you're new to the campus—"

"No, thank you," I say.

We walk north through Harvard Yard.

The sun is hiding behind some very gray clouds, and the air seems muggier than it was just a few minutes ago. The crowd of students, tourists, and residents seems, oddly quieter.

"Does anyone else hear that?" asks Hawkeye. "A splashing,

sort of. It's like a bunch of kids have jumped into the river and decided to fool around."

"I bet that's exactly what it is," says Tapper. "Kids will be kids, if you can recall."

Hawkeye shakes his head ruefully. "Not really."

We keep walking, intent on meeting Dr. Henry.

CHAPTER 22

THE CROWD THICKENS, then begins to move a little faster. The odd splashing sound is still in the air, and the sky begins to darken. All around us, young people have stopped to stare up at the sky, talking excitedly to one another. There's a sudden swell in the crowd, and it grows, becomes more jostling, as it seems everyone who was down by the river is now running away from it.

"Is something weird going on?" asks Tapper.

"I have no idea," I say. And, in fact, I don't.

The crowd grows as it gets closer to us and starts to move faster, packed, touching, polite but pushing and jockeying around for openings that don't exist.

"Joey! *Come on,*" a young woman next to me yells. There's real impatience in her voice. And maybe a touch of... fear?

The crowd is growing bigger, thicker. Now it's like a bunch of people herding together to get into a movie theater or a ball game, blocking our way.

"Lamont!" Tapper yells over the crowd, but we're being pushed away from each other.

"Meet up at Dr. Henry's office," I yell, hoping that Hawkeye can hear me as well. I can't see him anymore.

Now everyone in the crowd has noticed the change in the weather. A pleasant springlike day has turned into a heavy, humid tropical jungle. Everyone is hot. Everyone is sweating.

I turn to a young man trying to squeeze past me.

"Where is everyone going?" I ask him.

"Right now, we're just trying to move away from the river," he says.

"Why?" I ask, remembering the splashing sound. Is this some kind of party gone wrong?

"Because of *that,*" he says, pointing to the horizon.

Some kind of fog is floating up from the river, choking out Harvard Yard.

"That looks like steam," I say.

"The river is boiling!" a woman screams, her voice carrying in the dense air.

A man pushes through the crowd in a flat-out run, coming from the direction of the Charles River. The character of the throng changes, verging on panic.

I have to get to Dr. Henry's office. Now. Fast. I think I can snake through the crowd sideways. Total focus and total determination have always been my best friends. I'm on it. Tapper and Hawkeye will catch up with me at the rendezvous point.

CHAPTER 23

SQUEEZING THROUGH. MOVING roughly. Sideways, shoulder first, it takes me exactly six minutes to arrive at the recently unveiled Harvard Hall of Science. I turn back to look at the crowd, but they are lost in a fog bank, like smoke from a nearby town. I know it's the steam rising from the bubbling, boiling water.

The doors of the Hall of Science fly open as students, professors, and men and women in white lab coats all hurry out of the building. Most of them head for the river, carrying beakers and racks of test tubes. Inside, I stop three ordinary campus security guards who are rushing out.

"Have you seen Dr. Atticus Henry?" I shout.

"I don't know who the hell I've seen," one of them says. Then they disappear into the crowd.

I glance at the framed office directory on the lobby wall and learn that Dr. Henry has an office and lab on the tenth floor. The highest floor. The elevators have been locked down. Great.

I run up the service stairway to the tenth floor, a long hallway that's completely deserted. When I locate Dr. Henry's office, I don't stop to knock. I barge in and find a distinguished-looking white-haired man, perhaps seventy years old. This must be Dr. Henry.

Dr. Henry is calmly pressing some buttons on a handheld computer. He looks up at me and smiles.

"Ah, you must be my three-o'clock appointment. Mr. Cranston, I presume."

CHAPTER 24

DR. HENRY EXTENDS his hand. He bows slightly and smiles warmly. I'm wondering if it's possible that he doesn't even know that the Charles is steaming, even boiling, that people are fleeing. This doctor is no wild and crazy old scientist. He's very calm.

"You've certainly chosen an interesting time for your visit," says Dr. Henry.

"It seems so," I say. "I'm here to seek your advice on the events in Copenhagen and Kyoto."

Still smiling, he goes on. "Yes. Kyoto, Copenhagen... and now we seem to be having an interesting event occurring right here in Cambridge."

So Dr. Henry *does* know what's going on a half mile from his office. But if he's at all worried, it doesn't show. He motions me over to a large computer screen.

"Pull up a chair," he says, moving a steel workbench in front of the computer. "You will have a front-row seat to watch the end of the world."

I force a tiny laugh, assuming he's joking.

I am a smart guy. Some people even think I'm a sensitive guy. My history has certainly proven that. But I can't figure out what the deal is with Atticus Henry. Is he always so overwhelmingly calm, even with the horrors in Japan and Denmark? Even with a toxic river in his own front yard? Does he know something about these events that I don't?

"You are about to see a close-up of the destruction in Kyoto and Copenhagen," says Dr. Henry. He touches his handheld device and the big computer screen fills with a picture of murky brownish water.

"This is the bottom of the sea surrounding Copenhagen," he says.

"Off the coast of Denmark?" I ask.

"More or less. It is specifically the bottom of the Baltic Sea, off the coast of Copenhagen." He pauses, and for the first time he looks and sounds animated. "This is my first historical video. But there's more."

He taps a few more buttons. A new video begins.

"Look at that!" he says, and we both watch as the screen fills with huge bursts of orange and red and yellow. I'm not certain what I'm looking at. Insane fireworks?

Dr. Henry pushes a few more buttons. The screen dissolves to another scene—dry, cracking, splitting land. Massive pieces of earth tumbling and tumbling.

"What's happening?" I say.

"Hell is happening," he says. "Hell is coming out to visit.

An earthquake deep below the ocean itself has cracked open the ocean floor. Magma is spewing out from the very center of the Earth."

"Magma?"

"Molten rock that lies within the Earth. The heat is wildly intense. And the rupture here is the same as the rupture of the ocean floor in Europe. Ah, the power of magma! No wonder the Charles River is boiling!"

"But why? How?" I ask.

"The ultimate cause, I believe, is an attack of gamma rays hitting the Earth. When the extraordinary heat cracks the ocean floor, magma is released."

"And the gamma rays are coming from where?" I ask. Frankly, I am not merely confused and ignorant. I'm also starting to panic.

With a bizarre touch of mischief in his face, the professor adds, "It will be up to you and your merry band of helpers to figure out where the gamma rays are coming from. Is it the sun? Another planet? Another galaxy? Or are they being created by some malevolent fiend here on Earth?"

"Doctor, the best thing for you and me to do right now is to get out of Cambridge and move farther inland," I say.

He looks at me with a small smile, as if I am a child playing a game I don't understand.

I move to one of the windows and look out. The crowd of people I encountered on my short walk to the science building has thinned a little. It's fairly orderly but moving fast. From what I can see on their faces from the tenth floor, everyone seems anxious and scared.

"Dr. Henry, let's get out of here. Away from the river, away from the crowds," I say.

It's as if he doesn't hear me or doesn't care.

The older man saunters over to me at the window.

"Let me have a look," he says.

"It's hard to see with all the moisture from the steam on the window," I say.

"Yes, they have these windows hermetically sealed, but I have a self-invented contraption that can get them open," he says. He snaps a short steel piece into the side of the window, turning it. The gadget looks like a crude bottle opener. He stands at the open window and takes a deep breath.

"Ah," says the professor. "Good clean air. Enjoy it while it's still here, Mr. Cranston."

"I'd enjoy it more if we were outside, moving away from whatever that fog is."

He smiles broadly. Again, it's a facial expression filled with both pity and amusement. He looks out the window, from right to left, then back again.

I am going to make one more strong request for Dr. Henry to leave the building. If he refuses, I'm leaving anyway.

"Doctor, we've got to go now. We've got to save ourselves if we're ever going to have a chance to solve this!"

"Mr. Cranston, there is absolutely no way that this

horror can be ended. By you or anybody else. I'm a scientist. I'm sure we're all doomed."

Then, before I even realize what's happening, Dr. Henry lifts his right leg to the ledge of the open window. He pulls his body upright on the ledge.

Then he jumps.

CHAPTER 25

THE BOILING RIVER in Cambridge is huge news across the globe. Every country with a coastline or a river tries to organize some sort of protection against the possibility of more horror. But there are not enough sandbags or cement walls on the planet to protect against the Earth's waters.

And what about the other forces of nature, exploding mountains and billions of acres of land ready to split open? People everywhere are talking endlessly about the natural phenomena that might destroy humankind at any moment. It's as if the fabric of our planet has decided to move against us.

Thankfully, Hawkeye and Tapper made it out of Cambridge safely, but I don't know if anywhere on earth can truly be considered safe now.

Margo, Jessica, and Maddy keep pumping me for information and speculation. Unfortunately, the three people I live with are way, way too smart to fool. Expressions like

"Don't worry" or "Just stay calm" or "We'll figure it out" will not work with them.

And, yes, Maddy is one of those people, but because she's an emotional multitasker (God bless the training Dache has given her) she is able to fixate on the other challenge in her life.

CHAPTER 26

MADDY TURNS HER attention to Belinda and the girls she works with. She's determined to unravel the situation beneath the 59th Street Bridge, determined to help Belinda, determined to find Chloe.

Maddy has actually managed to squeeze some helpful information out of Belinda. She's learned that Belinda and the other girls get their marching orders from higher up, sometimes delivering privately to their clients, sometimes taking on the lower deals on the street. Some of the buyers who demand private delivery have favorite girls, and—to no one's surprise—there's occasionally a girl who sells more than what she's carrying, although Belinda assures Maddy that she's never traded on her body.

"Stay away from this shit, babe," Belinda tells Maddy. "You could end up in real trouble."

But Maddy insists. And finally Belinda gives her enough information that Maddy can create a sort of rough road map in her head.

"Third Avenue and 53rd Street is always cooking," Belinda says. "That area has been so busy for so long I bet you can get a contact high if you walk around barefoot."

Maddy finds out that Park Avenue is always busy when the stoplights turn red. Belinda clarifies: "There's a specific pickup stop at 73rd and Park.

"There's action in Spanish Harlem sometimes," Belinda adds. "You know, pick up some lemon chicken at Rao's and then grab your heroin a few blocks away."

"I never thought of pairing those," Maddy says.

And to her surprise, Belinda actually laughs.

Maddy smiles back, feeling the warmth of the connection growing between them.

Maddy can't figure it out.

The city blocks around Third Avenue and 53rd Street seem safer and prettier than Disney World. The usual cluster of Irish bars, singles bars, and bars for young folks who are missing their home state of Texas. There's a store that frames pictures, a store that sells ridiculously expensive window shades, a store that sells antique silver knives and forks.

As for the street scene: a young dad type with two little kids, twin boys, in a stroller. A teenage couple kissing so passionately, Maddy thinks they might smother each other.

Maddy wears a dark-blue polo shirt and a pair of old army-green cargo shorts. Her wardrobe goal was to look like a college student. Which she was until two weeks ago.

As she looks around, her observations become a bit more critical—"discerning" is what Lamont would say. Maybe the two very young women in jeans and down vests are not just teenage girls trying to figure out which bar won't check IDs. Maybe the unbelievably skinny young Black girl laughing as she gets into a taxi with a guy in sweatpants isn't out on a date.

Maddy crosses from one side of the street to the other, then back again. She glances through the window of a bar called the Naked Dog.

Men and women, boys and girls, come and go. Maddy watches the two pretty young girls in down vests who fit the profile of the girls in Belinda's circle. Clean-cut, conservatively dressed, nothing that would make a police officer look at them sideways.

Maddy is confused. The pickings in this neighborhood seem to be quite slim. In fact, she thinks, the pickings seem to be nonexistent. She phones Belinda, but the call goes to voice mail.

On the corner, a few doors down from the Naked Dog, is a CVS Pharmacy. Maddy goes inside the store and selects a ChapStick and a Special Dark Hershey's bar. As she waits in the checkout line, the young girl behind her—wearing a white T-shirt, black silk vest, and black jeans—smiles and cheerfully says, "I could eat a hundred of those dark chocolate bars."

Maddy grins back. "You must be an amateur. I could eat two hundred."

Maddy pays the cashier and returns to her spot outside the Naked Dog. She unwraps her chocolate bar and breaks off a piece, and as she's about to pop it into her mouth, she hears a voice.

"I don't think we've been introduced."

The voice belongs to a bland-looking forty-something man in a cheap gray suit. He's eating a greasy slice of pizza, which he's conveniently folded in half.

Oh, my God, Maddy thinks. *This guy thinks I'm working.*

"I'm just waiting for my friend," Maddy says.

"I'm sure," the cheap suit says. Then he nods in the direction of the two young women who've been talking together.

"You with Lisa and Randi?"

"No. Like I said, I'm waiting for a friend," Maddy says.

"Right," he says.

Maddy calls up her inner strength. As Dache has taught her, *You have depths within you that only you yourself can muster.*

"Listen," she tells the guy. "I don't know what your deal is. But I'm pretty sure I'm not what you think I am."

The man looks across the street at the two young women. One of them waves to him, tosses her chin in his direction. The other yells, "Bobby! Got a drop for you!"

Maddy has a very basic question—what the hell is going on here? But she knows from her criminology classes: just wait long enough and the person you're interviewing will start talking.

CHAPTER 27

"SO, HERE'S MY deal," the man says, clearly trying to impress Maddy as he chews the last chunk of his pizza crust. "I'm Detective Robert McCarthy. And this is a special strip in Midtown East. Very special. You see, I help the girls when I can, and they help me, and that's that."

"Well, I'm here to help also," Maddy says.

"Don't be a fucking idiot," McCarthy says. "You can't help. I can't help. This is not a nice place to be."

"Why not?" Maddy asks.

He answers. "You know how with doctors there are specialists—cardiologists and dermatologists and stuff like that? Well, the woman who runs the operation on this strip here is Carla Spector. She's a specialist, too. She knows how to move large quantities of H without anyone knowing, because she uses the right kind of girls."

"Like, what kind of girl?"

"See those two girls?" McCarthy asks, nodding across the street. "They look like trouble to you?"

"No, they look like—"

"Like nice girls," McCarthy interrupts her. "Exactly. The kind of girls who can walk around with their pockets full. Plenty to sell, and the cruisers move right past them.

"My only job is to make sure they each get into the right car, the client's car."

"And after they get in?"

"After they get in, they're on their own."

Maddy senses that some of those girls might be the ones who sell more than drugs to their clients, and she wonders if Carla gets a cut of that, too.

"Stay away from here, lady," McCarthy goes on, as if he's actually trying to do her a favor.

"This is no little deal. This is like a chain of stores. Carla's got this op running from here to Cleveland and Atlanta and some second-string cities you never heard of. Just get gone."

Maddy looks away from him, her eyes following the two girls across the street as a car pulls up next to them. They hug, and one gets in. McCarthy gives her a little wave.

"Can I ask you one thing, Detective?" Maddy asks. "Do you by any chance remember a girl by the name of Chloe?"

"Yeah," McCarthy says. "Chloe. Nice girl. Just like the others."

Maddy is anxious, nervous. Then she says what she wants to say.

"Do you know where she is now?"

McCarthy doesn't quite smile, but he doesn't quite sneer. Then he says, "Listen. That Chloe chick? She disappeared a long time ago. And that's what I advise you to do."

McCarthy puts his hand on Maddy's upper arm and rubs her skin softly. Maddy doesn't merely pull away from him. No, she snaps her fist into McCarthy's neck. He pulls back, gagging, clawing at his throat.

Then there's a flashlight coming toward her. Maddy looks up, terrified she's about to be arrested for assault. But it's being held by the same girl Maddy spoke to in the CVS. The light passes off Maddy to shine on McCarthy's face; he is still red-faced and choking.

The girl with the flashlight speaks loudly. "Leave her alone, Bobby. Don't be an asshole."

"Good advice," says Maddy.

"He's a cop," says the girl.

"Hey, JoJo, I told her who I was," says McCarthy, angry. "It's not like I'm a liar."

No, not a liar, Maddy thinks. But a dirty cop who takes money from drug kingpins and lets young girls be put in harm's way. Maybe he even thinks he's helping them out, like some of Belinda's clients. He might think of himself as a benevolent mentor keeping an eye on them while they work.

The girl looks at Maddy and says, "He's, like, one of the four NYPD guys we have to pay off. They never pull us in. It's a whole better deal for them. It sucks for us. But everything sucks for us."

"Put that fucking flashlight away, girl," McCarthy says. "I'm going but I'm not going far."

JoJo practically shrugs. "Like I care, asshole," she says.

McCarthy walks away. As he stumbles down the street,

Maddy takes a closer look at the girl. Her light brown hair is pulled back in a ponytail. She doesn't wear a speck of makeup.

"You're JoJo?" Maddy says.

"No. My name is Joanna, but Bobby thinks it's hilarious to call me JoJo. He's such a... Listen, can we move this closer to the CVS? I'm waiting for someone."

And, of course, Maddy realizes what the story is. She speaks slowly and cautiously. "Who are you waiting for?"

Joanna responds quickly. "A ride. Just a friend." She drops her eyes when she answers, hand fiddling with something in her pocket.

"Let me ask you one more question," Maddy says softly. "How old are you?"

Joanna still does not speak. So Maddy says, "You must be about fourteen, right?"

No answer. Maddy keeps trying. "Thirteen? Fifteen"

"Try twelve," Joanna says.

Maddy instinctively reaches toward Joanna and hugs her briefly.

"I got to go back outside the CVS," the girl says, hand still clutching something in her pocket. "I'll be in big trouble if I'm not there when my ride comes."

"Yeah, well. You're not going to be there when your *ride* comes."

"I've got to be," Joanna says, scared, teary.

"No. Not tonight," says Maddy. "Tonight you're going to be staying at my house."

CHAPTER 28

HAWKEYE, TAPPER, AND I escaped from Cambridge, but we are no better off than we were before. In fact, in my opinion, we are even more confused about the natural crises that are disturbing the entire globe. A plan? We have no plan. Hawkeye, Tapper, Burbank, Margo, and I meet in our conference room. Like bad gossip columnists, we must make something out of nothing.

"Our one source of information was Dr. Henry," I say to the group, "but he decided to avoid involvement in the most shocking way possible. However..."

Everyone looks up at me. Their faces are so full of hope that I wish I had a better announcement to make. But I go on. "However, Dr. Henry's suicide itself may be a clue."

"Well, sure," says Burbank. "I think we can deduce that the good professor knew this natural disaster situation is impossible, unstoppable. This was the old prof's way of not waiting to become a victim."

"We should try to hook up with someone at the

Environmental Protection Agency of the Americas," says Tapper. "Surely someone there will know something!"

"Or one of the undersecretaries at Agriculture," says Burbank.

Margo nods. Then she says, "Someone in this godforsaken world can solve this."

Then there's silence in the room. Deadly silence. No ideas at all. No good ideas. No bad ideas. The silence is relentless and infuriating and frustrating, and then... a voice.

"What a bunch," a familiar voice says; a low chuckle follows. "The only people who can solve this problem are right in this room!"

My heart feels like it's stopped inside my chest. I'm hearing a voice I thought I'd never hear again, a voice that had been removed from this world forever, lost under tons of dirt and debris in Kyoto.

Jericho Druke stands in front of us—alive and well.

Margo, Burbank, and Tapper all scream. Hawkeye, always quick with a reaction, can only stand and stare.

We are all thankful, yet we are stunned.

How did this happen?

CHAPTER 29

MADDY IS THE determined intern. R.J. is her by-the-book boss. This is not a match made in heaven.

She thinks that when she tells R.J. about her dealings with Belinda, Joanna, and McCarthy, he'll be excited that she's onto something big. But just the opposite happens.

"I send you to do a simple five-minute jail cell interview, and you launch a full-scale, totally unapproved, completely useless investigation. You're working here three days, and you've violated just about every rule in the book," R.J. says loudly and fiercely.

Maddy doesn't give an inch.

"I'm telling you that there's a major drug operation in the city using young girls as a delivery system, and that someone has discovered those girls make easy prey, and you start preaching about the rule book?" Maddy yells, equally angry.

R.J. is trying to keep himself under control. After all, Maddy saved his butt at Belinda's hearing when he showed up disheveled and unprepared. But he can't be controlled by that one event. So he tries to find some kind of middle ground.

"Look," he says. "You've got a lot of potential, Maddy, but you also have a lot to learn."

The cold, stern look on Maddy's face makes it clear to R.J. that's she's not buying this new, calm approach. And she's not going to let go. She speaks.

"Columbus, Ohio; Orlando, Florida; Scranton, Pennsylvania. That's how huge this setup is. It's countrywide! These girls are being used as smugglers and dealers, and who knows where that leads. For at least a few of them, I know it's led to being murdered."

"You heard all this from Belinda?" R.J. asks. And he seems interested for the moment.

"No. I heard it from the twelve-year-old girl I brought home last night. The girl I fed. I gave her a bed. I—"

R.J. jumps in. He seems to be both shocked and angry.

"You what? You brought a drug dealer into your house?"

"Oh, my God!" Maddy screams. "She's a child who's being taken advantage of!"

"Maddy," he asks, "what the hell is wrong with you?"

She looks at him and asks quietly, "No, R.J. What the hell is wrong with you?"

CHAPTER 30

MADDY HAS A lesson with Dache coming up. In fifteen minutes. Damnit.

Yes, she knows that to be taught by Dache is a unique privilege. Lamont has told her more than once, "Every class with Dache is a *master* class."

And while she knows all this is true, she's also in a really rotten mood, and that is not a good jumping-in point for lessons with Dache.

Since she was younger, years before she became a protégé of Lamont's, years before Dache took her into his intense training regimen, Maddy could totally chill just by high-speed running. Not jogging, but burnout running, the kind where you go until your body simply can't anymore. Her usual route these days was parallel to Central Park, pounding the pavement up and down Fifth Avenue.

Once, during a session with Dache, she hesitatingly

asked him about her homemade method of "centering" herself. The great Dache did not mock her for her running method, but he certainly didn't endorse it.

He told her, "The word *centering* is highly inadequate for what the practice actually is. What I teach you is far greater than 'centering.' I teach you control. Then that control leads to power, and the power produces strength for both body and soul. Then, and only then, will you carry the capacity for doing good."

Yes, Dache was right. Yes, she would learn. But for now Maddy is longing for a quick fix. So running at top speed up Fifth Avenue will have to do the trick.

When she reaches 72nd Street, Maddy turns into Central Park and keeps on running. But, damnit, her mind is not clearing. Her confusion is not diminishing.

R.J. is still a fool. Lamont still faces the most extraordinary challenge of his life. And Belinda is still living in a hovel while her friend Chloe is missing, with no one looking for her. And what about Joanna? After showering, eating, and staying at Maddy's overnight, she insisted on leaving the next day, returning to the street, claiming that she could take care of herself.

No, a high-speed run through Central Park won't help solve any of those problems, something Maddy quickly learns as her body begins to fail, but her mind is still spinning in circles. She slows down, then slows some more, then stops. She now stands at the top of the stone staircase that leads down to Bethesda Fountain and a crowd of people who are seated nearby.

Breathing heavily, she puts her arms above her head and walks toward the west side of the park, until she reaches the forestlike wild acre that sits close to Belvedere Castle.

Suddenly overwhelmed with fatigue, Maddy crouches down next to a boulder. She lifts her T-shirt and wipes her sweaty face. She is alone. Completely alone . . . until she isn't.

She hears a voice. The man says, "Ah, an accidental seminar."

It's Dache. He has found her. No one apparently can escape the great and gifted monk.

"You have ignored our meeting time, Madeline. Unacceptable. You know that."

She wants to respond intelligently, but all she can think of is *gimme a break*. But she knows that such a disrespectful phrase is also unacceptable. Finally, she simply says out loud what she is feeling inside.

"Everything I touch is falling apart. I haven't created any real changes for Belinda. I certainly can't find Chloe. Joanna ran out on me. I accidentally killed someone trying to help Lamont. And as for my boss . . ."

She stops talking. To her surprise she manages to hold back the tears.

Dache does not approach her. Dache does not try to soothe her. He is always beyond that sort of action. And he expects that Maddy should be also.

"I will give you one rule, and the rule is an insight to cherish."

Then, in the voice of an old-fashioned Sunday preacher, he says, "*Problems belong to all people. Solutions belong only to the chosen few.*"

Then Dache is gone.

CHAPTER 31

MY PERSONAL AND private cell phone is restricted to only the most confidential and approved-for-clearance messages.

That means that the phone is mostly for urgent communications from Margo, Hawkeye, Jericho, Burbank, or Tapper. Yes, the occasional world government sources will reach out to me on it—and whoever that caller might be is still identified by caller ID.

I'm still reeling from Jericho's surprise return from the dead, and the few times that he has called me on my cell since then, I've been overwhelmed with renewed joy. He was able to escape the building in Kyoto before it collapsed but had been so overwhelmed by the destruction and need of the people there that he considered it his duty to stay and help where he could. That accomplished, he'd come home as quickly as possible, not wanting to delay his return even long enough to give us some forewarning.

But it's not Jericho calling this time.

The phone buzzes, and the caller ID flashes a group of letters and numbers that completely confuses me. 744ADS455. I've never seen this combination before, and I'm very reluctant to connect. I press the Decline button.

Within seconds the phone buzzes again. Damnit.

I know it could be risky, but I also know that anyone who has this number likely has a very good reason for using it. Before I answer, I click to allow for video calling and see a harmless-looking young man staring at his own screen.

I say, "To proceed with this call, please identify yourself."

The young man says, "Please hold for Dr. DaSilva."

"Please identify *yourself*," I say sternly.

The young man complies. "I'm Kevin Forrest, assistant to Dr. DaSilva."

"Good start, Mr. Forrest. Now, if you could please identify Dr. DaSilva."

He doesn't hesitate. "Dr. DaSilva is a senior officer in the Townsend administration."

So, his office hasn't given up, even after I kicked the president off my property. They must desperately need my help in this crisis that could potentially destroy the entire world.

"This Dr. DaSilva. What's his role in the administration?"

He corrects me. "*Her* role. Her full name is Anna DaSilva, and she has been asked by President Townsend to speak to you regarding an issue of importance."

Enough of this telephone dance. "Put her on, Forrest."

He says thank you, and a moment later the young man

is replaced on the screen with the image of a pleasant, ordinary-looking woman, approximately fifty years old. Her silverish hair is cut short, simple, no-nonsense. I'm guessing that the white jacket she's wearing is a lab coat.

She speaks first. "It is such a pleasure—a pleasure *and* an honor—to meet you, Mr. Cranston. President Townsend is confident that you will be able to help us on a project of enormous gravity."

Her voice and manner are warm, but the "a pleasure and an honor" part is a little bullshitty.

I decide not to share with Dr. DaSilva that I think her boss, President Townsend, is among the most devious and unethical men I've ever dealt with.

"Thank you," I say.

"I think that the matter is so urgent that I'd like to begin briefing you immediately," she says.

"Of course," I say. "But I do want to tell you that I have some very specific thoughts about the matter at hand."

"The matter at hand?" she asks, looking a bit bewildered. "How would you know about this matter? I haven't told you anything about it."

"I don't mean to be arrogant, Doctor, but I've personally witnessed the natural phenomenon that is unleashing itself upon the world."

She nods, says, "That natural course of destruction of which you speak is indeed extremely troubling. But that is *not* the matter at hand."

I am surprised. No, wait. I'm shocked.

"No," Dr. DaSilva says. "We need you to assist with something else, something the public and press know nothing about yet. Something I think could turn out to be even worse than the environmental nightmare we're experiencing right now."

CHAPTER 32

"THERE IS AN extraordinary situation in Australia that its government does not have the ability to deal with. That's where we come in."

Dr. Anna DaSilva explains. Slowly, carefully, as if she's teaching a child in first grade.

"It is a new, never-before-seen virus. It is Ebola-like in its effects, but it has no known precedent in the medical world. And despite its similarities to Ebola, its chemical architecture is entirely different. That's one of the many baffling components."

Dr. DaSilva goes on to explain that the virus, whose current shorthand name is the Austravid virus, was restricted to a small rural area twenty miles outside the city of Perth, Australia. Now the virus is moving toward the city itself and will likely reach beyond Perth, even beyond Australia.

"There are two things you need to know. First of all, this disease causes deaths that are more painful than those caused by Ebola or COVID. In the early stages, black pimples, bruises, and scabs form on the victims' skin. These areas crack open to become large craters of brownish-black blood that ooze and send the patients into screamworthy pain. No amount of hydromorphone or fentanyl variations can ease the suffering."

Even with my prior study of science and medicine, I am stunned by this information.

"And the second thing you want to tell me?" I ask.

"At the moment we cannot trace the source to any animal or botanical substance. No pig. No wolf. No horse. And, by the way, I've heard all the inappropriate gallows humor about koalas and kangaroos."

I don't even smile.

"As a result," I volunteer, "we must assume that this virus is man-made."

Dr. DaSilva silently nods.

I decide to address the one point that Anna DaSilva has not mentioned.

"Doctor, do you think that this Austravid is related to the natural disasters that are plaguing the Earth?"

She answers quickly. "I am impressed that you don't think the connection is impossible. Most people do. But the fact is, we simply do not know. That's why President Townsend and I want you and your colleagues involved."

Now would be a perfect opportunity to tell her of my extreme dislike for President Townsend (not to mention his hatred for me), but that feels petty and foolish at the moment.

For the first time in this conversation I notice that her soothing schoolteacher voice has transformed into an efficient businesslike demeanor.

"The government will fund a research investigation on your part. It'll be you, me, and your chosen team in Australia. I hesitate to say that money is no object, but it really isn't. Will you do it?"

The assignment is over-the-top dangerous. Should I do it? *Can* I do it? There is just one person who can help me decide. One person who is wise, thoughtful, and totally devoted to my vision of what the world should be like. I need advice. As soon as I disconnect from DaSilva, I ask that person for advice.

"Of course you'll do it," Margo says.

CHAPTER 33

IT'S AS SIMPLE as this: I have never been involved in a crisis as challenging and frightening as the one I am about to embark upon.

I assume that the unmarked government plane that takes me and my team from Andrews Air Force Base in Prince George's County, Maryland, to Western Australia flew with the approval of President Townsend. When I ask the passenger service coordinator aboard if that was the case, he responds with a smile and a vague statement.

"That could be the case, Mr. Cranston. Meanwhile, what kind of beverage may I get you?"

Well, so much for that. A few minutes later the coordinator brings me a Diet Pepsi. It will be the first of a dozen Diet Pepsis I drink before our landing.

I know that the average flight time between the eastern coast of the northern Americas and the western coast of Australia is twenty-four hours. But I can't stop drinking soda. I'm chewing the ice from my last beverage when the plane begins its descent.

I check my watch. Wow. This trip has lasted only ten hours.

"What's the deal?" I ask the passenger coordinator. "I thought this flight was supposed to be twenty-four hours. Are we early?"

"Apparently, sir," he says.

Ask a stupid question...

CHAPTER 34

AS PROMISED, DR. Anna DaSilva is there to greet us. I did a quick investigation of Dr. DaSilva, but all I could find—along with a long list of medical and professional awards and accomplishments—was that she is fifty-four-years old and unmarried. Meeting her in person doesn't do a lot to fill in the blanks.

One striking fact of her appearance is that she is wearing a biohazard jumpsuit.

We shake hands, and I say, "I see you're dressed for work."

"I'm always dressed for work," she says, unsmiling. "My work—and yours—is a twenty-four-hour job." Her delivery isn't rude, but it is definitely no-nonsense. I'll need to keep that in mind, and I'd better warn Hawkeye and Tapper, two guys with a lot of talent but a penchant for wisecracks.

As Dr. DaSilva checks and rechecks her phone, I study my surroundings. Frankly, there isn't much to study. One landing strip, with our one and only plane cooling and resting on the tarmac. No one else other than my colleagues and I have disembarked. No pilot. No copilot. Not even the overworked passenger service guy.

At the end of the landing strip is a small aluminum building that looks like an art deco diner from a few hundred years ago.

"Where's the crew?" I ask.

"Why do you need to know?" Dr. DaSilva says. Her voice remains gentle, but I don't like the evasion.

"Look, Mr. Cranston," she continues, but I interrupt with, "Please, call me Lamont," in an effort to break some of the ice.

Her voice becomes soothing.

"Look, Lamont. This is a terrible situation."

"I understand that, Doctor."

"Please, call me Anna," she says. Then she continues.

"I am so deep into the ugliness and potential destructiveness of the Austravid that I don't know who I am, where I am, how we can possibly get through this. I try to avoid answering questions that are not connected to the disease itself. I'll soften up as we start working together. Because, Lamont, I am honored and excited that you have agreed to help out."

"That's all I want to do," I say.

She talks quickly now. "I know who you are. I know what you're capable of doing. President Townsend has enormous respect for you—"

I can't resist.

"Might want to run a quick fact-check on that," I answer.

"President Townsend said to me yesterday before I left, 'I've gotten you the best person. I've gotten you the Shadow. Use him. Make sure you allow him to be the boss.' Is that your understanding of the situation?"

Now it's my turn, and I choose my words wisely, and I mean them.

"If we do this job right, Anna, there will be no need for designating power or supervision. We will be a team. We will get it done."

She nods and says, "Good. You and I and your team have a three-hour ride ahead of us. We're going into the deep forest where the outbreak is disastrous. Your equipment and your men will ride with us.

"We'll leave in ten minutes. In the meantime, let's go into air headquarters," she says, gesturing to the strange aluminum diner at the end of the runway. Then she adds, "We'll get you into some clothing and shoes that are... are... what should I say?"

"Slightly more protective?" I ask, staring down at my street clothes while gesturing at her biohazard suit.

"Yes," she says. "Protective. The more, the better."

CHAPTER 35

WE ARE OVERWHELMED by the horror of it all.

Only Anna is not shocked by the sight of the tiny downtown area of Bullsbrook.

Two main streets run side by side, one muddy, the other deadly, dusty dry. The few stores that once existed—a general store, a liquor store, a butcher shop—are shut down. Anna tells us that Red Cross food delivery is once a week. This is sometimes supplemented with containers of dehydrated fruits and vegetables, courtesy of the Australian government.

As depressing as the landscape of Bullsbrook is, the condition of the people who live there is even worse. Everyone walks slowly and carefully, like patients recovering from terrible operations. Most horrifying are the huge black splotches that cover their skin. Anna tells us that these wounds are intractable and terribly painful.

She arranges for us to interview a select group of victims. That isn't the easiest thing to do while wearing full-body negative-pressure biosafety suits with thick plastic hoods, but we do the best we can.

While Hawkeye weighs and evaluates a twenty-year-old mother and her twin four-year-old sons, I ask questions. Unfortunately, I already know the answers to most of them.

"How severe would you rate the pain where the sores are festering?"

The woman's sunken, vacant eyes take on an unexpected glow.

"I would say it is the pain of hell," she says. And as if to verify her comments, one of her little boys, his neck and shoulders a field of black and bloody dots, begins to sob.

I turn to Hawkeye. "Hand me the lidocaine," I say, asking for the strong pain-relief cream designed for severe topical pain.

"You can keep it," the woman says, shaking her head. "Dr. DaSilva gave us all lidocaine some weeks ago. It does nothing for no one. It was no better than the plum jam my grandmother gives us for our bug bites."

Who knows why the medication was ineffective. Perhaps it was from an unreliable pharma manufacturer. Perhaps it was... hell, who am I kidding? Look at this jungle of screaming, suffering people. It will not be controlled with a tube of pain cream. Bleeding black sores. Children stumbling and weeping. An entire town on the verge of devastation.

More patients, all suffering victims, line up. I consider morphine doses. I consider fentanyl. But Anna told me on our video call that none of the usually reliable painkillers helped against this virus. What we need now is a bigger, better, newer solution.

I try to ignore my own jet lag and nausea.

I do not trust myself to draw blood for testing. I ask Jericho to do that job, and of course, as always, he proceeds with speed and efficiency. I am eternally grateful every time I see him, having thought I'd lost him forever.

I am even more grateful when, later in the day, he reports that a preliminary analysis of blood samples indicates that a faulty gene similar to the one that causes Huntington's disease may be at work here.

Could it be? Could Jericho be onto something?

Dr. DaSilva seems to think it's viral in nature, and she is a woman who clearly knows her own business. I don't want to discredit anything Jericho believes he may have discovered, either. The only answer is to keep searching until we don't have any more questions. With that in mind, I turn to my next patient.

CHAPTER 36

MADDY, R.J., AND Belinda head to the maze of courts and courtrooms in downtown Manhattan.

R.J. insists he will be handling representation of Belinda at this next hearing, which has been postponed and rescheduled twice already. Maddy carefully suggests that she might be better suited for the job, given her recent success at court. When R.J. is adamantly opposed to that, she surmises that he sees this session as a chance to redeem himself. He has on clean clothes this time, at any rate.

This final hearing is like a trial, but it is not actually a trial. It is what the City of New York terms a "preliminary jury," six men and women who listen, confer, and then give their evaluation of the situation to the judge. The judge can overrule the jury's advice, but that is rare.

Belinda and Maddy sit at a small table. Belinda is dressed like the president of a bygone high school's Young Republicans Club: loose-fitting chino slacks, simple white cotton button-down shirt, a dark blue scarf around her neck. Maddy helped her with her outfit, still befuddled by the conservative clothing these young drug dealers seemed to prefer.

Maddy and Belinda are extremely anxious about R.J.'s performance, given his initial stumble. But his presentation is smart, powerful, downright eloquent. Gesturing frequently to the well-groomed Belinda, R.J. calmly and carefully presents the story of a very young woman who was abused by her family and mistreated by the NYC social services system, and fell into the role of drug dealing, just one more victim of that long-running epidemic.

Maddy keeps her eyes glued to the members of the jury. All six appear to be listening with sympathy. One woman on the jury—a pudgy little grandma—even seems to nod slightly when R.J. mentions "the tender confusion of vulnerable youth, and the regret that can follow them for the rest of their lives."

All is going well until R.J. sits down and the prosecuting attorney stands up. He is an energetic young man from the DA's office. He begins by saying that he agrees with how R.J. has presented the situation.

"Yes," he says, "I would, under most circumstances, suggest that this young woman be given parole and entered into a society-rehab program."

Maddy is cynical enough to know that there's a big *but* coming.

The prosecuting lawyer continues.

"But these *are not* 'most circumstances,' as you will see

when I share this video recording of our young *victim* from January of this year on the corner of 53rd Street and Third Avenue in Manhattan."

The entire room is treated to a video of Belinda speaking to a man whom the prosecutor describes as an undercover vice officer.

Belinda cannot contain herself.

"That's Bobby McCarthy!" she shouts.

The judge tells Belinda to calm down, and the video continues. Everyone watches as Detective McCarthy slips both his hands inside Belinda's unzippered jacket, emerging with two baggies, which he holds above his head, taunting her as she tries to get them back. Then the video abruptly stops.

The lawyer smiles. "The tape don't lie, man."

R.J. stands up quickly and speaks fiercely. "No, it doesn't lie. It's abundantly clear that this girl was robbed and attacked by a full-grown man."

The prosecutor, his voice dripping with sarcasm, says, "That's one point of view."

"Any other pertinent statements?" asks the judge, and when there are none, the advisory segment goes to the jury.

Belinda and Maddy are thrilled that R.J. actually came through for them. Now there's nothing left to do but wait for the jury to decide.

CHAPTER 37

IN SPITE OF R.J.'s eloquence and Belinda's let's-go-yachting costume, the advisory jury takes only twenty minutes to return with its advice. Ironically, the jury comments are delivered by the grandmotherly woman Maddy thought would be a slam-dunk sympathetic vote.

"It is the advice of this group that the offender under consideration be assigned to the youth detention facility for mental health and social rehabilitation, in Harriman, New York, for an amount of time deemed appropriate by New York City and this justice."

Maddy turns to Belinda and says softly, "Don't worry. I'll take care of this."

Maddy is about to do what she did previously: use her mind-control powers to influence the judge's thinking. And why not? She is certain she can get the judge to ignore the advice of the jury.

Belinda, hands shaking, eyes watery, looks at Maddy and says, "Don't. Don't do anything."

"I've got to do something. I can't let you go to that place," says Maddy. "You don't know what—"

"No. Absolutely not. Stay out of this," Belinda says, shaking her head.

Then they hear the judge say, "Person in advisory will report to New York City Circuit Court at a date within the next three weeks, a time to be assigned specifically by this court. I believe a residency at Harriman will prove beneficial to both the young woman and the community."

Belinda bows her head. Maddy shakes her head. Both of them, totally unplanned, speak together in a loud stage whisper.

"Bullshit."

CHAPTER 38

THE THREE OF them stand outside the courthouse on Centre Street. Maddy is angry. R.J. seems confused. Belinda shows no emotion at all.

"Why? Why in hell did you refuse to let me help you?" Maddy asks.

"I thought you were catching on, but you still don't get it, do you?" Belinda shoots back. "I'll be safer there than I am on the streets."

Maddy and R.J. look at each other, confused.

"Damnit," Belinda says. "Think! You saw the video. McCarthy is a piece of shit. Undercover, my ass. He might be put there by the NYPD, but he's on Carla Spector's payroll as well. He's making money off both sides, but the only person he's looking out for is himself."

Maddy nods, astonished at her own naive view of the situation. She thought she was the savior. But Belinda, the victim, is the wisest person there.

"We kids are disappearing," Belinda goes on. "Chloe's

gone, and she's gonna stay gone. And now my buddy Travis is missing. Somebody is stalking us because they know we're easy to get. Carla will just replace us. McCarthy isn't interested in protecting us. Jail is my best bet to stay alive."

Now Belinda begins to sob. Maddy embraces her. R.J. puts his hand on her shoulder.

"Who's Travis?" Maddy asks.

Belinda swallows, rubs her eyes. Then she speaks clearly.

"I had this friend, Travis. He was a skateboarder that ran drugs for Carla, sweet as sugar. Now he's gone, too, disappeared. I hate the idea of Harriman, but at least no one can murder me there."

There is a sad silence as the three of them stand on the crazy-busy street of downtown Manhattan.

Then Maddy says, "I know I've let you down, Belinda, but..."

"You haven't let me down. You did your best. You couldn't do anything better," says Belinda.

"No," Maddy says. "I can do more. I'm going to extinguish this monster. And while I'm doing it, I'm going to find Chloe and Travis and anyone else who—"

"That's kind of a big offer," R.J. says, his hand dropping from Belinda's shoulder, his face slipping into disapproval.

"Do you really think you can?" Belinda pleads.

"Yes." Maddy pauses for a moment, then says, "And I know just the people who can help make it happen."

CHAPTER 39

THE SAME PLANE that brought Burbank, Tapper, Hawkeye, Jericho, and me to that hellhole of a village in Western Australia takes us back home, at least temporarily. At least until we get organized. And the sooner the better.

I'm a perfectly capable manager, but I really don't enjoy organizing and leading a team. Being the Shadow and destroying evil is a great privilege. But people management? Not so much.

That's where my mind is as the plane takes off. My team and I are sitting at the airplane conference table, which is covered in papers and computers and sandwiches and cookies.

"Here's the situation," I say to my gang. "The two phenomena—the ongoing natural disasters and the strange, novel Austravid virus—may be related. I have no powers that allow me to predict the future, so we have to rely on old-fashioned groundwork.

"I'd like to hear what experts from other parts of the world are saying, not just those from the Americas," I say. "The Biomedical Engineering and Healthcare Technology Research Centre at the University of Johannesburg is the top biomedical research institute in the Southern Hemisphere. Hawkeye, immediately after we land at Andrews Air Force Base, you will travel to South Africa on our behalf. Speak to as many specialists there as you can, and *learn* as much as you can—fast."

"Great," Hawkeye says. "Nine more hours on an airplane. Looks like I'll be destroying evil and defending the good by drinking seltzer and eating chicken salad sandwiches."

Everyone laughs. Then I address the general group.

"As frightening as the virus is, I fear it's only a matter of time before it becomes a worldwide plague. But in my opinion the natural disasters are an even more imminent and dangerous threat."

Jericho asks, "How can you even differentiate which one of these horror stories is the scariest?"

"I cannot make a truly informed judgment," I say. "But I am smart enough to know that we have to dive in now. And you, Jericho, are the most qualified member of our team when it comes to earth science. So I'm sending you to join an ad hoc committee of amateur environmentalists meeting at the University of North Carolina in Chapel Hill."

Jericho grits his teeth to form a sort of I-should've-kept-my-mouth-shut expression as I continue to speak. "To be perfectly frank, I have some information that indicates that earth-formation testing near the University of Virginia and the University of North Carolina is showing signs of core soil erosion. So it's a good and dangerous place to be."

Burbank, the wise guy of the group, can't restrain himself. He looks straight at Jericho and says, "Ah, both good *and* dangerous. You should fit right in."

I let the laughter subside before I take the perfect opening to tell Burbank *his* assignment.

"Burbank, you will be headed to the Kyoto destruction site to sift through the rubble. Take multiple samples and calculate causes as to what—or who—is behind the geological disaster of the ages."

"With honor," says Burbank, who seems to know that the time for jokes is over.

"Excellent," I say. "And you, Tapper, will do the same with the sea around Copenhagen."

But Burbank's personality can be held at bay for only so long. Before Tapper can respond to his assignment, Burbank interjects with, "I just want to say that surveying an entire city sounds like a very big job for just one person... even if that person is me."

"Don't worry," I tell him. "Margo and I will be there with you."

"But I'm going to handle an entire sea on my own?" asks Tapper.

"You won't be alone for long. After we finish our work in Kyoto, we'll *all* join you as soon as we can."

CHAPTER 40

DACHE HAS NEVER been generous with praise to anybody. So Maddy, during this most recent training section, is astonished to hear him say, "I observe, Madeline, that there is significant improvement in your development."

"Yes, uh, thank you, sir," Maddy says.

They are concentrating today on one of the most advanced abilities—shape-shifting. This allows an ordinary person to actually transform their body into something else. A human being with this rare power can become a vicious writhing snake, a twenty-foot cement wall, an insect, a race car...whatever best fits their situation.

Dache has taught Maddy to immerse her entire body and soul into a different mental state, a state so flexible and strong that she's able to bring herself into a new plane of existence.

"This is not fantasy, Madeline. This is not the banal art of hypnosis. This is so much larger, a new reality. It is a reality that exists beyond who you actually are," he says.

Maddy thinks she might be ready to try. It has taken many lessons to override her own logic, to believe that her body can transform into something else. It's a perspective shift that can take years to master. Margo—who'd only been able to influence the minds of others when Maddy first met her—could harness the ability over the past few years, thanks to Dache's rigorous instruction.

Whenever Maddy feels doubt, the ability abandons her. But when she pushes herself, when she meditates so strongly that her mind seems to actually leave her body, then—and only then—can she become a speedboat, a leaf falling from a maple tree, a grain of sand, a raging wild horse, a child's toy.

Dache reiterates today what he has said during other lessons. It is Dache's mantra, and Maddy knows it must become her own.

Problems belong to all people. Solutions belong only to the chosen few.

When this most recent lesson ends, Maddy is a mass of nerves and pain. Her head aches and she wants to fall into a swimming pool of icy water to recuperate.

She lies on her bed, unable to sleep. She keeps hearing Dache's mental proverb over and over in her head, until she suddenly grasps the full meaning of the words: Like Lamont, Maddy is one of *the chosen few.*

She must seize the power. She must fix the problem. Lamont and Margo, Burbank, Jericho, Tapper, and Hawkeye are all busy literally trying to save the world. She can't ask them to drop everything to help with her problems. She must become the solution herself. She knows she can only succeed if she actually plunges into Belinda's grim world. She must go undercover. She must join them.

CHAPTER 41

HERE'S A PIECE of wisdom that I should permanently embed in my brain: just when you think you've seen it all, you can be almost certain that you haven't even come close.

That is certainly true when we disembark after landing in Kyoto. Margo, who has joined Burbank and me for the Japanese leg of our trip, literally freezes in place as we stand on the tarmac. That is how shocking the devastation is: mountains of rubble. No. I don't exaggerate. Mountains. Billions of pieces of concrete and marble and steel piled high into the air.

Our driver, Mr. Fujita, apologizes for the absence of a welcoming committee. He explains that so many people in Kyoto have been displaced or have disappeared that the city is barely functioning. In fact, Kyoto's famed super-speed railways have totally vanished. What few streets exist are narrow; the sparse traffic is slow. With so few people left to drive around, I'm not surprised.

"Look at this car I am driving, Mr. Cranston," says Mr. Fujita. "It is not even a car."

He's correct. The four of us are riding in a sort of a jerry-rigged tank, half jeep, half bulldozer. Few people walk the streets, and those who do, walk with their heads bowed. Some look sad. Some look angry.

For me the most astonishing sight is this: actual tunnels have been carved through many of the massive rubble piles, passageways for the few cars out on the streets.

"I thought nothing could beat the horror we saw in Australia—the death, the suffering, the chaos," Burbank says. "But this is even worse."

"Nightmares are often not the same," says Margo. "But they all frequently have similar components."

"Yes," I say. "And those components are exactly what you just said, Burbank: 'the death, the suffering, the chaos.'"

We stop suddenly at one of the huge mountains of destruction. I have no idea what separates this pile from the hundreds of others we passed along the way. Mr. Fujita, of course, notices the confused looks on our faces.

"Kyoto University stood here," he says. "But do not fear, an even greater one will rise once more."

Looking at the pile of broken concrete, twisted metal, and rusted rebar, I marvel that Jericho was able to get out alive.

"I admire your strength and energy, Mr. Fujita," says Margo. "How can you be so optimistic?"

"How?"

He pauses, then he speaks gently.

"I have hope for the future because Mr. Cranston is here with us."

I'm flattered, but I am also terribly, terribly scared.

CHAPTER 42

OUR ESCORT PARKS the not-quite-a-jeep and tells us to follow him through a man-made tunnel. We do as we're told, a journey of barely a few hundred feet. Both Burbank and I are carrying unwieldy pieces of sensitive equipment for surveying and managing the rubble. Margo and Mr. Fujita help as much as they are able, all of us struggling to keep a foothold as rocks slide out from under our feet.

We emerge on the other side of the tunnel and see a group of eight Quonset huts forming their own little island of peace amid the enormous mountains of debris. The one-acre area surrounding them is clear and clean but completely covered with thousands of dark red pebbles.

A carefully lettered sign is attached to a wooden post that rises from the ground. It might easily be a traffic sign or a historical marker. Mr. Fujita reads the Japanese characters aloud for us.

"It is a sign of hope," he begins. Then he reads, THE FORMER

AND PRESENT SITE OF KYOTO UNIVERSITY. ADMINISTRATION OFFICERS PRESENT IN OFFICES. ALL ACADEMIC INSTRUCTION LOCATED IN NORTH CAMPUS AREA.

Fujita explains that the North Campus now also houses a group of Quonset huts, located about a half mile from where we stand.

"But for now, Acting President Myoki anxiously awaits your visit in office number 3."

I realize that he expects us to follow him to the Quonset hut close by, but Margo, Burbank, and I are all so fascinated by the beautiful red stones covering the ground that we do not move. It is hypnotizing.

"Just a moment, please, Mr. Fujita. Before we meet the president, may we ask where the tiny red stones come from?" I say.

"They were natural remnants from the clearing of the debris, presumably from inside the rupture of the ground," he says. "When they were first distributed around the small temporary campus in the wake of the disaster, they were a light brown, some of them a dark beige. But one day, we awoke to see they had turned pink during the night. A few days after that we awoke to see that the pink had transformed into red."

Burbank, Margo, and I all nod and exchange glances with one another.

Mr. Fujita says, "Let us hurry now to go and greet the honorable president."

"Please inform the acting president that we may be a few

minutes behind schedule," I say. "We need to take this scene in, to understand it."

Luckily Margo understands and respects the importance of courtesy in Japan.

She adds, "Please tell the *honorable* president we sincerely regret the delay and send our deepest apologies."

CHAPTER 43

AS SOON AS Mr. Fujita leaves to alert the acting president of the postponement, Burbank removes a sonic measuring rod and its high-frequency evaluation screen from the equipment case he's been carrying.

"You've read my mind, my friend," I say to him.

"As did I," Margo says. "It's incredibly rude to keep the president waiting, but you just couldn't wait to get started, could you, Lamont?"

"Not when this could be an important discovery," I say, shaking my head. "And on our first day, too!"

Margo and I watch as Burbank forcefully but carefully pushes the control stick into the earth.

"How far can the extendable probe go?" Margo asks.

"About three meters," I answer.

Burbank does the math. "That's about ten feet," he says.

"Thanks for that," Margo says, sarcastically.

I am holding the information screen in my hand. It will soon be communicating the levels of pyroxenes and feldspars. These are the minerals most common in earth samples everywhere in the world. Sure enough, there are high levels of each.

"I'm pretty much totally extended. Let me try to get a little deeper with manual force," Burbank says as he pushes the testing probe deeper, until it is almost flush with the red pebbles.

"Right now I'm getting a water reading," I say, the excitement clear in my voice.

"What's the reading?" Burbank asks.

"I'm getting a notice of illite," I say. "That's just clay. Damnit. What the hell is going on?"

Leave it to Margo to have the answer.

"Rice," she says. "We're in Japan. Rice is farmed everywhere. Clay, along with the mineral illite, creates the best soil for growing rice."

Of course, after over two thousand years of rice growing, the entire Japanese chain of islands contains millions of tons of clay.

So much for a lucky break.

I stare at the screen. If only my mind training could force greater information onto this screen. But I'm an arrogant fool for even fantasizing such a possibility.

"Should I reel in the probe, sir?" Burbank asks.

"You might as—" I begin, but then there are three quick bright flashes on the screen. After each flash the screen continues to register the illite reading. What the hell is going on? I keep my eyes glued to that screen, and I'm rewarded with three more flashes. I tell Margo and Burbank what I'm seeing.

"I've seen that happen in some lab work," Margo says. "It usually means that there's a danger of radiation."

And then it all comes together—gamma radiation. Of course. That's precisely what Dr. Henry believed was happening in the natural disaster in Cambridge. The gamma radiation created waves of power at the nearby epicenters.

I share this theory with Margo and Burbank. They both think it makes sense. We wait a few seconds more. We hope for more information, and I hold my breath as the screen darkens, then brightens. Then the screen tells us something new.

NO POWER

The screen goes dark.

Yes, there must be some connection between the disaster in Cambridge and the disaster that took place here in Kyoto.

A clue. A good clue. An important clue.

But what the hell do we do with it?

CHAPTER 44

IF THE ACTING Kyoto University president, Mr. Myoki, is angry with us, he certainly doesn't show it. No, not at all. He tells us how grateful he is for our especially knowledgeable presence. He tells us that he and his family and staff are completely at our service and that the eminent doctor and professor Anna DaSilva claims I am the finest power in all of the Americas.

Satisfied as I am with Dr. DaSilva's glowing endorsement, I protest humbly to President Myoki that he should not get his hopes up.

"This is an extraordinary test," I tell him. "The challenge of a lifetime."

For the next two days, with the assistance of the staff, which truly is completely at our service, we test and retest square-acre areas of the land. Our industrious Japanese assistants use power shovels and front-end loaders to extract half-ton units of deeply buried land. Margo establishes an examination laboratory in the largest available Quonset hut. Because of the equipment we've sent ahead, she has managed to create a level of excellence that would be celebrated in any industrial pharmaceutical lab or university science hall.

But Margo and her new team fail to come up with any discoveries of their own. They concentrate on the red pebbles, all of which resolutely fail to change color inside the laboratory. Ultimately, the lab scientists tag them as common gravel. But, of course, that defies logic. They just can't be ordinary, but... what the hell are they?

Meanwhile, while Margo, Burbank, and I all appreciate the devotion and skill of our Japanese colleagues, it becomes clear that many of them are suffering from some form of PTSD. At least half of them will sporadically stop working and begin sobbing uncontrollably. The weeping seems to be strangely contagious. Work on any given site will end abruptly because the power-drive operator turns off his engine, bows his head, and begins shaking with tears. Within thirty seconds, scientists and dirt diggers and medical assistants join in the crying. We urge everyone to relax, take time out, rest. But we have no pill to give them, no mind-control ability to share.

So we face our frustrating jobs.

No hints. No clues. No progress.

Dr. DaSilva texts: I send my complete understanding for your problems. I am not surprised at your lack of advancement. Toughest challenge I've ever encountered. Keep at it. Should I join you?

I know Dr. DaSilva means to help, and that Burbank and Margo are here with me, but...no, no, no. That's not how Lamont Cranston rolls. I will do this. I will do it successfully. And I will do it myself.

CHAPTER 45

I FEEL COMPELLED to report to Acting President Myoki that we have made very little progress in identifying the source of the devastation to the Kyoto University campus. The look on his face clearly registers grave disappointment.

He says, "But, Honorable Mr. Cranston, we were so very much expecting success from you."

The most awkward silence possible follows. No doubt he's thinking that Dr. DaSilva's ringing endorsement has proven false.

What he doesn't know is that I'm afraid our lack of success may predict even more tragedy. With Kyoto and Harvard already demolished or devastated, what's next? Who's next? Oxford? The Sorbonne? Stanford? And what of the medical chaos in Australia? Is there, as we suspect, a connection between the earthly destruction and the virus poised to ravage the world?

Myoki, his eyes wet with tears, speaks softly.

"Tomorrow morning at dawn is the Shinto-Buddhist memorial service for Dr. Wellington Nakashima, former chairperson of our university science departments. Dr. Nakashima and his wife were both victims lost in the disaster. My hope was that we might have an answer to protect the living. I was hoping to announce a breakthrough as an honor to Dr. and Mrs. Nakashima, as well as the thousands of other faculty and students who are dead. But we will pray. No matter what, we will pray."

Talk about making a guy feel lousy. Both Margo and I bow our heads. Then I tell Mr. Myoki that we will work through the night but that it is unlikely we will uncover anything.

Mr. Myoki says our devotion is praiseworthy, but that Margo, Burbank, and I should rest to renew our hearts and minds.

"Tomorrow you should direct yourselves to the memory of the dead," he says. He turns away for a moment. I am certain that it is because he does not want us to see him weeping.

He turns back and adds, "Please honor my direction. My own heart tells me that you long to work, but my lips tell you that rest and prayer are what we all need."

Our arms and legs and backs are aching. Our minds are tormented by our fruitless endeavors. But we obey Myoki's advice.

We go to our Quonset hut. We try to sleep. We cannot. Margo and I discuss whether we should use our mind power to approach sleep, to control it, to fall deeply into rest, but we quickly agree that such an exertion for personal comfort would be selfish. Our powers are best saved for the demanding work ahead of us.

We nap. We wake. We nap some more. We wake again.

As the early morning sun begins to brighten our room, Margo has a suggestion.

"The memorial service should be starting just about now," she says. "We should go."

CHAPTER 46

FOUR GUARDS STAND at the double hut where the service for Dr. Wellington Nakashima and his late wife is about to begin. Because all of them have been working on our exploratory teams, they recognize us and bow slightly as we enter. We bow in return and join the fifty or so people who are already inside.

The room is beautiful, peaceful. I might call it holy. A sad celebration with a thousand white chrysanthemums and a hundred sticks of incense burning on the far side. Men and women bow to one another. Men wear black business suits; widows are dressed in black kimonos. So many of the mourners clutch prayer beads.

Margo and I join the line of people waiting to sign the large gold memorial book to honor the dead. As we step closer to the table where the book is resting, we see a handsome young Japanese man. He speaks and bows to each person who approaches.

"I think that's Dr. Nakashima's son, Jason. I've seen photographs of him on the internet," Margo whispers.

Then it is our turn to sign the document of mourning. Immediately the welcoming smile that greeted other guests disappears from his face. Because he does not bow to us, Margo and I bow to him. He does not return the gesture. Instead he yells—loud and angry.

"Your presence for mourning has not been requested!" he shouts. His words are loud, and his English pronunciation is impeccable.

Margo, Burbank, and I look at one another, not understanding the reason for his anger.

"What do you mean?" I ask.

"*YOU HAVE NOT BEEN INVITED!*" he says, shouting now.

As is often the case, I consider using mind control to calm the young man. Margo takes a wiser and less radical approach: sympathy and understanding.

"Please, honorable and sorrowful son, forgive our discourtesy. We are ignorant in the customs of Japanese funeral rituals. But..." Margo looks at me. Her assumption is that I will complete her thought. Miraculously, it comes to me. As always, the truth is easy to welcome.

"But we mourn your loss. We open our hearts out of respect to your father and your mother. If our presence disturbs you, we shall, of course, leave. But with your permission we long to stay and pray."

As cold and angry as his face looked, now everything changes. His eyes fill with tears. His lips quiver slightly. He bows, long and deep.

"Forgive me," he says. "You both honor my late parents with your presence. Please stay."

CHAPTER 47

THREE HOURS LATER Margo and I are having tea with Jason Nakashima. We are seated on the floor of his very small, very simple Quonset hut. Burbank returned to the disaster site to continue collecting soil samples after we paid our respects at the funeral.

"I must continue to apologize for my angry outburst," he says as he pours tea into our pale green cups.

"You must understand," he goes on. "This is particularly painful for me. Not only because of the death of my beloved mother and father but also because I... I could have... might have... could have been able to prevent it."

Margo jumps in immediately. "Nothing could have prevented what happened here. The destruction of Kyoto and the university was an incredible catastrophe of nature."

I add, "Even now we have no idea what caused it. We do not even know how we might prevent it from happening again."

"I know. But let me explain my role in this matter. It

may help you to understand the depth of my sorrow," Jason urges, seeking understanding.

I'm concerned about what his role might have been. The wide-eyed look on Margo's face tells me that she is also anxious for the explanation.

Jason begins his story.

"My father, as chairman of the science department, taught only one seminar, nothing more. Only five students, the smartest of their study levels, were admitted to the class."

"What was the subject of your father's class?" Margo asks.

"Whatever he wanted," says Jason. Then quickly: "My father was so brilliant that anything he had to say was valuable—the history of DNA enhancement, the future of space science, the application of Buddhist philosophy to medical healing—no topic was off-limits. His students respected him, even loved him."

"Yes," I say. "I understand having such a relationship. I have one with a teacher myself."

Jason nods and continues.

"A few weeks before the disaster, my father told my mother and me that he had been receiving disturbing anonymous emails and text messages from someone he believed was a former student of his at Kyoto. He described this student as very smart but socially off-balance, some-one who would often argue with his classmates and disrupt sessions. My father was not merely a brilliant man; he was also a kind man. He tried to reason with the student privately, but to no avail. My father's only choice was to ask him to leave his seminar."

Margo asks, "Do you have copies of the emails and texts he received?"

"Of course," Jason replies. He taps his phone and begins reading random messages:

Your ignorance and arrogance will cause the downfall of this school.

The blood that will flow through Japan will be on your hands. Your phony British name is a tragedy for Japan and you.

The mountains will crumble. The rivers will rise higher than the mountains. The pain will be unbearable. And you will be the cause.

"My father was unsure whether to inform the university president of these communications. He asked us for advice. My mother believed that this information needed to be shared. And as for me, I told him it was the foolish ramblings of a disappointed egotist, and that paying attention to him would only encourage him. I urged my father to ignore the messages."

The more Jason tells us, the more distraught he becomes, guilt clearly plaguing his conscience.

"Let's go for a walk, Jason," I suggest. "This tiny room feels like it's closing in on all of us."

We drink the last of our tea and walk outside.

CHAPTER 48

THE THREE OF us find one of the tunnels near the closest mountain of debris. Unfortunately, my suggestion to escape the small hut also exposes us once again to the stench of rotting flesh that permeates this place. We all begin walking more quickly.

"Did your father respond to any of the messages or emails?" I ask.

Jason shakes his head. "He listened to me. He ignored them."

"Did he ever identify the student by name? Do you have any idea who it could be?"

"None at all. My father taught thousands of students over the years and did not want to surmise his identity, for fear of smearing an innocent person's name."

I tell Jason that I'll need to investigate all of his father's electronic equipment, that my colleagues, especially Burbank, will be able to unlock information stored on his father's machines.

"Unfortunately I don't have any of my father's equipment. After the tragedy, I did what I should have done much earlier. I spoke to the police investigation unit and told them about the deranged student. They immediately confiscated anything electronic, as well as hard-copy messages, from the equipment he kept at home," says Jason. "Of course, everything that had been in his office was lost to us."

"We can talk to the investigation unit," I say. "Or, if need be, we can have Acting President Myoki intercede for us and have all of your father's material released."

Jason laughs, the bitter kind that has no humor at all.

"Both Mr. Myoki and I have already asked for the return of the confiscated equipment," says Jason. "The commissioner of the investigation told us to come back in fifty years. That's when it's scheduled to end."

He says all material related to the investigation has been handed over to the military police. All pertinent matter—at least what survived—is being stored and guarded in a secure locker.

"It's impossible to break in," Jason says.

My response is simple.

"Impossible for anyone else, perhaps."

CHAPTER 49

AT THREE IN the morning Margo and I approach the four connected Quonset huts where Jason told us the Japanese government's investigation is housed, along with their files and equipment. It's cold and rainy, and the smell of decomposing bodies hangs heavily in the air.

Although the small complex of huts has no identifying signage, it stands out from the others. It is surrounded by six armed guards; the four men and two women carry rifles and electronic equipment. They all wear suits made of the Japanese-manufactured chemical compound Ganko, a virtually impenetrable material made from a combination of elastomers and advanced polyurethane.

"This isn't going to be easy," I say to Margo.

"Then why do you look so happy?" she asks, a smile of her own pulling at her lips as we approach the guards.

I am always amazed by how well Margo knows me, as if we are on the same wavelength. She's right. The delays, the setbacks, the lack of progress on this trip, have me frustrated.

Right now, I believe we have a chance to learn something, and that does make me happy, danger be damned.

I turn to her, my smile spreading. "As much as I like how you look, I believe it may be time for a change."

"Ah, what did you have in mind?" Margo asks. She knows I'm not talking about a new haircut or color. We're about to use our shape-shifting powers. Right here. Right now.

Worms, snakes, roaches, and rats all have exceptional invasive powers, yet none of them has the strength and power necessary for hand-to-hand combat.

Margo suggests the Japanese scarab, one of the few insects that Dache himself taught us to inhabit in order to utilize the scarab's powers of flight and speed, not to mention a nasty set of pincers.

But today we need something different. Nothing large, nothing noisy, nothing flashy.

Would it be too challenging and risky to change into another human being? A new guard? Yes, we agree that it will.

As we are debating, one of the guards shouts out in Japanese, "Examination of weapons."

Each of the six guards twists a small lever on the magazine release of their gun, then clicks it back into place.

The man who gave the original order shouts again, "Number Two! Test!" One of the guards, presumably Number Two, fires the weapon into the air.

Margo and I reflexively cover our ears but soon discover that we don't need to. The weapon is absolutely silent.

The test over, all six guards return to their positions.

Margo turns to me and speaks quietly but with a note of excitement in her voice.

"Pika," she says.

"Pika?" I repeat. "What the hell is that?"

CHAPTER 50

MARGO EDUCATES ME quickly: a pika is a small furry creature that lives in the mountains of Japan, like a koala bear, only smaller and nowhere near as cute. Because of the destruction of the mountains, the tough little animals have fled to the rubble-strewn cities of Japan to join other animals—dogs, cats, and pigs—in a desperate search for food. Their hunger has made the pikas vicious.

It's a bit of a struggle to transform myself into one of these obscure mountain terrors, since I don't have the best idea of what they look like. But once Margo has shifted, it's much easier.

"You are definitely as cute as a koala bear," I inform her, before I shift my own form.

Once inside, we return to our normal selves, and for the first time on this mission we experience a bit of luck. In front of us is a door marked with a sign: EVIDENCE ROOM. Inside, we find boxes of hard drives and stacks of files, as well as ten personal computers lined up in a row like the stone monuments at a cemetery. A home for the dead? No way. We soon discover that the room is very much alive... with information.

Margo is the first to make a discovery: a handwritten note on a piece of thick elegant paper:

> Ignore my messages as you see fit, but you are foolish to do so

As Margo continues to read aloud the contents of hard-copy messages, I snap a hard drive labeled *Nakashima* into my personal handheld computer.

> You can ignore my brilliant ideas. My algorithms. My theorems. My biochemical discoveries. But you cannot ignore my promise, a promise to disrupt and destroy you and everyone in your domain.

The threats, the tone, the absolute coldness of the notes, are all the same. Although Jason told us earlier that his father did not know who was sending them, Margo and I see that both these messages have been signed with the lowercase letter *h*. Indeed, as we quickly sort through other emails, notes, and texts, we discover that this simple one-letter signature closes them all.

We keep reading as fast as we can, disturbed only when we hear an occasional noise from outside. When we hear the shouts for another weapons check, we realize that we are pressing our luck by remaining here.

"Just a few more minutes," I say.

"Fine," says Margo, "but we have to enter into the pika shape-change soon. We can't be caught in here. You're a highly recognizable person."

She's right, but I'm too intrigued by a new message I've found to listen. "Look at this one," I say as I hold up my screen.

"It's totally encrypted," she says. We are both looking at a long jumble of English letters and Japanese characters. There are a few images that we can identify—some numbers, a question mark, a ridiculous smiling emoji—but beyond those things, the document is gibberish.

"We've got to get this deciphered by Burbank or Jericho," I say.

"Which we can't possibly do if we're caught," says Margo pointedly.

I pause and look around the room; Margo's eyebrows go up.

"Just give me a second to enjoy myself," I say. "We're finally onto something."

CHAPTER 51

MADDY IS READY to go undercover. Really undercover.

Wardrobe and makeup are an easy fix for her. She's a very young-looking twenty-one-year-old to begin with, so eliminating makeup and leaving her hair loose is all that's needed. This accentuates her soft, pale skin. When she looks in her bedroom mirror, she smiles at her image. Maddy could pass as a cheerleader for a junior varsity football team. An inexpensive gold chain, a pair of faded not-too-tight jeans, a snug white T-shirt. The crowning piece of the costume is an old favorite, something that she wore almost daily when she was in middle school—a faded olive-green shacket from Forever 21.

But she realizes that this is no Halloween costume party. This is the real world, and her intrusion into a very dark part of it is truly frightening. She has to admit to herself that she's scared. Yes, she keeps reminding herself that she's worked hard with Dache, that he's even assured her (in his own stern way) that she has mastered the teachings of the master. But Dache is still a man in a man's world, and Maddy is about to wander into the worst place to be a female.

She's got to do it. Belinda and the other girls need her. No matter what she encounters, she has to remember that they live like this, with no hope of escape. Her undercover is their everyday.

At one o'clock in the morning, Maddy joins a group of young people gathered at the 59th Street Bridge.

The start of her adventure begins badly. In fact, it begins very badly.

Maddy arrives quietly and leans against the side wall of a luxury apartment building. A few yards away from her is another girl, clearly working the same job as Maddy. They exchange a glance, and after a minute or two the other girl walks quickly toward Maddy.

"You're Belinda's friend," the girl says.

"How'd you know that?" is what Maddy says.

"Belinda told me a few days ago that her new 'guardian angel' was thinking of joining us," says the girl. Then she adds, "So, you're a cop, right?"

"No," Maddy says. "I work for the public defender's office, but I'm here on my own."

"Bullshit," says the girl. "Here on your own for what? You tried, girl, but everything you're wearing is expensive labels. You don't need a dime, and you ain't here for—"

"I want to help," Maddy says, quickly cutting her off.

The girl's eyes narrow. "Like I say, bullshit."

The girl yawns and smiles just a tiny bit. Then she says, "No difference to me, you want to take a walk on the wild side. Just get off my corner. You filch my customers, I'll tear that expensive hair out by the roots."

So much for caring about others, Maddy thinks to herself, as she slinks away from the girl.

CHAPTER 52

HEADLIGHTS FROM TRAFFIC on the bridge above give the area below, the area where the girls are waiting for drop-offs and pickups, a weird theatrical glow. Shadows come and go rapidly, the lights in the surrounding apartment buildings flicker on and off, car horns blare, and tires screech. People on the nearby streets shout to one another, and sirens add an even greater sense of madness to this New York, this job, this place.

Maddy has become both a participant and an observer. She notices two SUVs arriving, leaving, and then returning to the area at least five times. Sometimes they pick up girls; sometimes the driver hands them packages through the window. Then the girl checks it—for an address or a name, Maddy thinks—and heads out on foot. Both these vehicles are black BMWs. One is driven by a bored-looking middle-aged man. The other BMW is driven—to Maddy's surprise—by a very beautiful Black woman. How a fellow female can allow these girls to live on the edge like this is beyond her. But she quickly realizes that her surprise is actually naivete. Hadn't Detective McCarthy himself told her that the person at the top of this operation was a woman, Carla Spector?

Maddy stands near a filthy loading truck stinking of rotted food. On the other side of her sits a sparkling-clean yellow snowplow. She wonders why, in late summer, a snowplow is sitting, all set to go, under the 59th Street Bridge.

"I've never seen you here before," a whisky-raspy woman's voice says. Maddy turns around and sees a woman who looks like she's probably forty-something but is trying hard to look half that age. Lots of white makeup, lots of cheap black hair dye, thighs squeezed into red tights. She's clearly working a different kind of job than the underage drug mules, participating in the world's oldest line of employment.

"Yeah. It's my first time up around here," says Maddy, surprised at how calm she is when she speaks to this tough-looking woman.

"Listen, hon. It's crowded enough up here." Her eyes trail up and down Maddy's clothing, then one side of her mouth curves. "Never mind. We're not selling the same thing, are we?"

"Doubt it," says Maddy, who suddenly realizes that if she should be approached by a buyer, she has nothing to sell—which could land her in a serious problem.

"You got a new friend, Mama-Girl?" one of the girls asks, coming to the prostitute's side.

Mama-Girl? Who is this woman? Some weird street sorority mother?

"We've got a loiterer," Mama-Girl says, still eyeing Maddy. "Too well-dressed to be one of you. Too, well… *dressed* to be one like me."

Remembering the very specific threat from the first girl on the street, Maddy asks, "You're not going to tear my hair out by the roots, are you?"

The woman and the girl look at each other, then break out into laughter.

"Aw, hell no," the streetwalker says. "Women got to look out for each other out here; that's how I roll."

"Especially now," the younger girl says, her eyes cast down.

"What do you—" But Maddy doesn't get to finish her question, as the BMW with the male driver slows down near them.

"Oh, great, Gerard the asshole," says Mama-Girl, her voice suddenly tight.

"Who's Gerard?" Maddy asks, trying hard not to sound frightened.

"I just told you. Gerard is an asshole," says Mama-Girl.

"He's one of Carla's enforcers," says the girl. "Makes sure we get to where we need to be, on time." She starts to backpedal, clearly not wanting to be seen.

As soon as she says that, Gerard spots her, and his face contorts in anger.

He jumps out of the car and grabs the girl, throwing her up against the vehicle.

"You fucked up again, Kailyn. You fucked up big time. That fat-ass Doc Katz was expecting you at the Soho Grand at midnight. On the dot," Gerard shouts. "I texted twice to remind you. But you was too fucked-up to remember, am I right?"

Two other girls move to join the scene, one of them brave enough to speak up. "Nah, man, Kailyn's clean. Just, like, her phone was dead, or something."

Mama-Girl steps forward, lightly caressing Gerard's bulging biceps. "How about you drop the child and pay attention to a real woman?"

"A carcass, you mean?" Gerard shoots back, still pressing Kailyn against the BMW. "Nobody wants your worn-out ass, Jennifer. Now, get out of here before I stomp you."

At least they're trying to help their friend. Maddy doesn't know what the hell to do. But she has a sense that the fan is going full blast, and a dangerous pile of shit is about to hit it.

CHAPTER 53

"YOU'RE HURTING HER," Mama-Girl shouts, dropping any attempt at seduction as she slaps at Gerard's arms. "Let go of my girl!"

But Mama-Girl's shout just seems to make the attacker squeeze Kailyn even harder. As she screams, another huge BMW screeches up to the scene. Maddy is expecting the female driver. But no. Instead two very large men jump out of the car.

For a moment Maddy thinks they might actually be NYPD. But as soon as they shove Mama-Girl to the ground and one of them slaps the young girl who tried to intervene, Maddy's hope is totally shattered.

What isn't shattered, however, is her almost crazy determination to handle the situation.

Of course, she thinks. If she can do something, she sure as hell better do it now.

The intense training she received from Dache—his stern instructions, her own tough determination—is no longer theoretical. She is not in the safety of her bedroom or backyard. This is the real world. These are real people. Villains? Innocents? Enemies? Friends? What the hell difference does it make? She's got to get on it. Like those cheap greeting cards: LIFE HAS NO DO-OVERS.

Maddy concentrates until she hears Dache's voice inside her head.

Dismantle and eradicate all other mental interference.

She tries with everything inside her to honor Dache's directive.

And to her own astonishment, she feels she might succeed.

Embrace the talent that embraces only you. Focus, Madeline.

Madeline! She's begged Dache not to call her that, but it is that infuriating word that sets her free.

Her entire body snaps spontaneously into judo position. Effortlessly, she thrusts her right leg upward and executes a brutal upsweep kick to Gerard's back. He immediately drops Kailyn. Then, as the two other men run at her, Maddy executes a perfect ankle throw. Both men tumble to the ground.

Maddy senses that everything she does from here on out is going to be absolutely perfect. She has become another person, another power. Is this how it feels for Lamont?

The men and Gerard struggle to rise. Maddy isn't frightened, but these guys clearly are. All three make a break for their vehicles. They stumble. One falls. Before they can get to their cars, Maddy gets to them.

Using the speed and strength of her mental hands, she grabs them by their shirts and flips them hard against the concrete.

She hears Mama-Girl yell out, “Kick him in the—”

But she doesn’t have to hear the end of the sentence to know what Mama-Girl says, and she does exactly as advised, Gerard letting out a rough *whoosh* of air that moves the pebbles in front of his mouth.

Dache might not approve of that last part, but he’s never had to walk the streets at night as a woman.

CHAPTER 54

THE SUNNYTIME DINER would fit perfectly in, say, Kansas or South Dakota. The place has five twirling counter stools covered in fake-marbled plastic. There are four booths for customers, and there's not only a Coca-Cola dispenser but also one devoted exclusively to Orange Crush.

But Sunnytime is not in some faraway state. No, Sunnytime is at 59th Street and First Avenue, a little more than a block east of the bridge.

At three o'clock in the morning, six people are squeezed into a booth designed to accommodate four.

This is an impromptu event arranged by Maddy, the person who only two hours earlier was demonstrating her extraordinary skills as a fighter. Some of the young drug runners working the 59th Street Bridge area were afraid she was an NYPD decoy. Now they don't know what to think. One thing is certain, though—they want Maddy on their side.

Maddy has a tale to tell, and Mama-Girl suggested they

move away from their "office" and settle in Sunnytime... what she calls "the break room." Then she adds, "A good story is always improved by a plate of great flapjacks and shitty coffee."

Everyone agreed, and the group is about to collectively destroy twenty-five pancakes and three carafes of coffee. When Maddy surveys the crowded table, she can't keep herself from counting that among them all, they're about to consume twenty-five pancakes.

Although Maddy is paying, she's not eating. These girls need the food more than she does, and besides—her job here is to talk.

CHAPTER 55

"YOU ALL FIGURED out by now that I'm not police. I'm just an ordinary person like the rest of you."

Kailyn immediately interrupts.

"Don't go spoiling everything by starting to lie, girl. You're no ordinary person. We just saw you wipe out one of New York's ugliest, toughest groups of scumbags ever. So don't go saying—"

"Okay, so I have a few special skill sets," Maddy admits. "I want to use those skills to do something that needs doing. To help you. All of you."

She takes a big gulp of Sunnytime's particularly lousy coffee, then continues talking.

"I know that some kids in your line of work have disappeared. Two of them that I know about are a girl named Chloe and a boy named Travis."

Interruption time again. A girl Maddy vaguely remembers—a tall, skinny red-haired girl with a concerned look on her face—speaks up: "They're only the tip of the hot dog. And don't fuck with me, I'm being funny. I know it's supposed to be 'iceberg.'"

"Shut it up," says one girl. "This is serious stuff. Plus your joke sucks."

"The only person here that sucks hot dogs is me," Mama-Girl says, her fork in the air. "But Jacine is right. It ain't just Chloe and Trav. There's been Rosella, Jada, and Melissa and maybe even five or six more."

She leans in toward Maddy. "I could go on and on. Listen, I try to watch out for these girls, but the men who run this show are brutal, and the woman at the top is even worse. You want to know where Trav and Chloe are? Try the cemetery. Try the Gowanus Canal. Try heaven."

It suddenly seems that no one is interested in their food anymore. All forks are down.

With all the very real sincerity that's inside her, Maddy says, "Then, help me. I can't do anything to protect you if I don't have information."

And they do. Slowly at first, with one girl speaking, then another nudging her friend, who also chips in. The group gains momentum, and soon they are interrupting one another, contradicting and teasing. But they are talking.

They all agree that right around the time Chloe and Travis disappeared, there was a Cadillac that had been driving around the bridge for quite a few days. Not one of their regular drivers or drop-offs.

"And not any of the usual johns," Mama-Girl chimes in.

"Was it a big Cadillac?" Maddy asks.

"No," says one of the girls. "It was a small SUV, like the Cadillac XT4 from back in the 2020s."

"How do you know so much about cars, girl?" says someone.

"There's lots of stuff I know that you don't know I know. Ask me state capitals. Go ahead. Ask me. Nevada, Carson City..."

Maddy jumps in. "What color was the car?"

No arguments. Everyone agrees that it was dark green. And, no, no one thought to write down the license plate. And, no, since the car windows were shaded dark, no one has any idea what the driver looked like.

Or so it appears, until a pretty girl with a southern accent says, "I don't exactly know what the man looked like. But I was kneeling behind a pile of stacked-up traffic cones one night, trying to hide from that piece of shit McCarthy. I saw the car door open up, and some white guy stepped out and took a pee."

"Can you tell me what he looked like?" Maddy asks, but the girl only blushes. Kailyn is the first to catch on.

"Since you were kneeling you saw his dick, but not his face, am I right?"

"Wonder if I would've recognized him," Mama-Girl says, brow furrowed in concentration.

"Yeah. That's right," says the southern girl, still blushing. "But I heard him talking on his cell. He had, like, a French accent."

"Like, how'd it sound? Try it out on me," says Mama-Girl.

The southern girl tries on a French accent. She ad libs, "I'm on my way back now, or something like that."

"You sound like you always do, like a girl who just got off the airplane from Atlanta," says Kailyn.

The southern girl says, "Well, shit, I don't know. Maybe it was more like German?"

French? German? Maddy knows she's not going to get an accurate sound description.

"It's okay," says Maddy quietly. She can see that the girl is embarrassed that she can't mimic the accent. "You've all helped a lot. I've got way more to go on now than I did a few hours ago."

A green car. A man with an accent.

It's not a big start. But it's something.

CHAPTER 56

OUR BODIES ACHE. Our brains ache. But Margo, Burbank, and I carry with us a tiny bit of hope as we travel from Kyoto to Copenhagen.

Copenhagen, like Kyoto, is an extraordinary site of damage and destruction. But each of these cities is distinctly different in its kind of physical ruin. While Kyoto was a mass of stones and concrete and dirt, Copenhagen is a swamp of battered buildings. Rivers flow where streets once were, and sad citizens paddle along in makeshift rafts.

We are greeted by a seriously despondent Tapper. After our discovery of the warnings to Dr. Nakashima in Kyoto, we asked him to find out whether anyone who'd been present the day of the tidal wave had received similar messages. He has been trying with little success to uncover any threats that might have been sent to academics in Copenhagen.

"Here's what I have, and it isn't much," says Tapper. "I went through hundreds of messages, maybe a thousand, received by personnel at a bunch of schools: Technical University of Denmark, Roskilde University, even the Royal Danish Academy of Fine Arts. I examined the files of professors, visiting professors, student teachers, even the correspondence of maintenance workers and secretaries."

As the list grows, energy leaks out of Tapper's tone. Then he stretches out his arms in a kind of despair. "What in hell do I have to show for it?" he says loudly. He is clearly a man on the brink.

I am all too familiar with Tapper's sense of frustration. I've been there. I *am* there right now. But I have neither the time nor the urge to play baby nurse and dispense comfort to my colleague.

"Exactly," I say, somewhat sternly. "What the hell *do* you have to show for it?"

"That won't take long," warns Tapper.

He snaps some buttons on his electronic device and shows me four messages that may be pertinent. Like the messages sent to young Jason's late father in Kyoto, they are threatening and harsh. They promise tragedy if they are ignored.

Margo reads them as well, then leans back. "The first thing we have to do is speak to the people who received these messages. Who are they? Did they survive the tsunami?"

"One is a revered Danish botanist. Another is an honored female professor of ancient Scandinavian literature. The last is a Swedish teaching assistant who had only been in Copenhagen two weeks—and they're all at the bottom of the Baltic Sea."

What can I do? What can I be? We can shape-shift into deep-sea diving creatures and scrape the bottom of the sea. But we have no ability to bring the dead back to life.

"But there is one other thing," Tapper says.

Margo, Burbank, and I glance up hopefully.

"What? For God's sake, what?" I say.

"There is one survivor. I was about to tell you—"

"Tapper!" yells Margo. "Dear God, don't you know the proper order in which to relay information?"

I reach out, covering her hand with mine. "He's not married," I remind her. "He hasn't had that kind of training."

"Well, *get* married," Margo snaps at Tapper.

"Or," Burbank suggests, "just go ahead and share the good news."

CHAPTER 57

"HER NAME IS Langi Singh," Tapper says. "She is originally from Pakistan. Now she is a professor of physics at the Technical University of Denmark. That's the good news." He looks carefully at Margo, as if checking if he can continue. She waves him on.

"She's currently in the intensive care unit of Rigshospitalet, the most respected hospital in Copenhagen."

Tapper tells us that her survival was miraculous. Thousands died in the tsunami at the awards ceremony, but for reasons that no one can discern, Ms. Singh, a thirty-five-year-old woman who had never even learned to swim, made it through. She was found unconscious on the penthouse roof of an apartment building in Nyhavn, a fashionable section of the city. The woman was alive, but both her legs had been broken, and she had lost total hearing in her right ear. Equally serious, her right lung was filled to near capacity with water, dirt, and grit.

Burbank joins Margo, Tapper, and me in the small intensive care room where Langi Singh lies, hooked up to two IV drips as well as an oxygen nose clasp. Her legs are swaddled in large casts and suspended by wires from above her.

Ms. Singh's eyes are closed when we enter, but she must feel our very presence, because as we approach her bed, her eyes open.

Margo, with a gentle voice and authentic concern, speaks. "Good morning, Ms. Singh. Are you feeling well enough to talk?"

The injured woman replies with her own question, her voice surprisingly strong.

"Are you doctors?" she asks.

"No," Margo says. "We are here to investigate the great tsunami, the one that you managed to survive."

"If you call this survival," Ms. Singh says, nodding slightly toward her bound and bandaged body.

"We understand, but if you could, we are hoping you might answer a few questions," says Margo.

The woman in the bed asks simply, "Danish?"

"No, we're American," I say. "Why do you ask?"

"Can you *get* me a Danish, I mean," Langi says, a smile curling the edge of her mouth as she nods toward a side table. "My arms work, so I can feed myself," she says. "Just can't reach them."

We all laugh along with her as Margo hands over the pastry. This woman clearly will be able to survive.

Carefully, in between bites, she begins to tell us her story.

CHAPTER 58

ALMOST A YEAR ago, Langi Singh received a research proposal from a man who told her that he was constructing the largest and most powerful microwave radiation generator the world had ever seen.

She pauses, a pastry halfway to her mouth, to side-eye us all. "Do not imagine a huge microwave for one of your midwestern potlucks. No. This man was constructing a weapon of mass destruction."

The writer was submitting parts of his plan and proposal to Professor Singh anonymously. This was, of course, for reasons of confidentiality and self-protection, but also because when he had previously shared his idea with a few colleagues, they had mocked him. Because of Singh's successes in the same field and her reputation as a forward-thinker, the anonymous writer thought she might be interested but still wanted to be very cautious. He worried that his idea was so great, his blueprints so perfect, that others would steal it.

"Frankly, I was intrigued," Langi Singh tells us. "Not that a male academic would be worried that his idea was so brilliant someone would steal it. No, that's pretty standard," she says. Then she holds up her index finger, biting another pastry in half before she continues to speak.

"It was," she says, "an outlandish idea. At that moment, I was working on a molecular research project designed to modify and access the benign atomic particles in simple coal, and I simply did not have time to deal with a new project. I emailed back to him and said as much."

Langi then tells us that this refusal caused a flood of dramatic and frightening communications from the passionate inventor. They were so unnerving that she can recite them even now—and they are identical to the threats that Dr. Nakashima was sent in Kyoto, holding promises of destruction and annihilation.

She answers, unprompted, the question that I am about to ask.

"He always signed the communications with the letter *h*," she says. "Until he began signing them 'Hephaestus.'"

"Hephaestus," repeats Tapper. "That's a Roman god."

"Not quite," Professor Singh corrects him. "A Greek god. The god of fire and volcanoes, among other things. Hephaestus was also incredibly ugly, so I found it to be an odd choice."

None of us needs further interpretation to make the connection between the recent natural disasters and the power of Hephaestus. The similarity is obvious, maybe *too* obvious.

Now Langi Singh begins the most astonishing part of her story.

She says that on the morning of the Copenhagen awards ceremony she received a text message that has haunted her ever since the tsunami, the words never leaving her mind.

> Ignore me today and you will never ignore me again
> My plan will succeed today. You will see and suffer
> At the award service all attendees will be awarded with pain

As we all confront the content of the message, the hospital room becomes silent except for the soft whirring buzz of the medical machinery.

Finally, Margo asks, "So you avoided the award ceremony because of the message you received?"

"Perhaps that text was the reason," she says, shrugging. "I am a woman in a competitive field. Threats are not unknown to me. I hated the idea of bowing to him, or even giving this madman enough credit to take him seriously. I had my own studies to concern me, and so I chose to skip the ceremony and proceed with my work instead."

"A wise choice," I say. "And one I am glad you made."

CHAPTER 59

OUR DILIGENCE AND energy are leading to some lucky breaks, but they are not truly *breakthroughs*. What to do but keep on trying? What to do while the world stands on the very brink of destruction?

As the four of us ride toward Kastrup, the main Copenhagen airport, Margo says, "The world is completely on hold. People are frozen in decision-making. Should we have a baby? Should we plan a holiday? Should we get married? No one is planning their future, because they don't know if any of us has one."

As we all pass through the private government security gate at Kastrup, I receive a text from Dr. Anna DaSilva: Conditions in Australia worsen. Deaths increase. Confusion reigns. Talk very soon.

Dr. DaSilva's news is so simple and so depressing that we barely discuss it as we take our seats on the plane.

A few minutes later an attendant approaches us, I assume to take our beverage order.

Instead she says, "The captain is coming back to speak to you." Sure enough, the captain appears within seconds.

"Mr. Cranston. We have been blocked from takeoff. I have no special information, but air traffic has informed me all aircraft must stay grounded. This is a worldwide order, because of a dynamic breakout of Newbola—"

Burbank interrupts. "Newbola? What the hell is that?"

"It's the virus spreading—that is on the verge of becoming a pandemic. You don't know about it?"

Margo says, "Yes, we know about it. We just didn't know it has a new name. I thought it was called Austravid."

"The media must have rechristened it as Newbola," I say. Then I ask the captain to continue.

"The Newbola virus has shown up in Venezuela, Detroit, Honolulu, Moscow, Melbourne, Tokyo—it's everywhere. So far, the death toll is low. But no one wants to take any chances. Nobody is being let in or let out of anywhere. The world has been shut down."

As I look at my companions' faces, I know they are having the same thought I am—we've recently been in some of those places.

"Is it possible that we could receive some sort of special clearance?" I ask the captain.

"Queen Margarethe is sitting on the tarmac a few thousand yards away from you," the captain says in answer. "She's supposed to be on her way to an audience with the pope."

Well, if the queen can't get off the ground, I'm sure Lamont Cranston can't, either.

CHAPTER 60

DACHE DOES NOT talk very much when he is training Maddy. But when the great man does speak, Maddy knows that it's bound to be important. As a result, his words are the only ones she ever writes down with an actual pen in a paper notebook. One of his rules now comes to mind:

Your power does not exist for your own convenience. It exists only for the good of others.

Maddy remembers this as she stands outside a locked wrought-iron gate at the state-run youth rehab center in Harriman, New York, the current residence of her friend Belinda.

Should she press the Visitors button, even though there is a sign underneath that warns SUNDAY ONLY? Even if they allow her inside the building complex, Maddy knows there will be an avalanche of paperwork for her to fill out if she wants to see Belinda.

She keeps turning Dache's words over and over in her mind.

Only for the good of others.

She decides to chalk this one up to the good of Belinda. Maddy isn't there to do something wrong like help her friend escape. She's not bringing Belinda contraband. She just wants to see her and tell her about the progress of her unofficial investigation. Anything Belinda might know about a green car and a man with an accent would be welcome, as well.

Maddy looks through the locked gate, as if she is hoping that Dache might magically appear and give her his point of view on the subject of breaking and entering. No way. She's on her own. She looks up toward the sky, then she tightens all of her muscles. *Focus, Maddy, focus. Be someone or something other than yourself. The smaller, the better.*

The guard manning the security cameras thinks nothing of it when a small, adorable gray squirrel scurries under the base of the wrought-iron gate and heads for the main building.

CHAPTER 61

"YOU'RE CUTE, BUT if you shred my pillow, I swear—" Belinda begins, then shrieks when Maddy transforms from a squirrel back into her usual self.

"Holy shit!" Belinda screams, jumping to her feet, holding the aforementioned pillow above her head, and smacking Maddy in the face with it.

"Unhelpful," Maddy says, rubbing her nose.

"Sorry, I just..." Belinda looks from Maddy's face back to her feet, as if expecting her to suddenly shrink back into a furry animal again.

"We've had every form of vermin in this room. Rats, mice, cockroaches. Not to mention a perverted gynecologist. But, man, we've never had a squirrel that turned into a woman. What the hell, girl? You holding out on me?"

"Let's just say I have some special skills," Maddy says.

They laugh. They hug. For all their terrible arguments and emotional disagreements in the past, they embrace each other tightly, and for a good long time.

"Nice place you got here," Maddy says. Her voice has only a mild, teasing note of sarcasm, because it's not *that* bad. Maddy was expecting a prison cell with a toilet in the middle of the room. But Belinda's room looks like it could be any college dorm. That is, if the students were forbidden to add any decorative touches. No photos. No pictures taped to the wall. No comfortable visitors' chair. No video. Only two twin beds, each covered with a coarse gray blanket, and one closet without a door.

Maddy gestures to one of the beds and asks, "So, who's your lucky roommate?"

"Oh, just a mass murderer and part-time serial killer," Belinda says. "Good work if you can get it."

They settle down for a visit—a visit that could immediately force Maddy back into her disguise if a guard or matron or roommate comes along, so they talk quickly.

"I wanted to *see* you, not just talk to you for three minutes on a cell phone." Maddy pauses, then adds, "And I've got to say, you are looking terrific."

"Amazing what three square meals a day and a good night's sleep will do for a girl," Belinda says.

Then Maddy turns serious.

She tells her that she's been gathering information about the scumbag who is kidnapping and possibly killing Belinda's friends.

"I uncovered some very specific information over coffee with Kailyn, Mama-Girl, and a few others. They said—"

"Wait a fucking minute, lady," yells Belinda. "You had coffee with Mama-Girl? I'd like to have seen that. How many pancakes she put away?"

"The equivalent of half my paycheck," Maddy says. "But it was worth it."

Maddy tells Belinda about the green Escalade; Belinda remembers it well.

"Yeah, that's right. I saw that car about a million times. The one with the darkened windows and the hula dancer bobblehead on the dashboard," she says.

Maddy's entire face brightens.

"Cool. Very cool. You just gave me a piece of info—the hula bobblehead—that I never had before. I should come here more often."

"Yeah, you do that," Belinda says. "Come on Wednesdays, that's when the hairdresser is here. She can trim up that tail for you. Is that how you got Mama-Girl and the pack to trust you? Showed up as a little furry animal?"

"No," Maddy says. "I impressed everyone with an incredible display of power, strength, fortitude, and judo."

Belinda stares at her blankly.

"I kicked three guys' asses at the same time," Maddy simplifies.

"Bet the girls liked that." Belinda laughs.

"I did, too," Maddy says. "I know you think I've been bullshitting you, but I care about you, about them, about Mama-Girl. None of you asked for this life. You fell into it, or were forced there. No one deserves to live like that, not you, not these young girls, and not even a tough old hen like Mama-Girl."

Belinda looks down at the floor. Then she looks back up and holds the palms of her hands against her eyes, not wanting Maddy to see her cry. After a few moments' silence she speaks.

"You are really doing what you promised you'd do. Helping us. You're just about the only person who's ever made a promise to me and then kept it."

"And I'm going to do more than that," Maddy promises, but she is interrupted by the sound of voices coming down the hall.

Belinda speaks in a loud whisper.

"You got to get out of here."

Within a few seconds, Maddy—back in squirrel form—scurries away.

"Damn," Belinda says, staring at the spot her friend had been in. "That is one cool-ass trick."

CHAPTER 62

MARGO AND I, along with Burbank and Tapper, are back in the living room of our hotel suite in Copenhagen. All four of us have that awful feeling of being both anxious and bored at the same time. Burbank and Tapper are having a sandwich-eating contest that Tapper is losing, due to a dislike of herring and a mix-up with room service.

Trapped and unable to work, we distract ourselves by theorizing if any of us might be carriers of the Newbola virus. Eventually our minds are at ease. We wore biohazard suits in Australia, and there was no one ill in Kyoto. Still not satisfied that we aren't vectors for disease, Margo devises a simple but precise blood-droplet test that uses sodium azide to detect the presence of viruses. We have all been tested three times since we left the airport, and are all absolutely free of Newbola. Still, I don't want to take chances.

"Don't get angry, Margo," I say, "but is it at all possible that your homemade test is not accurate?"

"Blueberry muffins are homemade!" Margo snaps. "Moonshine is homemade! This is a simple laboratory procedure, using ingredients that I carry in my biomedical travel case. If you think—"

"Sorry, sorry," I say, quickly putting my hands up in surrender. "I'm not questioning your capability."

"Neither am I," Tapper says, glancing up. "But *does* your bag happen to have the ingredients for moonshine? Because if so—"

"Stuff it, Tapper," Margo says.

Then she looks at me calmly, all her anger vented. "I'm sorry, too," she says. "Doing nothing is so frustrating and infuriating."

Our laptops and phones have been silent since the worldwide quarantine began. So when my handheld device signals a communication, we all perk up.

I read aloud a string of messages from Dr. Anna DaSilva.

Aware of worldwide delay

Crisis here exploding

Stay safe not your fault

The moment I finish reading the text from Dr. DaSilva, Tapper flings one of his sandwiches violently to the floor. Then he jumps up and speaks very loudly.

"I can't stand this. We worked our butts off. We traveled a million miles. The goddamn world is falling apart. And we're sitting here in an expensive hotel room eating fish sandwiches. We're doing nothing!"

I nod. "We all feel this way," I say.

"So?" asks Burbank.

"So, I'm going to do something. We're going to get out of here and get to work. We're going to get back to the Americas."

"I'm sure you can get there by swimming the Atlantic Ocean, Lamont, but what about the rest of us?" asks Tapper.

"We are all going. You'll see," I say.

"Great," says Margo, watching me closely. "Now answer Tapper's question. How?"

"Don't worry," I answer.

"What's the plan?" asks Tapper.

"Well..." I say. Then I pause, and the pause is alarmingly long.

Shit. I've got to come up with a plan.

CHAPTER 63

I DECIDE TO play it by ear.

If Dache ever heard me say that, he'd be through with me. If he thought for a moment that I might give that same advice to Maddy, well…I can't even imagine what he might say—or do.

But in the horrid confusion of the visits to Kyoto and Copenhagen, with the terrifying knowledge of a global plague, I've got to come up with something.

I tell my team that this might be a risky undertaking, but they are all in. As Tapper puts it, "Doing something is better than doing nothing." I don't dare let on that this is not always the case, especially when the *something* could get us all killed.

We exit through the back stairway of our hotel and end up on an empty side street. But no one told the hungry dogs and rats of Copenhagen that the entire world is on lockdown. The starving animals are out in full force and seem just as desperate as we are. We keep moving.

I mentally summon a taxi's ignition remote from the pocket of a sleeping driver. With almost no traffic on the streets, the ride should take only twenty minutes. With an added microelectronic engine boost from me, we'll be at our destination in two.

We arrive at an empty airport, no people, no noise, no loudspeaker. Margo looks around, her voice echoing when she says, "It's not normal. It actually scares me."

I tell her, "None of this is normal. The entire world is not normal. This night, this moment is not normal."

The arrivals board is completely blank. The departures board lists only three destinations, all of them showing the same status.

FRANKFURT, GER canceled
MILAN, IT canceled
AMSTERDAM, NETH canceled

We walk quickly from one terminal to another. But we are lost in this vast auditorium of luggage carts with no luggage, and food counters with no customers. Every few hundred yards exit doors promise TAXAER, but we don't need a taxi, we need a miracle. And that's sort of what happens, although I must say that this miracle is a very *minor* miracle.

A sign over a huge steel door declares KUN AUTORISERET PERSONALE. I've seen this same sign so many times and in so many languages that I know it translates as "authorized personnel only."

We ignore that warning, of course, and we find ourselves in a terminal of the Copenhagen airport marked AIR CARGO. This terminal is as empty and creepy as the passenger terminal. Through one of the loading gate windows I can see a plane, near a stack of shipping containers on the ground, waiting to be loaded. I'd gamble that it's a plane that was gassed up and ready to roll, only to be halted like the rest of us.

I head through the exit door that I've strong-willed open with my mental forces, and tell my group to follow me onto the tarmac. Inside the plane, I use the same mind strength to unlatch the cockpit.

We're inside. On the copilot's side of the controls the screen is frozen, but a piece of information lingers on the display. It shows a weather and route map with a very simple heading.

DESTINATION: NEW YORK CITY.

Suddenly, finally, my jumpy, crazy-nervous brain is able to create a plan, a real one this time.

It will, of course, be dangerous.

But the Shadow prefers things that way.

CHAPTER 64

I ASSUME THAT the Earth is still turning. But if so, that's the only thing that has kept moving during this lockdown. As we make our ascent in the stolen airplane, I look down at the highways and byways below.

No cars are driving. No trains are moving. No planes are flying. I take that comment back. There is *one* plane flying, and it has quite a lot going for it—fold-down cots for napping, microwavable food, and about fifteen bottles of a decent burgundy, to name a few.

We've been in flight twenty minutes when I ask Burbank, "How do you think we're doing? Are you feeling sure of yourself?"

He answers calmly. "Number one, I'm doing fine. Number two, I'd feel more sure of myself if I could see the friggin' fuel gauge. We've either got a full tank or we're going to have to call an audible for a landing in Greenland."

My own flying ability is practically nonexistent. I try to conjure up some hidden brain power that could help. I'm coming up with nothing. We're traveling too far over open ocean for me to chance using my mind powers to give the engine a boost.

Tapper and Margo are buckled into the swivel pods behind us. In case they couldn't hear our conversation above the engine's roar, I turn to reassure them. "Everything is going fine."

Margo, resting on her cot, rolls her eyes. "No, it's not, Lamont. I heard Burbank say that the fuel indicator is out."

Caught. In a lie.

"Let me look," she says, unlocking her safety belt.

The lights all over the control panel make it look like the Christmas tree in Rockefeller Center to me. But Margo stoops over, looks back and forth, up and down, and says, "Burbank, this is a 'partner control' fuel indicator. You've got to press the Vision Clarification button at the same time you press the Current Allotment Fuel switch."

And that's exactly what she does.

"Almost totally full," she says.

Unable to embrace humility, I say, "Ah, yes. I forgot about that. I must be tired."

Margo gives the tiniest smirk and says, "Despite having slept most of the time we were trapped in our hotel?"

"Yes, despite that," I say.

CHAPTER 65

I HAVE EVEN more time to rest during our entirely automated eight-hour flight, but I can't. I'm way too nervous about the last, most problematic part of my plan—which is how to land this damn thing...

Burbank, as our captain pro tempore, calls the three of us to attention.

He cups both his hands to his mouth, and, pretending to be an announcer on a loudspeaker he says, "This is your captain speaking. For your information, we are approximately thirty minutes from our destination."

Then he adds, "I hope."

His joke is far from funny, and I might be the only one who knows exactly how far. I've had a plan jumping around in my head for the entire flight, but it's risky—and I have just thirty minutes to share and execute it with Margo, Burbank, and Tapper.

"I also have an announcement to make," I say.

"Does it have something to do with how we're going to

land at a deserted John F. Kennedy Airport without any air traffic controllers?" says Tapper.

"Well, funny you should ask," I say. "While I've been sitting here next to Burbank on this flight, I've thoroughly examined the self-landing capacities on the board. I believe that everything I've calculated is ready to go. We've all got to work together if my plan is going to be successful, and"—I pause here, perhaps a bit too dramatically—"if we're all going to survive."

I try as hard as I can to ignore the mixture of dread and confusion on all three of my friends' faces. I talk some more.

"As Burbank has already informed us, we will soon be over land. I have set all phases of the computer's self-navigation mode to route our flight, as much as possible, over Cape May, the last land location on that little peninsula on the southern tip of New Jersey."

Margo stands up. "At which point I assume we'll still be at least ten thousand feet in the air. Is there a plan for getting us the rest of the way down?"

I look down at the floor. I stop talking for a moment. I brace myself. Then I speak.

"The four of us will evacuate the plane when I give the signal."

Tapper speaks loudly, his voice quivering. "What the hell?"

"Let me finish. There is a ram-air parachute under every seat and cot. Please take yours out and—"

It will be a scene of interruptions.

"No," says Tapper. "I can't do it. I won't do it."

Margo's voice quivers as she says, "I don't know if that's actually a plan, Lamont. That's just jumping."

"And crossing our fingers when we do," says Burbank.

"Just keep one hand free to pull the chute," Tapper says.

Then I say, as firmly as I can without sounding panicky, "Yes, you will do it. It's what we must do. Surely what's happening to the rest of the world is more important than our individual fears."

"That's easy for you to say, Lamont. You have capabilities we don't have," says Margo.

"I understand that. But this is what we must do," I say. "It's the only viable plan."

"And what about this plane? It'll just crash into Cape May, killing people?" Burbank asks.

"Of course not. I would never allow that. The plane is programmed to continue beyond the peninsula and dive sharply into Delaware Bay, which will, I assume, be deserted at this time."

I tell them that the ram-air design of the parachutes is the safest launch-and-landing gear that exists. Of course, that does absolutely nothing to calm anyone.

Then I add, "I will use my mind strength to try to build a power connection between the four of us as we fall. But I make no guarantees."

My team has lived a life of no guarantees for a long time. Still, I can't help but sense a growing feeling of resentment as they slip into their gear. If anyone is hurt. If I lose anyone...

"Cape May is coming up in a few minutes," says Burbank. "I'm bringing the flight height down. Down. Down. No further adjustment needed."

Margo unfastens the three security bars on the door.

"Get ready!" I shout. "On my signal!"

Mentally I add—*And God help us.*

CHAPTER 66

MADDY HAS LEARNED a lot in her brief undercover experience. She has come to understand quickly that absolutely everything about her work is dangerous. Yes, Mama-Girl watches out for them. Carla Spector quietly pays off the police regularly, whenever a girl gets picked up. She even supplies the girls with decent medical access. But she can't protect the girls from clients who want more than just drugs from the girls, and smack them around when they don't get it.

Maddy has, of course, confined herself to playacting, walking the streets but never doing any deals. But even as a nonparticipant she's been spat on, grabbed, chased, threatened, and called names that are astonishingly creative, as well as disgusting. Through it all, there's no sign of the green car and the man with the accent.

One night—rainy and humid, with dirty water splashing her from cruising cars—Maddy catches a small break.

Two big guys, each of them with a round face and an

elaborate beard, slow down when they catch sight of Kailyn, who is working the street across from Maddy. The car suddenly brakes, then makes a U-turn. When it comes back around, Maddy can see that it's a green Escalade.

Maddy steps deeper into the shadows and throws a warning look to Kailyn, who spots the car and immediately heads for the relative safety of the bridge, where Mama-Girl can at least keep an eye on her.

There's a screech of tires as the driver accidentally drives up onto the curb, his neck craned as he scans the street for Kailyn. The Cadillac has flattened the stop sign at the intersection. Through the windshield, Maddy can see the driver swearing and slamming the steering wheel, his passenger still scanning for Kailyn. Maddy takes the opportunity to memorize the Cadillac's New Hampshire license plate number:

LT4 63Z2

Maddy turns, moving quickly into the dark recesses of the alley. On the other side, a few yards away, everything is brightly lit by streetlights. She can see two of her fellow workers standing in their usual spots.

Relieved, Maddy takes a few steps toward them but is stopped when a strong gloved hand comes from behind her and covers her face. Unlike the goons under the bridge, these men expect Maddy to fight back and are prepared for her counterassault. Unable to take them by surprise, she's lost her advantage.

While she struggles to escape, the attacker forces her

head back. Of course, it is terrifying. She moves her eyes and sees that there are two of them.

Surprisingly, they're not the same two guys she saw in the Cadillac. These are new attackers. They both have ski masks pulled down over their faces and woolen scarves pulled up high around their necks and chins.

As one guy holds her head in place, his partner thrusts an aerosol can into her face. She's about to squeeze her eyes shut against the coming spray, when a third man appears. He is dressed exactly like them—ski mask and scarves totally obscuring his face. But he's clearly not a friend. Maddy feels the man holding her tense up at the sight of him.

"What the hell?" he says, and is blown backward off his feet. His buddy follows, both of them thrown out of the dark alleyway and into a dumpster across the street. The third man, with almost impossible speed, removes his mask, scarf, and jacket.

"Dache!" Maddy yells.

She cries. She is terrified and happy. But Dache appears to be stern, angry.

"Listen to me! And listen well!"

Maddy shakes her head up and down. She is shivering, shaking.

Dache continues. Intensely. Firmly. "I will not always be here to help you. You must understand that. This is your final lesson. This is your most important lesson. *You must learn how to save yourself!*"

CHAPTER 67

THE PARACHUTES ALL deploy; I wait to jump last and see all three balloon into life below me. The jolt of the chute after I pull the ripcord feels as though I'm being yanked roughly upward, knocking the air from my lungs. After that, it's almost pleasant. I glide through the air, taking in the New York City skyline.

But that all changes when I realize what's about to happen.

The cargo plane shudders on, dropping rapidly as it is programmed to do. I keep my eye on the three chutes below me, unable to tell who is who. One of them hits the water, the chute floating for a moment—then sinking. I can see a human figure flailing, and then it goes under, dragged down by the chute.

"Shit, shit, shit," I say. But I can't fall faster.

I concentrate deeply, then send an enormous amount of mind power in their direction, pulling the sinking person above water. I see their hands scrabbling—I don't know if it's Margo, Tapper, or Burbank—but they are able to free themselves from the chute and swim away as their gear sinks once again.

The plane, meanwhile, has rapidly lost altitude. It hits the water of the bay, sending up an enormous wall of water that is only going to give the swimmer more trouble. But that's not the biggest problem. Margo was right—the fuel tanks on the plane were quite full, and the plane explodes on impact, sending a percussive wave of hot air in all directions.

I'm immediately blown out to sea, and I spot the other two chutes struggling as well. One of the jumpers cuts themselves free of their gear and free-falls the rest of the way to the water. I steady my own chute with my mind powers, watching as the last chute makes it to the water and the human figure swims away, safe.

Now I can see all three of my team below me, swimming for the shore. The mind connection I'd built between all of us is strong, but in some ways it's only making matters worse. I can feel their pain, their fear, and the weakening of their bodies as they try to make it to land. I send a last pulse of mind power at the trio, creating a small wave that pushes them to the shore, just as my own feet hit water. I slip easily from my chute and glide to shore, feeling the collective relief of my team as I do. I gain my feet and walk to them across the surf.

Margo, Tapper, and Burbank are wet and shaking from the cold, but no one seems to be hurt, thank God.

Margo even manages a smile for me. "Next time, Lamont—a better plan would be nice."

It's a miracle that we all survive, and it turns out that New York City, in its own way, is also a miracle. The city has so far remained untouched by the horrors that are destroying so many other parts of the world. New York has no beds full of sick and dying people like in Australia, no half-mile-high tons of rubble like in Kyoto, no rushing water flooding the streets like Copenhagen.

"Who would have predicted that New York would turn out to be a beacon of stability and peace?" says Margo as we make our way back to our home.

"Too soon," Tapper says, as he comes to an abrupt halt.

It seems that Margo and the rest of us misread the situation.

A crowd of about fifty people are gathered directly in front of our house. They all push and shove one another, trying to get as close as they can to the entrance of my home.

Burbank is first with the obvious question. "What the hell is going on?"

Then we get our answer. Sort of. One man in the crowd points toward us and yells, "There they are. It's Cranston and his people! They're right here! They can't hide!"

Suddenly, the crowd moves toward us. Everyone is yelling. Questions pepper the air.

"How did you let this all happen, assholes?"

"Do you have a plan to fight back, to stop it?"

"How could such a holy redeemer do such an awful thing?"

I cannot figure out the meaning behind these questions. And I certainly don't have time. I've got to get us through this mini-mob. We've got to be safe if we're going to fix anything.

I force my brain into a strict, structured control mode, even though I'm already so weary from saving everyone during the water landing.

Damnit. I need this to work. Fast. *Keep it going, Lamont. Keep it going. Stay focused.*

Finally, a narrow pathway seems to be forming through the crowd. People are suddenly, unexpectedly, backing up. They look surprised, taken aback by their own movements, which isn't all that shocking, considering they aren't in control of their bodies anymore—I am. The four of us take advantage and walk quickly through the newly cleared pathway. But the screaming does not stop.

"Cranston, do you accept the responsibility for this plague?"

"Responsibility? Are you insane?" I yell back.

Another voice. "Are you planning to destroy the world, just so you can save it?"

The voices gather, coming together in unison, shouting, "*Damn Cranston! Damn Cranston!*" I see another crowd of maybe a hundred people approaching from the other direction, all of them carrying cameras and microphones.

"Oh, great," Margo mutters. "Reporters. We've got to get through before they block us completely."

One of the marchers, a woman, breaks from the group and rushes toward us. She seems to be aiming at me specifically. I've never seen a professional running back this determined or vicious-looking. As I move out of her way, I hear another reporter shouting at us.

"Just tell us the truth, Cranston. What's your plan?"

"Funny," Burbank says under his breath. "We were asking the same thing just an hour ago."

We are only a few feet away from the entrance to the house when the front door suddenly opens. Jessica holds the door, beckoning for us to make a break for it to escape the mob.

The four of us rush inside. Tapper slams the door shut. Bando runs through the group, giving Tapper and Burbank inquisitive sniffs, rubbing against Margo's legs, and panting happily in my direction.

"Welcome back to New York City," Jessica says. "You may find your reputation here is greatly changed."

CHAPTER 68

THE CROWD OUTSIDE is terrifying. The news inside is worse.

Jessica immediately brings us up to date.

She begins by saying, "I can't believe you haven't heard about what's going on."

Burbank says, "Pardon me, ma'am, but between the four of us, we have been continent-tripping the past few days, and we even hit some of the water while we were at it."

"So I see," Jessica says, eyeing our wet clothing.

"What's more, there's been a universal shutdown," Margo says, "although the monsters outside our house don't seem aware of it."

"Oh, they know they should be following the mandates to stay sheltered and safe inside, but these folks are so worked up about things that they're ignoring the rules." Then she adds, "And with the police on their side, they can do what they want."

Then she explains further...with details that absolutely stagger us.

"Where to start?" Jessica asks, tapping her chin.

"With the mob outside my front door!" I practically shout. "Why are they here?"

"Ah, yes, we'll start there." Jessica clears her throat. "That's because almost everyone in the world thinks that you, Lamont, have been spreading this god-awful virus!"

I cannot contain myself. "That's insanity," I shout. "Who's saying that?"

"Everyone. Absolutely everyone," Jessica says. "Up until last night, when they were still sending out news flashes, everyone—politicians, preachers, doctors, everyone! They're all saying—"

Then she gives up trying to explain, thrusting her hand-held video device toward my face.

Jessica pushes a button and we see a checkerboard screen of six speakers. Three men, three women. They all seem to be speaking foreign languages. The translation scrolls across the bottom of the screen.

THE LEADING BIOCHEMISTS AT UCLA, OXFORD UNIVERSITY, AND PIRO-GOV RUSSIAN NATIONAL RESEARCH MEDICAL UNIVERSITY AGREE THAT THE PLAGUE KNOWN AS AUSTRAVID SPREADING AROUND THE WORLD IS

DUE TO THE CROSS-INFECTION CARRIED BY REVERED HERO LAMONT CRANSTON AND HIS COLLEAGUES. BEGINNING IN A TINY BACKWOODS HAMLET IN SOUTHERN AUSTRALIA...

The newscast rattles on and on. When the checkerboard layout cuts quickly to a single screen, President of the Americas John F. Townsend, his brow sweaty, his sleeves rolled up over his elbows, is speaking.

"The inhumane villains fostering this plague will be found and brought to an end. An end as horrible as the disease they are spreading. A disease created to destroy the world."

I toss the electronic screen to the ground. I yell. I sputter. I spit. I cry.

"We are trying to save the world, not destroy it! This is madness! This is unbelievable!"

Margo says, "But clearly people *are* believing it."

"Yes," I say. "Scum like Townsend, sure. But there must be someone who—"

"Only a few people disagree, Lamont," says Jessica. "A scientist in Morocco, that doctor friend of yours—"

"Dr. Anna DaSilva," I say.

"They interviewed her, I remember. She said it was impossible that you're involved."

"At least one friend is left, I guess," I say.

Then Jessica, perhaps the strongest, toughest woman I've ever known, begins to cry.

Margo asks what Jessica is too tearful to put into words.

"What can we possibly do, Lamont?"

"Everything in our power. Anything we need to do to overcome evil."

But for the first time, I wonder if we will.

CHAPTER 69

THE HARSH REPRIMAND from Dache has the intended effect. Maddy decides that from now on she will move forward with intense caution and care. Yes, she has extraordinary powers, and, yes, she certainly has self-assurance, but, *no,* she cannot be a one-woman army in her quest to locate Travis and Chloe and any other kidnap victims from under the 59th Street Bridge.

Logically, Lamont or Margo would be her best adviser. But she's seen the news—they've got their hands full. Besides, Maddy wants to prove to Dache—and to herself—that she can handle the job alone.

Belinda is locked up and has no idea about what's going on in the outside world now that she's in Harriman. Mama-Girl does what she can as the guardian angel of the young gang and has promised to let Maddy know if she spots the green Escalade again.

But for now, Maddy is on her own.

Or maybe not.

The slimy, tough face of Detective Robert McCarthy pops into her head. Yes, he's worked against her. Yes, he's the scum of the earth. But he might have some inside information. After all, he's been walking the same streets the girls have. McCarthy could be a big help if Maddy plays her cards right. The only problem is this: Maddy knows that she is playing with a very lousy hand.

CHAPTER 70

MADDY IS FAIRLY surprised that McCarthy allows her to walk right into his office at the 17th Precinct police station in Midtown East. He's the same smug, self-satisfied asshole she remembers, but she's even more repulsed when she notices the framed family photographs on the credenza behind him. Pictures of a pretty red-haired woman on a beach somewhere with twin boys, also redheads. She hardly recognizes McCarthy as the grinning, wholesome-looking dad standing with them.

Worse than the photo is the fancy framed document hanging next to it, with a large inscription at the top that reads: 17TH PRECINCT NYPD DETECTIVE OF THE YEAR. ROBERT MCCARTHY. It's signed by the mayor.

McCarthy gestures toward the chair opposite his desk, and Maddy sits, pushing hard to summon a smile and make herself agreeable.

"I was curious when they told me that a 'good friend' was out at reception asking for me," McCarthy says. "I certainly wasn't expecting you. Maybe one of the girls from the police academy, or some chick I met at one of the local watering holes... but never you."

"I'm glad it was such a pleasant surprise," Maddy says. The fact that he refers to full-grown women as *girls* and *chicks* makes it hard for her to keep her smile in place, but she manages.

McCarthy stands and moves to the front of the desk, directly opposite where Maddy's sitting. Then he sits on the edge of the desk, way too close, and rubs his hands firmly up and down on his thighs. Maddy's smile remains in place, but she nearly has to summon her mind powers to make it happen.

"Look, I know I'm jumping into the deep end here. But I need your help," Maddy says.

"You need my help?" McCarthy says, with a laugh that is just short of a snicker. "Girlie, you might not have noticed, but I'm not sure you and I are playing on the same team."

"I don't think we have to be on the same team to share the same concerns. I've seen you at work; I know you want to keep the kids at the 59th Street Bridge safe."

Maddy knows nothing of the kind. In fact, she's certain McCarthy takes kickbacks from Carla Spector in order to keep her business running, therefore putting the girls directly in harm's way.

But she remembers what Belinda told her—some of her male clients have actually convinced themselves they're helping her. Maddy has no doubt that McCarthy has cast himself as a hero in his own head: the Patron Saint of Lost Girls.

He makes sure they get in the right cars and get the drops into the right hands so that they can get their paychecks. And she's right.

"Of course I want them to be safe," McCarthy says. "Why do you think I let them play that tape of me at Belinda's trial? She's in no danger now, is she?"

Maddy doubts that McCarthy *let* the prosecutor do anything, but she continues.

"You probably already know this," Maddy says, not above stroking his ego. "But quite a few of the young people from that group have gone missing."

"And?" McCarthy says.

"And I'm going to bust my ass trying to find them." She lets the insinuation that he should be doing the same thing hang in the air between them.

McCarthy stops smiling. The brightness disappears from his face. Maddy removes a small folded piece of paper from her pocket.

"This is the license plate number of a car that's been trolling for kids. It's a New Hampshire plate, number LT4—"

At that moment Robert McCarthy stands up from his desk and holds out his arm, flashing a stop signal with his hand.

"Maddy, let me tell you something," he says.

"Yes?" Maddy asks.

"Get the hell out of here!" he yells.

Maddy's head snaps backward a tiny bit. Damnit, she promised herself she wouldn't let him intimidate her.

"Listen, Detective," she tries again, but he quickly rounds the desk, almost knocking her chair over. He grabs her by the arm and pulls her up, propelling her toward the door. He snarls one last thing in her ear before he tosses her into the hallway.

"Get out of here before I kill you."

CHAPTER 71

TWO STORIES HAVE taken over the headlines in all news media.

First, of course, is the scourge of the Newbola virus. What was once only an unverifiable prediction is now exhaustively reported: the hideous illness has worked its way across the entire world. No country has gone untouched. No city is free of plague.

Grandma Jessica shares that in our absence she received a package from Dr. DaSilva that contains a trial vaccination for Newbola. The good doctor sent along a note saying that there were no guarantees it would be effective, but it was the best chance she could offer us, as soldiers on the front lines against the spreading illness.

Second, I am sorry to say, is this: When the media reports on the spread of the virus, they invariably mention my team and me and continue to spread the enormous lie that we are leaders of a conspiracy to destroy the world.

Communication networks like TMZ and Fox News

can't get enough. Priests and preachers sermonize about the devils among us. The ERs of almost every hospital on earth are packed with patients who are fearful that their colds and flus are early forms of the illness.

The Americas seem to have benefited the most from the travel ban. Though cases of Newbola are being reported everywhere, there has been no severe outbreak as of twenty-four hours after our arrival home. Essential workers such as those in health care and food services are allowed to return to work. The rest of us are being *asked* to shelter in place...but we're not necessarily being *told* to.

Meanwhile, my team and I, as well as Margo and Grandma Jessica, spend an enormous amount of time discussing the situation. Hawkeye barely managed to get out of Johannesburg before the air travel shutdown and had to make his way to us surreptitiously, hoping not to be recognized as a member of one of the most hated groups of people on earth at the moment. He's tired and let down after discovering nothing new in South Africa, but he's the first to ask something critical.

What Hawkeye asks is the biggest question: what's our next move?

Most importantly, we need to clear our reputations, which will not be an easy job with so many in the media relentlessly undermining us. But if we're attacked by an angry mob every time we leave the house, there is very little we can do to help contain the virus. Burbank and Tapper agree that if we can find a way to connect the virus to the natural disasters, it will help lead us to whoever Hephaestus is—and hopefully move the wrath of the entire world off our shoulders and onto his.

There is another problem, this one personal, totally unrelated to the Newbola chaos. That has to do with Maddy.

Where the hell is she?

She hasn't been sleeping at home. Yes, she's texted and we've spoken to her. While I can't detect any hint of lies in her answers—*No, I'm not with a guy. Anyway, I'm a Dache-trained adult*—I'm not buying what she's selling.

Now we all sit in our tech room, each with our own worries. Burbank, Tapper, and Hawkeye are entirely focused on somehow tying the virus to the natural disasters, while Margo, Jessica, and I try to focus on the same thing, while not letting worries over Maddy distract us. We are making no real progress when, all of a sudden, a communication emergency alert buzzes.

The largest of the four screens in our conference room lights up.

A name appears.

Dr. Anna DaSilva

This is followed by a notification labeled *communication priority*. A few seconds later the word *URGENT* flashes on the screen, followed by a close-up video of our friend and colleague Dr. DaSilva—who does not look particularly happy. In fact, she looks as stern and angry as I've ever seen her.

"Lamont, we need to talk," she says.

It takes me a few seconds to adjust to the coldness of her greeting. Apparently, I'm wasting time. She repeats, "Lamont, I said that we need to talk. That means I need you to respond."

All I say is, "Yes, of course."

Then Dr. DaSilva begins. Intense. Irritated.

"I am astonished, not to mention furious, that you are involved in this immoral, disgusting attempt to spread the Newbola virus," she begins.

"Hold on, Dr. DaSilva. You are as ill-informed as—" I interrupt. But she talks over me, speaking harshly.

"I do not know how you could have seen the devastation of the virus here in Australia and purposely chosen to smuggle it out of the country. Maybe you thought you could study it, maybe you thought you could beat me at finding a vaccination and become an even more heroic figure. Whatever you had in mind, it's completely backfired, hasn't it?"

I try to interrupt again, but the good doctor cannot be stopped. She rants on. Meanwhile, my personal device lights up with an email from Jericho, reporting in from North Carolina.

"I plan on discussing this extraordinary matter with President Townsend. I'm scheduled to speak with him in the next hour. I know your relationship with the president is shaky at best. It's about to get worse."

I am usually a reasonable and courteous teammate. But not now. Now it's my turn to explode.

"Just stop it, Anna! Just stop! Townsend is the last person you should trust and confide in. If you do, then you're a bigger fool than everyone who has fallen for this media lie, hook, line, and sinker."

She strikes back. Her delivery is emotional, angry.

"I have devoted my life to improving the health of people everywhere," she says. "I, sir, am no fool."

Now it's time to play my ace. I speak calmly and seriously.

"Prove it," I challenge her. "Show me that you're not part of the misled mob once I share with you the new intelligence I've received from the team member who just spoke to me from North Carolina."

A slightly calmer but still slightly suspicious Dr. DaSilva asks, "Who's that?"

"Jericho," I say. "He's shared with me some very alarming—but very helpful—information that he picked up in North Carolina."

"Tell me everything," she says. Then she adds, "Please."

"Yes, I'll tell you everything, Anna. But first, I'm going to tell the people who trust me. People whose names have been dragged through the mud along with mine. People whom I'm sure you yourself have smeared."

"But I want—"

"I don't care what you want," I say, and cut the feed.

CHAPTER 72

THEY SIT AND listen. I stand and talk.

"I want to communicate and clarify everything about Jericho's trip to Chapel Hill, North Carolina. But first I must begin by correcting a misimpression that I put forward at the very beginning."

They look at one another. Confused? Annoyed? Upset? I've got to slow down.

"Let me put it to you simply...I lied to you," I say, then backpedal when I see anger flash across Margo's face. "Well, I lied a little." When I gave out the assignments, I said that Jericho was going to the University of North Carolina to attend a meeting of amateur environmentalists to brainstorm about the recent problems around the world.

"The official name of the meeting was given as International Study of World Health Data." But the real purpose was to bring together three of the world's most important epidemiology experts to report on any insight that might be helpful in solving the question of how Newbola is spread. All three of the academics gathered there had been doing secret, independent research on the subject."

Hawkeye speaks up. "And yet you sent Jericho? He's not a public health expert."

Strongly and slowly I speak.

"Let... me... finish."

And I bring them up to date.

"I sent Jericho as an observer, a reporter, a notetaker. I think you'll agree that among all of us, Jericho is the best at knowing when to listen and not talk."

"Completely agreed," Tapper and Burbank say at the same time, effectively proving my point.

"He spent two days sitting in on these meetings and was able to make some very important observations about the workings of Newbola."

I press a key on my device, projecting what Jericho shared with me via email onto a large screen.

The most compelling conclusion is clearly this: the Newbola virus is transmitted in a very different manner than most quickly spreading contagions, which are typically transmitted via a cough, that is, airborne.

This contagion is more similar to some forms of hepatitis: THE BASE VIRUS MUST PHYSICALLY ENTER THE BLOODSTREAM.

This is most effectively accomplished by injection, transfusion, or sexual contact.

I stop reading. I look at the group. "That means that it would be impossible for any of us to infect so many people across the world with Newbola."

"Especially me," says Tapper. "I can't even remember the last time I had—"

"In any case," I interrupt. "Whether it is merely a media frenzy, or if there is a dark guiding hand that wants the world to point a finger at us is yet to be discovered."

"I'd like to advise that we *not* be the ones who inform the entire world that they should stop having sex," Hawkeye adds. "We're unpopular enough as it is."

"Yes, let's leave that to the WHO," I agree.

"I say we make Dr. DaSilva do it," Burbank says. "Make her public enemy number one, since she was so eager to believe it of us."

Margo's device goes off with an alert, and she glances down at it.

"Regardless of if we're being framed or not, Newbola is definitely spreading. An outbreak was just reported in Texas. With that in mind, I think it would be wise for all of us to take Dr. DaSilva up on her offer of the vaccine."

"Absolutely not," I say immediately. "I'm not injecting myself with something if I don't know exactly what it is and don't completely trust the person it came from."

"Lamont," Margo says quietly, "it's safe."

"How can you possibly know that?" I ask.

"Because Grandma Jessica is just as suspicious a person as you are. She injected herself the moment the box arrived to determine whether or not there was some trick involved," Margo says.

"You did what?" I ask, turning. "That's insane."

Jessica nods at Lamont from her seat.

"No," Margo says. "It's what you do when you care about people—you put yourself last. Which is why I won't be taking a dose."

"Why the hell not?" Burbank asks.

"Because there are only five syringes left," Margo says. "I will save Jericho's syringe for when he returns."

"But—" Tapper begins, and she puts a hand up. I know the gesture well.

"Don't bother arguing," I tell him. "You won't win."

I turn to Margo. "Fair enough. If you could prepare the syringes, I agree that we should be vaccinated. What's more, now that we know how difficult it is to transmit the virus, it's clear that the initial outbreak was caused *deliberately*," I tell them.

"Now all we need to find out is: who the hell did that?"

I am not surprised that the group is bursting with ideas, procedures, insights, and even anger. They talk with enthusiasm. They gesture with excitement. I am gratified by their passion. Without this team, I'd be lost, but I also know that all of the Shadow's investigations ultimately begin and end with myself.

Margo reenters the room with the prepared syringes just as I get an urgent incoming text. I hate that I have to leave so quickly after we've found our stride, but someone I've been trying to contact has agreed to meet me.

What I don't tell them is that my next meeting is as important as—perhaps even *more* important than—the one we're having right now. I've got an appointment to speak with a brilliant geological professor from the University of Peru. We've just made some headway with the virus. Maybe now the mystery of the natural disasters will be laid to rest, too.

And if I'm lucky, we can link them, bringing us one step closer to Hephaestus.

CHAPTER 73

MADDY HAS BEEN trying for the past three days to connect with Belinda at the state-run youth detention facility for mental health and social rehabilitation in Harriman.

Even though Belinda isn't allowed to have any tech, she's always connected with Maddy via the facility's phones during visiting hours. That hasn't happened lately, and when Maddy calls in, a nonemotional guard simply tells her that Belinda is not available.

Maddy is so frustrated that she even asks her volatile boss, R.J., for his help. R.J.'s response to the request is delivered in the sort of impatient style that is so typical of him.

"How should I know what the problem is? Maybe they're on lockdown because of the outbreaks. Maybe she put your name on a do-not-call list. Maybe—"

But Maddy doesn't want to hear any more of his maybes. She wishes she could put R.J. on a do-not-talk list.

Maddy just wants to bring Belinda up to date on where things stand with her case. Maddy has learned that Belinda may be offered a reduced rehab sentence if she shares some inside information about Carla Spector's drug ring.

So Maddy decides to create her own solution. She tells R.J. that she has to head to the evidence room for a few hours of paperwork, and instead drives to Harriman in person.

Maddy arrives during visiting hours and tells the guard at the lobby desk that she is there to see Belinda. The guard looks at his computer screen, pushes a few buttons, and within a few seconds announces, "Sorry, the person you're asking about has been transferred to a different facility."

"Where to?" Maddy asks.

The guard doesn't even bother to look at the computer screen.

"It doesn't say where they sent her," he says.

"Could you please check?" asks Maddy.

He barely glances at the screen.

"It doesn't say," says the guard.

"Is there someone you can ask who might know?" Maddy asks.

"Yeah, sure. I'll ask the governor later tonight when we're having dinner."

"Give me a break, buddy," Maddy says.

"A break," the guard says. "What a great idea." He then

swivels around in his chair and faces the computer screen, pressing a button on his keyboard.

The screen flickers and he begins an online poker game.

"Nice," Maddy says, then turns her back to walk away. She's halfway to the door, using her mind power to monitor the guard's game, when she calls over her shoulder, "Bet you wish you'd kept that three of hearts, am I right?"

She doesn't see him tip over in his chair, but she does hear the crash.

Smiling, she lets herself out.

CHAPTER 74

MADDY COULD CONTACT Lamont. Or she could connect with Dache. If she were really desperate, she could try again with R.J.

When it comes to her next move, Maddy has a lot of choices. But she also realizes that any of the three will lead to some unpleasant conversations, not to mention loads of "here's what you should have done" advice.

Feeling stuck, she decides to use the drive home to clear her head, but it's almost impossible. The lack of traffic on the roads should make her less stressed, but it only serves to remind her about the Newbola outbreak and how everyone is blaming Lamont for it. Her usual playlists can't even calm her mind. She snaps the music off with irritation, and a live news update takes its place on the radio.

The drug wars in Bolivia are raging. The economic update from President Townsend is packed with lies. Nuclear drones are flying over Malaterra, the country that was formerly called Mexico. Everything is falling apart. It's all so frightening.

She decides to find a classical music station, something from a less-chaotic time period. But before she can turn the dial, the newscaster's voice rises in volume with a breaking update.

"To the astonishment and concern of the entire medical community, the spread of the dreaded Newbola virus is overwhelming the resources of the world everywhere. From East Africa to northern Canada, Newbola is ravaging every area of the earth."

Maddy snaps off the radio, not wanting to hear the expected follow-up—blaming Lamont for everything.

Suddenly, a huge green Cadillac swerves in front of her and purposely slows down. Maddy yells, slamming on her brakes. Her entire body is tense as she braces for the impact, but she manages to stop right before rear-ending the larger vehicle. It's so much higher than her car that the license plate is directly in her face when she comes to a stop.

LT4 63Z2

"Oh, shit!" Maddy yells, just as the Cadillac gasses it.

Maddy accelerates as well, not wanting to let the car out of her sight.

Suddenly, the Cadillac's trunk flies open and spews a small flood of bright blue liquid onto the roadway. Maddy's car is now completely out of her control. She skids off the road and onto the muddy embankment.

Ahead of her, the Cadillac does a U-turn and comes back in her direction, stopping with its nose only two feet from her ditched car. Three masked men jump from the green car and rush toward her.

Panicked, she tries to think what Dache would tell her to do right now. Calm down. Concentrate. But that's the last thing she's capable of right now.

Should she shape-shift? Into what? A German shepherd? A poison arrow? She tries. She tries so hard. But her powers fail her. She cannot grab calm from out of terror.

The masked men pull her from the car and drag her to the Cadillac. They push her in, zip-tying her hands in front of her, as well as her ankles. One of the men presses a blue handkerchief to her face. She tries not to breathe in but can do it for only so long. The first whiff of chemically laced air puts her out. But not for long.

When Maddy comes to, she does not know how many miles they have traveled. It could have been five miles; it could have been five hundred. All she knows is that she is awake, alive—and abducted.

She is inside a moving vehicle, but when she stretches her legs out, she meets no resistance. Much too roomy to be the trunk of a car, even a Cadillac.

Her eyes adjust to the dark and Maddy looks around. A simple little room, sheetrock walls, nothing else inside there but Maddy herself and a modest wooden trunk. Her mind is churning with anxious possibilities.

It could be she's being transported in a different vehicle.

Maybe they've transferred her from the green car to a truck, a van, or even a trailer.

It's dark, but not pitch black. A farm animal odor. Strands of hay are on the floor. Yes, it must be a trailer of some kind.

She focuses on the wooden trunk. Maybe there's something helpful inside. She calls upon her shape-shifting powers, but they don't appear. She calls upon her superior-strength abilities, but, for all of her work with Dache, they don't take hold of her.

Maddy decides wisely to use her innate physical powers. She wriggles and twists, her bound limbs aching, to make the very short journey to the trunk. She squirms to her knees, gingerly edging the tips of her fingers under the lid of the trunk. With her hands bound, she's unable to lift it very far. Slowly, she lowers her head to glance inside. It takes a few seconds to adjust to the low light inside the trunk.

She looks. She registers the contents inside. She pulls her hands away. The trunk snaps shut.

She cannot believe what she's just seen.

CHAPTER 75

I AM SCHEDULED to have a top secret one-on-one meeting with Dr. Carl Laksa, one of the world's top geologists. Dr. Laksa, Indonesian-born, has just completed a virtual three-day seminar with three other geologists at the University of Peru; they have come to the same conclusion as my team and I—these natural disasters are most likely man-made in origin. After they agreed on this, the four seminar participants became fearful for their lives, and Dr. Laksa informed me that he believes he is being followed.

For this reason, Dr. Laksa did not want to let me know his current address, no matter how secure I assured him my own personal devices to be. Right now, I'm waiting at the Hunts Point bus station, where I was told he would meet me.

When an unshaven middle-aged man wearing a filthy once-white ski jacket and equally filthy brown gaberdine trousers that bunch at the ankles stumbles toward me, I'm not particularly frightened, because I see right through his disguise. Dr. Laksa may be an eminent geologist, but he's no actor.

"Mr. Cranston?" the make-believe bum asks, leaning in.

"Yes," I say. "Dr. Laksa?"

"Yes," he says. Then he immediately adds, "Please try to look disgusted and repelled by me. Someone is probably watching us. Now... get ready to yell at me."

Then, in a loud voice, Laksa says, "C'mon, man, a dollar. A dollar. I gotta get some food."

"Leave me alone," I say sternly.

"Just a dollar," Laksa says.

"Get the hell away from me."

As Laksa staggers away, he speaks quickly and softly.

"Shamrock Hotel, 650 West 42nd Street, room 201. In thirty minutes."

The Shamrock Hotel, far west on 42nd Street, is disgusting. A small lobby contains one severely ripped leather sofa and a matching chair covered with the random crusts of a pizza party. No one is manning the shabby front desk, so I take the back stairs to room 201, where I'm greeted by Dr. Carl Laksa.

Dr. Laksa is now dressed as the perfect example of a college professor: rimless eyeglasses, brown and gray plaid wool sports coat, brown corduroy pants.

"I almost didn't recognize you out of costume," I say.

Laksa neither laughs nor smiles. Obviously this is going to be a serious meet-up.

"Welcome, Mr. Cranston," says Laksa. "I realize that this room is a less than ideal meeting place, and I apologize for the playacting on the street, but at least nobody can spy on us. The only ones watching us will be the cockroaches and an occasional rat."

Then he says, "I brought these."

I am expecting him to produce elaborate plans, or, at the very least, a file full of hot information. Instead, Laksa reaches into his small metal briefcase and takes out two large cans of Pellegrino water. He hands me one of the mineral waters and says, "I brought my own, as the Shamrock Hotel room service leaves something to be desired."

The professor goes on. "I'm going to give you a verbal report, Mr. Cranston. Hence, we will not leave any confidential data information behind for enemy sleuths."

My body tenses as I prepare to hear Dr. Laksa out. How much more bad news can a man be asked to stand? The destruction of the Earth by disease? The planet slowly falling apart? How many disasters can collide in my world at once?

"I'm counting on you, Professor. I'm really counting on you," I say.

"Very well," says Laksa, and I can't help but notice a note of satisfaction on his face. He is a man who is accustomed to being treated as important.

And what an extraordinary font of important material he is.

"On the second day of my video conference with my esteemed colleagues, I received a message from a former student of mine. His name is Glenn Ambrose."

"He was a student of yours in Peru?"

"No. I am on sabbatical at the moment, which is how I came to be stranded so far from my home during a pandemic. Two years ago I was a visiting professor at UC Berkeley. Glenn Ambrose was one of the four students in my geological philosophy seminar. Ambrose was the absolute brightest of this very bright group."

Laksa takes a long gulp of his mineral water, sighs deeply. Then he tells his story.

"Ambrose submitted his course paper on the theoretical possibility that by using satellites to create radiation waves, we could generate unlimited green energy by tapping into the Earth's molten core.

"I saw the possible execution of this idea as a great advancement for humankind—for environmental salvation and general medical well-being. I even helped guide some of Ambrose's research."

Then Laksa adds a wildly important piece to the story. Quite simply, he watched his student—a certifiable scientific genius—become seduced by the idea of power. He explains that Ambrose began talking about how wealthy and famous he would become. Then, suddenly, his research went in a different direction entirely. Ambrose was determined that his invention—which he arrogantly called Terrageddon—could be transformed into a superweapon, not an energy source. Dr. Laksa was devastated that so much work and intelligence could be diverted to such an evil end.

"Meanwhile," Laksa continues, "Ambrose became completely unhinged. He babbled. He failed to bathe. He had actual fistfights with anyone who challenged his thesis. The university had no choice but to dismiss him."

As expected, Ambrose was insanely angry. He sent university administrators and Dr. Carl Laksa messages threatening revenge.

"Then Glenn Ambrose just fell off the grid," Laksa says.

"But," I say, "not for long."

"Correct. When I was virtually attending the summit with my colleagues, I once again began to receive threatening messages. This time they were signed *Hephaestus*."

I do not want to interrupt Dr. Laksa's story, so I do not tell him the same signature appeared at the end of the messages sent to the late Professor Nakashima, as well as Dr. Langi Singh.

"After the incidents in Kyoto and Copenhagen occurred, I had my suspicions," Laksa says. "But I also knew how far Ambrose's machine—the Terrageddon—would be from completion. It seemed impossible to me that he could have finished his work so quickly, especially given his mental state. After the shocking incident at Harvard, I became more concerned. When my colleagues asked to meet and shared their beliefs that the natural disasters were of human origin, I had to confront the facts. I shared what I knew with them, and now I'm telling you." He pauses. I say nothing. Laksa takes a deep breath. His opens and shuts his watery eyes very quickly. His lower lip quivers.

"After I spoke with them and conveyed Ambrose's identity, they, too, began to receive threatening messages from this Hephaestus. For this reason, I think Ambrose may be monitoring my emails and devices, which is why I've gone to such extremes to meet you in secret."

Then Laksa says, "I am afraid, Mr. Cranston. I am very afraid."

"I'm also afraid, Doctor. But you know what?"

"What?"

"We haven't got the time to be afraid."

CHAPTER 76

I HAVE LEARNED from experience—perhaps more experience than I ever wanted—that if you are working against time and evil, there is just one thing to do: make a plan. Dache taught me long ago that the best plans usually have the highest risk. And the best way to proceed is to accept the risk.

I've got Dache's words in mind as I imagine how to capture Dr. Laksa's terrible acolyte, Glenn Ambrose. But I can't help but remember Margo's words after she swam out of Delaware Bay: *Next time, Lamont—a better plan would be nice.*

But with the fate of the entire world on my shoulders, and time of the essence, I also need to come up with something fast. If I can capture and destroy this horrid genius, I can ultimately stop him from using Terrageddon.

High risk. High reward.

My plan? With the travel ban scheduled to end, I will convince Glenn Ambrose that Laksa is traveling to the Scientific University of the South in Peru.

Then I will have the college officials evacuate the campus. With the false information we've provided, Ambrose will believe that Laksa is back in his office in Peru. Once he's made good on this threats by unleashing Terrageddon on an empty campus, we will track the satellite's route and, hopefully, discover Ambrose's location. Poland? Norway? Samoa? Ohio? Wherever.

We will find him. We will destroy him. We will... Well, we will save the world.

I, of course, discuss this idea with Laksa, and to my surprise and satisfaction, he agrees to participate without hesitation. He is willing to be the bait. I realize for certain that I am dealing with a person who is both extremely smart and extremely brave.

First, I ask Burbank to use his superior skills to tap into government travel databases. I know he can do that. He will create an entirely false flight to Peru, which will appear as completely booked to anyone else who might be trying to travel into the city. Then he will fabricate plane tickets in Laksa's name and send them via email, where Ambrose will be sure to spot them.

Then I give Margo the task of writing bogus emails to be sent out as if they were actually written by Laksa. Margo has the creative skills to monitor Laksa's old emails and then mimic his tone and style. The mix of phony emails filled with serious, official-sounding phrases, interspersed with ordinary everyday messages ("I am wondering if the antique Picasso lithograph is still available?") will be meticulously constructed so that it appears Laksa has no idea he is being monitored. I know Margo can do this.

It's a very risky plan. My companions and I will have a very short time between the evacuation of the campus and Ambrose's launch of the geological disaster. During that time, Burbank, with Jericho helping remotely from the UNC campus, must find and identify the specific satellite signal Ambrose uses to deploy Terrageddon, so that we can track his location. It could be coming from India or Indiana, China or Cheyenne, anywhere on earth—and maybe even beyond.

Now I know what Dache meant by *high risk, high reward.* Gotta go. Gotta do it.

We are fortunately off to a good start.

Within twenty-four hours, Burbank has the tickets delivered to Laksa's inbox, all while Margo keeps a steady stream of emails coming from the account. By all indications, Laksa is leading life as normal, with no suspicions he is being monitored.

My job is to convince the dean of the Scientific University of the South in Peru that his entire campus needs to be evacuated and shut down. I expect resistance and have a string of arguments prepared, but the dean is happy to comply—none of the major institutions of learning across the world wants to be the site of the next tragedy.

Then it happens. The fake flight to Peru takes off. Will this plan of mine actually save this sad, threatened world of ours?

CHAPTER 77

IT TAKES MADDY only a second to recover from the shock of finding Belinda inside the trunk. With extreme effort, Maddy is able to lift the lid high enough for Belinda to squirm, stretch, and struggle in order to climb out.

The two bound young women twist and flop around on the floor of the van like two freshly caught fish tossed onto dry land, then come to their knees. Maddy brings her bound hands up to her face, raising a finger to her lips and signaling to Belinda that she needs to be quiet.

Maddy realizes she may have a small surge of mental energy inside her that can help them.

She imagines Dache's stern stare as she tugs at her restraints. No luck.

She takes two slow, deep breaths, searching for peacefulness and concentration, just as Dache has taught her. Maddy tries forcing her ankles apart. Not enough force. Not enough strength.

Has Dache deserted her? Has he been a bad teacher?

Impossible. Has Maddy been a lousy pupil? Hmm. A possibility.

As she struggles with her useless efforts to harness her powers, she and Belinda look at each other. Maddy sees the fear and anxiety in her friend's eyes, and, more than ever, she longs to be able to help. But her own fears have made it impossible to engage in the deep concentration necessary for her to access her powers.

Maddy's frustration brings her close to tears. *Get a hold of yourself!* she thinks. Then she finds the determination to stay focused and strong. At least her innate grit has not evaporated.

She tries something new. She manages to free the index finger on her left hand with a painful yank. But suddenly the trailer swerves to a halt. Brought up short, the girls are tossed against the wall.

The roar of traffic stops. The abrupt silence is eerie. The two young women are almost on top of each other.

A loud scratching noise. Within seconds, Maddy and Belinda realize that the locked door to their traveling prison is being opened.

CHAPTER 78

BELINDA LOOKS SURPRISED and confused to see the two men who enter the van. Maddy, on the other hand, is not at all shocked to see that one of them is the repugnant Robert McCarthy. She doesn't know the other one, but he has the same sneering mouth and blazing eyes as the sleazy detective.

"Sorry we had no seats available in first class, ladies," says McCarthy, almost as if he's being serious. "I hope business class was acceptable."

While McCarthy doesn't laugh or even smile, his companion—whom Maddy has already silently nicknamed the Stooge, supplies a nauseating, loud guffaw.

"We thought you two divas could use a little fresh air," says McCarthy.

The Stooge chimes in. "And if you need a bathroom break, you've got the whole forest." He gestures to the open trailer entrance. Yes, it is wooded and green. Maddy assumes they've parked on the side of some highway.

"I've got to take a wicked piss myself," says the Stooge.

"Hold on," says McCarthy. "Let's do the other thing first."

The other thing? Maddy is genuinely terrified and knows that Belinda must be as well.

Then both men kneel down—McCarthy near Belinda, the Stooge next to Maddy.

As soon as the men come close, Maddy notices that both kidnappers are wearing something strange on the sides of their ears. Small white electrodes are protruding from just above their sideburns.

Each man's device is attached in the back with a slim gray wire. The devices themselves emit a tiny blue flash every few seconds. Maddy does the one-Mississippi count and discovers that the blue light appears every four seconds. What's this all about?

Communication orders from a central location?

Whom are they getting their instructions from?

Carla Spector? Someone even more heinous?

McCarthy and the Stooge get to work. They are each holding a small hypodermic needle. The Stooge forces Maddy's head onto the floor.

Seeing her savior about to be attacked, Belinda seems to have had enough. She bends her knees and aims her bound feet at McCarthy, giving him a kick that does nothing more than knock him aside.

"Bitch!" he screams. Then he looks at the Stooge. "Let's do it!"

At that moment both men plunge their syringes into their victims' necks.

The two young women quake uncontrollably, and within moments they both pass out.

CHAPTER 79

BURBANK, WITH HIS extraordinary technological skills, has set the trap for Glenn Ambrose impeccably.

Jericho, newly returned from North Carolina with his own set of skills, has set up a tracking system that is mind-boggling, so we can monitor for the satellite signal that deploys Terrageddon.

We're off to the races.

We watch the video displays, but…damn…it looks like we are *not* off to a particularly great start at all.

The two Peruvian government security agents who have committed to aiding us in this project have notified the Scientific University of the South in Lima to begin a rapid evacuation of the campus. These agents know that any person left on campus will be destroyed should we be unable to thwart Ambrose's launch of Terrageddon.

The first big problem? The rapid evacuation of the UCSUR campus is not rapid, not very rapid at all. Despite the dean's willingness to comply, the campus has been on general lockdown as a precaution to avoid the Newbola virus. First being told to shelter in place, and now being told to evacuate immediately has people confused, some of them skeptical of this new, opposing order.

I watch some people make slow, meandering paths off campus, some of them hugging or prolonging their goodbyes. *Move! Goddamnit! Move fast or be killed!*

Burbank, controlling the various visual mechanicals, remains calm. His only comment on the campus scene in Lima is "Give the idea some time to breathe, sir. We've only just begun."

It's great advice, wise advice. I should be able to take it. Strength, order, serenity, are at the basis of my very existence. Yet, try as I might, I am becoming not merely nervous but also extremely angry.

"Why can't people do what they're told?" I say hopelessly and sadly to Margo, Burbank, Tapper, Jericho, Hawkeye, and Grandma Jessica. Bando whimpers from beside my feet.

I close my eyes tightly. I clench my hands to my chest. I consider the thoughts and teachings of Dache.

When the initial evaluation is inaccurate, the best path is reevaluation.

Is it that time? Time to reevaluate?

"Move! Run! Get out the hell out of there!" I yell at the screens as if the people might actually hear me.

“Careful, boss,” Tapper says, clearly alarmed at my loss of temper.

Even as I yell, in the back of my mind is the vital question:

Should we abort the plan?

CHAPTER 80

SHOULD WE SIMPLY abort this plan?

At the moment my answer is a resounding... "I'm not really sure."

After all, there are literally millions of human lives at stake.

Concentrate, Lamont. Meditate, Lamont.

Yes, I am the vessel of the unique powers taught to me by Dache. But I don't need those superpowers right now. I need the power that exists in every single one of us—the power to dig deep inside and take control of our emotions.

I need to give myself a violent attitude adjustment. This is life and death we're dealing with here. *Get a hold of yourself, Lamont.*

Keep going. Concentrate. Meditate. Adjust.

And so I do it. I cross over to courage.

Just in time.

Burbank's monitors showing images of the campus are filling with tremendous close-ups of thick gray clouds and tiny patches of blackish-blue skies. Our fake flight is scheduled to land at Jorge Chávez International Airport, just outside of Lima.

At the time when the nonexistent plane should be descending, Burbank sends a message from a device cloned from Laksa's cell phone that states: landing with joy in Lima. Gracias a Dios.

"What's the plan now?" Hawkeye asks.

It is clear from his tone that he is overwhelmed with fright.

For lack of a better response, I say, "I don't have a plan at this specific moment."

What a cowardly response. What an unsatisfying account.

"We'll have to wait and see," I say.

This doesn't stop Margo from commenting, "That's what we're doing, Lamont. We're waiting *and* we're seeing. But we are not moving forward."

Now the screens are filled with even darker clouds. The gray sky has turned black, which at least has made some of the crowd still on campus begin to move faster. Jericho fidgets and stands, turns a few dials and presses some buttons, monitoring the skies for any unusual satellite signals.

Then Jericho makes an announcement that sounds like it's coming from a man who's falling off a cliff—loud, echoing, desperate.

"I've got something!" Jericho shouts, pressing his headphones to his ears. "I've got something!"

I do not say what I am thinking—if Jericho has picked

up a signal, then Terrageddon has been unleashed . . . and a glance at the screen tells me there are far too many people still gathered on campus.

We prayed for the best. We hoped for a small amount of luck and safety. But we have failed—and when the blow lands, it is much stronger than expected.

"Oh, shit," Tapper says, switching the screen to a view of the airport.

Burbank manipulates the video, causing the screen to widen as the view ascends. We now have a bird's-eye view of the land below, from a high enough vantage point that we can see the actual outline of Peru.

Then we see what we never, ever wanted to see.

Mile-long chunks of the Peruvian coastline begin crumbling into the ocean. The devastation moves inland, so fast that it will soon destroy the nearby cities of Callao and La Perla. It is only a matter of minutes until it will consume the city of Lima. Thousands of people will die. Great chunks of land fall away from the continent.

The campus is not safe. The airport is not safe. Peru is not safe.

Terrageddon has been unleashed!

CHAPTER 81

I TAKE A deep breath. I hold Margo's hand.

Together we make a video call to Dr. Laksa. The good doctor is inconsolable. His friends, his former colleagues and students—in fact, much of the country he called home has been destroyed. Laksa speaks haltingly through his tears.

"My heart is breaking, but I do believe... I must believe... that the people who died did so for a good cause. I will keep telling myself that."

I, too, will keep telling myself that, for I know that to be true. Then I tell Laksa that we do have one piece of positive feedback from our effort.

"Out of the chaos and tragedy, there is one piece of very helpful, very good news."

The doctor looks up at me. I see some hope in his face.

"And that news is... ?"

"Jericho and Burbank have just told me that they have

been able to trace the signal of the satellite that coordinated the attack on the country of Peru."

Burbank, bursting with enthusiasm, cannot help but intrude on the conversation.

"At first, it seemed that the launch point might actually have been coming from Pyongyang in North Korea, but then the satellite began moving farther east," he says.

Okay. Fine. Interesting. Now let us know where it truly came from. But Burbank doesn't stop with his background story.

"North Korea would have been a perfect location from which to initiate the Kyoto disaster. But that proved unlikely when—"

I simply cannot wait a second longer for the answer.

"Damnit. Get on with it! Where the hell is Terrageddon coming from?"

Burbank and Jericho answer in perfect unison.

"Africa," they say. Then Jericho adds, "Possibly Dakar, the largest city in Senegal."

I have to stop for a moment and visualize a map of Africa in my mind. Senegal. Senegal. Senegal. Then, there it is. A small country on the northwestern coast of Africa.

Now Laksa speaks: "Of course, West Africa. That would be a perfect location to set up a fortification for a nuclear launch. I should have considered that.

"So, you think this is all happening in Dakar?" Laksa asks.

Jericho responds, "I said *possibly* in Dakar."

"Wait," I say. "Did you just use the word *possibly*? We need a specific location."

Burbank says, "Forgive me for sounding arrogant, sir. But it's amazing that we were able to pinpoint the country of Senegal."

I know he's correct.

"You're forgiven," I say. I crack my first tiny smile of the day. "Dr. Laksa and I appreciate the miracle you've given us."

Laksa is about speak. But suddenly we are interrupted by alerts as multiple internet news outlets report on the extraordinary disaster in Peru.

The news saddens me, of course, but it strangely and unexpectedly strengthens me. There is much to do.

"We'll connect very soon," I say to Dr. Laksa. "Let's hope for a positive outcome."

"I hope so, too." Then he adds, "I only wish that I might live to see a happy ending."

"Why would you not, Doctor?" I ask.

"Think about it, Lamont. Just think about it," he says. "Ambrose clearly wants me dead and was willing to destroy almost an entire country to see it done."

Then he adds, "But for the moment I bid you thanks and farewell."

CHAPTER 82

AS SOON AS the conversation with Laksa has ended, Margo says to me, "He's scared, isn't he?"

I am not surprised at her intuition—she's always been remarkably accurate with her emotional insight. But I sense that Margo herself is nervous, as if she is as frightened as Laksa.

"Lamont, look at the situation," she continues. "We know a lot more about Ambrose than we did a few minutes ago. But it's also true that Ambrose knows a lot more about us, about our incredible intrusion on his plans. And when he learns Laksa isn't dead, he'll know someone has foiled him—and that we're tightening a noose."

"Of course, you're right, Margo," I say. "I've thought from the beginning that Laksa could end up being a victim in all this, but I guess I put that aside because I was so pleased that we succeeded in locating Terrageddon. Isn't that the larger goal, and worth it?"

I realize, of course, that while I am the cause of Dr. Laksa's jeopardy, I can also be the source of his safety. I know that Laksa cannot be protected by guards with guns or locked rooms with steel-and-granite walls. A madman like Ambrose will track down Laksa easily. He will destroy him handily.

So I try mightily to connect with the most dependable source of safety in the world. I send psychic signals with my greatest possible strength of concentration. Margo can sense what I'm seeking. She does not cower, but she does close her eyes and hold my hand.

I am not certain if it's taken a minute, an hour, or even a lifetime for a successful mental connection to be made. But when the powerful process of double presence finally occurs, I see Dache standing before me.

"Your wise and good friend. Laksa. About him you will speak, and I will listen," he says in a voice that is at once strong and soothing.

I begin.

"We owe him his safety. He deserves that. And we deserve his wisdom, his knowledge." Dache gives no response, so I continue.

"Laksa will only be safe if he is in your care. With the power of shape-changing and your stunning instincts for sorting good from evil, you can cross the guarded borders with him; you can guarantee Laksa's safety. Then the remainder of us can swiftly begin our work."

Do I see Dache nod? Is he even moving? Do I hear

something, anything? Is there even a murmur of agreement? I wait, and Dache remains still and silent.

Finally he speaks. "You have spoken. I have listened. I will comply."

Then he pauses once again. He has only one more word to speak.

"Tibet," he says.

I nod. I know there is one place Dache can keep Dr. Laksa completely safe. The great monastery hidden in the mountains of Tibet where I once trained. Unfindable and untraceable. The presence of Dr. Laksa will not be detected by Ambrose and cannot invite his fury onto another unsuspecting location.

Dache dissolves into another world. Now the room is empty except for Margo and me. Yet even in Dache's absence, the great man's aura of hope and strength remains.

CHAPTER 83

THE SHARP-EDGED, SUPER-STREAMLINED plane cutting through the sky is an aeronautic design masterpiece created in the year 2055, an evolutionary variation of the NASA X-43. There is no faster, finer aircraft in the world.

Right now, in the two-seater front section of the vessel, sit two angry, unhappy passengers. They are tightly buckled in, with twine and cables binding their hands and feet. They are being nourished by feeding tubes, which are looped around their seatbacks. The ramjet engines are so loud that conversation is completely impossible, even without their gags. The two very unhappy passengers have been informed the flight time is three hours from takeoff to landing.

Suddenly, the plane makes a dive-bomb descent. It feels like a crash landing is about to occur, but then, within seconds, the plane lands softly on the ground. From the small windows, the two passengers see only endless miles of sand and bright sky.

In less than a minute, the plane doors open and the two

passengers appear on the landing strip. It is not Laksa and Dache; they are safely in Tibet already. It is not Lamont and Margo. They are still in New York, anxiously hatching a plan for moving forward.

The two passengers are Maddy and Belinda. They emerge blindfolded and handcuffed, accompanied by Detective McCarthy and three other men Maddy continues to think of as stooges. She can hear them all talking to one another even though she can't see anything. She assumes the two new men—whose voices are unfamiliar—must have been sequestered in the rear section of the plane.

All four men shove the women out onto the tarmac. Maddy estimates that the heat level surrounding them is 110 degrees Fahrenheit at minimum. The air is so dry and hot that when she takes a deep breath, her throat and nose are filled with pain.

"Move fast and watch your pretty little heads," says one of the new stooges. Within a few seconds Maddy and Belinda are pushed into an RV.

"Now that you are safely on board, we can remove the blindfolds," they hear McCarthy say. "Let them enjoy the scenery during the ride."

Two stooges remove the blindfolds, then unlock the handcuffs. To Maddy's surprise, all four men then exit the vehicle. The only other person in the RV is the driver, a young man with a mustache and beard, wearing a black helmet.

As the RV makes its way along at an insanely high speed on a deserted highway, Maddy and Belinda begin to talk.

Belinda asks, "Do you have any freaking idea where we are?"

Maddy begins to answer. "No, it could be the moon for all I know. Maybe it's—" But she is interrupted by the driver's voice on the intercom.

"Kindly shut the hell up. We have work to do." Maddy and Belinda trade looks of confusion with each other.

Then the driver talks again.

"I call your attention to the plastic bags under your seats, one each. There you will find fresh clothes to replace what you are wearing."

Belinda and Maddy reach under their seats. The bags they find contain normal-looking street clothes.

"What the hell?" says Belinda. "How did you know my size?"

Maddy looks at her own outfit—a fashionable yet nondescript outfit that any young person her age could wear on the street and blend right in—exactly like the girls who were selling drugs under the bridge back home. It looks like Belinda and Maddy have been relocated for work—probably because Maddy let on to McCarthy that she knew the green Escalade was involved in the disappearances of kids like Chloe and Travis.

In the middle of a desert, in a locked speeding vehicle, in a horrible new world with crazy people and killers, Maddy invokes her lessons from Dache. If she connects with her mental powers she can control the driver and force him to take them somewhere safe. Not...wherever it is they are going.

She tries hard for major mind clearing and concentration. She can feel her muscles begin to spasm mildly, then more vigorously.

She remembers that Dache's lessons have not always helped her. Yes, she thinks, the power has often eluded her. Yet at other times it has helped her splendidly.

Yes, it's happening now. Maddy will put an end to this terror.

Her arms strengthen. Her leg muscles tighten. She stands, feels power flooding her.

But then...damnit all...then...she starts to feel weak. She starts to feel dizzy. Her legs betray her, and she falls to the ground. She is not collapsing, but she certainly is not connecting with her power.

What the hell? What did McCarthy and the other goon inject them with?

"Belinda," Maddy asks, her voice weak. "How do you feel?"

"Feel?" Belinda repeats, astonished. "Like a kidnapping victim, that's how I feel."

"No," Maddy says. "I mean—"

The voice of the driver, on the intercom, comes through loud and clear.

"Girls! Stop screwing around. Just put on your clean clothes. Right now!"

CHAPTER 84

I AM DETERMINED that Margo and I will not sit like two weak and wounded animals after the partial collapse of our Peruvian plan. Dache and Laksa are safe in exile. My colleagues are depressed and confused. Margo and I are in a holding pattern while we decide what to do with the information that Ambrose is located somewhere in Africa. This is a huge leap forward, but the question remains—what do we do now? To truly conquer the scientific capabilities of Glenn Ambrose would take an air force and perhaps a navy of monumental strength. Even Dache—and certainly not me—cannot conjure up that kind of extraordinary power.

Margo takes the opportunity to administer the last dose of the experimental Newbola vaccine to me. It had completely fallen off my radar after meeting with Dr. Laksa, and our ill-fated Peru mission had clouded my spirits even further, driving it entirely from my mind. When Margo mentions it, I offer no argument. Since none of the team suffered any ill consequences, I believe it's safe. I even try to convince her to use it for herself, but she refuses.

After she injects me, Margo sips very hot basil-mint tea. I try to meditate, unsuccessfully. Grandma Jessica stays alone in the tech room trying to trace and track the actions of Glenn Ambrose long after the other members of our group have gone to their rooms for the evening.

Finally, Margo breaks the silence between us.

"We can sit here until the end of time, but it won't help," she says.

"You're right," I say. "But the end of time could arrive in the next few hours or the next few days."

Margo smiles and says, "It always helps to have a sense of humor."

"I wasn't being funny," I say. The fact is, I actually mean that.

We remain silent for a few more minutes, and then Margo speaks again.

"You know that there *is* an alternative, something we could do right now," she says.

"I know what you're going to say," I tell her. "You think that it's time to get in touch with President Townsend."

"Yes, I do. No matter what you think of him—traitor, monster, dictator—he and this nation have the means at their disposal to help us."

"Don't you think I know that?" I ask, trying not to sound angry.

"Of course you know that," Margo says. "But what I need to see you do is act on that knowledge."

"No. I'm not going to involve Townsend until that becomes our very last chance," I say.

"And when will that be, exactly?" says Margo, who has clearly run out of patience with me. "You just said yourself that the end of time could arrive in the next few hours."

I prepare myself for a long, tough argument with the person I care about the most in the world.

But that possibility is eradicated the moment Grandma Jessica walks into the room. She is clearly nervous and upset.

"Maddy's car has just been found abandoned on the side of the highway."

CHAPTER 85

MADDY AND BELINDA are locked inside a luxury suite in a luxury hotel in what is perhaps the luxury capital of the world.

They are in Dubai.

Maddy sees from the tourist information on the multiple television screens in their suite that they have been imprisoned in the most expensive hotel in the world—the Burj Al Arab, a wonderland of fountains and restaurants—and surely plenty of people looking to buy drugs.

Maddy and Belinda both realize that they have likely been recruited to provide exactly that service.

Damnit. Just damnit.

Maddy is still weak and deflated after being unable to tap her powers earlier.

Belinda, however, feels fine. And although she is tough and jaded by her days working the streets of Manhattan, she is naive enough to think they might be able to escape.

"Shape-shift, Maddy. You can do it. Remember when

you became a squirrel? You could become a lion or something, right? Eat everybody and we can escape."

Maddy sighs and admits her inability. "I have tried, but I couldn't summon even an ounce of power on the car ride here. Whatever they injected us with is affecting me very differently from you, maybe because I have special abilities and you don't. It feels like I'm connecting, but, no. I'm as powerless as—"

Belinda finishes Maddy's sentence.

"You're as powerless as I am." Then, tough as she can be, Belinda begins to weep. Big, heaving sobs.

"Even if we got out, where would we go, what would we do? I don't know anything about Dubai. We don't have a way to contact anyone, either."

They both walk to the window. They look out at the huge clutter of skyscrapers, man-made waterways, and parks. They see the cluster of islands that make up Palm Jumeirah, home to the iconic Atlantis hotel. They watch. They cry.

Then they hear a noise. The door is opening.

They turn around quickly to see Robert McCarthy standing there, along with two of the goons.

"Meet your new boss, ladies," says McCarthy.

McCarthy and his posse step aside and reveal a very short, very fat man who is dressed in a long white robe Maddy somehow recalls is known as a kandura. Flabby little lumps of flesh cover the man's face. The bumps and wrinkles are so plentiful that Maddy cannot even discern what the man's expression might be.

Then one of the stooges says, with mock formality, "You will be honored to meet Karnama Alsamida."

Then the stooge adds, "Please, show your respect to your new employer by bowing."

Neither Maddy nor Belinda moves. They are paralyzed with a combination of disgust and fear.

Louder, the stooge shouts, "Bow!"

Maddy and Belinda both bow. The sheik smiles, clearly pleased with his new employees.

CHAPTER 86

MADDY IS FEELING weaker and weaker. She can barely stand up straight. She can barely think.

On the other hand, Belinda seems to be fine. Although she has nothing inside her that even comes close to being superior physical and mental power, she is brimming with anger. Maddy can feel the girl's hostility crossing the space between them. She only hopes she won't do anything foolish while Maddy is incapacitated and unable to help her.

The sheik sternly addresses the two goons who entered with McCarthy.

"The medical analysis! Now!" he shouts.

"Of course. The Newbola testing," says one of the stooges. He immediately grabs Belinda and throws her to the ground. She squirms and screams and tries in vain to fend off her attacker.

At the same time, the other one grabs Maddy by her shoulders and pushes her down to the floor. Maddy feels so weak that she offers no resistance at all.

The Newbola test consists of an electronic device with a short bloodletting spike inserted quickly and sharply into the lower stomach. A few drops of blood are extracted. The blood specimens are smeared on individual small devices. As soon as the blood-to-machine connections are made, both testing devices emit a loud beeping sound.

"Both girls are exactly where we want them," says one of the men. Then he adds, "If you'd like to interview your new employees now, we can give you some privacy."

The man nods and waddles over to Maddy when the three men leave, and as she feels his eyes on her, she hopes there truly is an interview coming, and not a more sinister reason for him to desire privacy. And what did it mean when the goon said that both girls were exactly where they wanted them after they were tested for Newbola? Is that what's wrong with Maddy? Is that why she is so weak? Does she have Newbola?

"You will please stand," he shouts at Maddy.

A pause. Too long a pause for him to tolerate.

"I can't get up," says Maddy. "I'm too . . . tired. I'm exhausted."

He nudges Maddy impatiently with his fat foot, then kicks a little harder when this gains no response. And it is that kick that inspires a human explosion from Belinda.

Belinda may not have studied with the great Dache. Belinda may not have unique preternatural powers. But on the tough streets of New York City, in one of the most dangerous jobs in the world, she has learned how to defend herself—and her friends.

Belinda springs from the floor, delivering a strong kick into the man's stomach. Then she gouges both of the fat man's eyes with her index fingers.

He screams out in an animal kind of pain. Belinda screams in victory.

Her blows are not especially strong, but she has a compensatory talent: she has the anger of a girl who has been abused for her entire life and is propelled by rage. The man falls to the ground and lets out yet another strong yelp of pain.

Belinda turns her attention now to Maddy.

"Get up, Maddy. You've got to get up. You can. I know you can," Belinda yells. She kneels next to her friend while she steals glances at the quivering mass of flesh that was supposed to be their new boss.

Maddy staggers to her feet. Her knees are weak. Her head hurts. She takes a deep breath. Maddy leans on Belinda, and they walk toward the dining room. From the dining room to the kitchen. From the kitchen to the service entrance.

As they open the service door, they hear a loud screech from the room behind them, then the sound of footsteps as the goons respond to the man's cry.

They hear someone yell, "Those bitches! Those goddamn bitches!"

Those bitches make their way down from the suite via the employee elevator. They've outsmarted the kidnappers. They've immobilized a drug kingpin of Dubai. Now all they have to do is deal with a very unfamiliar city that neither of them knows anything about.

CHAPTER 87

THE PROBLEMS OF the world are drowning Margo, Jessica, and me. Even Bando's mood is low. The worldwide infestation of the Newbola virus. The terrifying prospect of the destruction of the entire planet by the insane powers of Glenn Ambrose.

Can anything be worse? Yes and yes and yes. We are overwhelmed with misery and panic at the disappearance of our beloved Maddy. Maddy, the tough and trained inheritor of my personal crusade for peace and justice. Maddy, a human vessel of kindness and intelligence, wisdom and joy. *Maddy, where the hell are you?*

When Grandma Jessica brought the news, we immediately exhausted all investigative skills at our disposal. I contacted every ally I've ever had—the premier of Canada, the London School of Science and Technology, the holy Buddhist monks still remaining in the Maldives.

They, and others, are attacking the mystery with full force. But no one can find even a hint of knowledge of

Maddy's whereabouts. There are no limits to my pursuit. I even have the audacity to contact Dache. His only response is "I have a sense of her absence, but there is no communication from her—not even a weak signal. I share your fear. I will employ all my skills to assist."

This is horrible news. If Dache cannot succeed, then none of us...But as I ponder this impossible situation, a message appears on my personal handheld device.

I study the words intently. It seems vaguely Arabic or Iranian, languages I am usually able to read and speak, but I am unable to translate the script in my current state.

Grandma Jessica shouts out, "It's Arabic. I know it is. It doesn't really make sense. But...but...It just sounds foolish, something about a town or a place—" Confused, she furrows her brow, then a light dawns in her eyes.

"If you read the sentence backward, it says, 'I am lost in a very big city.'"

I am amazed and, I must admit, jealous that I was too blocked or stupid to unearth such a simple solution.

"Could it be from Maddy?" Margo says. "But why so cryptic? Why so vague?"

I theorize that Maddy is confused, frightened, perhaps even weak. I call in Burbank from the adjoining room and ask him to calculate the location of the sender.

With merely a quick glance at the screen and a few clicks, he says, "It's coming from Dubai."

"Of course," says Grandma Jessica. "I should have known by the incorrect use of the nominative case."

I am gratified that both Burbank and Jessica cracked the case so quickly, but I am also angry that I, someone who speaks so many languages, was unable to solve it. What's happening to me?

"Everything else is on hold until I get to Dubai and bring Maddy home," I say.

Jessica, Margo, and Burbank agree that this is the wise and proper way to proceed. I ask them for a moment alone to gather my thoughts and make a plan.

I initiate all my psychic abilities to find and commandeer a flight to the United Arab Emirates. I make no connections. I keep trying, but with no success. In fact, my intense concentration is rewarded with a wildly severe headache. My temples are throbbing. My eyes are stinging. What is happening to me?

I continue to work at making a mental connection. After a few seconds my headache and eye pain vanish. They are, however, replaced with a weakness in my spine, my knees, my shoulders. I am tired. I am also off-balance. I am too weak to rise from my chair. I am too frail to find Maddy, to save Maddy.

What's happening to me!?

CHAPTER 88

HERE'S THE DEAL that I decide to make.

And, yes, I know that it is horrid and frustrating and humiliating. But I must.

I cannot halt the spread of Newbola. I cannot prevent Glenn Ambrose from destroying huge pieces of the world. Worst of all, I cannot get to Dubai to help Maddy.

So I do what I never, absolutely never, wanted to do.

I make arrangements to meet with President Townsend. He welcomes the opportunity to meet with me, his highly troublesome enemy. But I cannot think of any other solution.

I am steadily growing physically weaker, and I have no idea why. I am steadily losing my intellectual ability. Much as I detest Townsend, I don't have a viable alternative.

So here I am, standing in the presidential office. When Townsend was illegally elected president by an illegal vote in the illegal world congress, one of his first acts was to rebuild the Oval Office as the Square Office. A simple redo, all that was needed was four new walls, arranged to hide the historic curved walls of the past few hundred years.

Another "personal" touch from Townsend was his portrait enshrinement of the former presidents whom he particularly admired: Richard Nixon, Marjorie Taylor Greene, Andrew Johnson, and, predictably, Donald Trump.

"How do you like the place?" Townsend asks me.

"It suits you," I answer. We both know, of course, that this is my first visit to the presidential Square Office since Townsend was elected.

"Certainly took you long enough to get here," he says, extending his hand for me to shake and then motioning to the armless visitors' chair abutting his desk. Seated there I feel like a recent college graduate on his first job interview.

Although I am having difficulty breathing, and although there is significant pain coursing up and down my spine, I present myself as a friendly, hearty sort of guy. Townsend does the same thing. If you were to watch us together you'd think that we were the closest of friends. But Townsend and I know otherwise.

This is an act. Our smiles are too wide. Our handshakes are too firm. Our voices are too high and happy.

Then, as if we have cut to a brand-new scene in a movie, the warmth and friendliness are sucked out of the room.

"So, my instinct and my sources inform me that you are here for a very specific reason," Townsend says seriously.

"Then you'll be glad to know that your instincts and sources are correct," I respond, and I am as somber as Townsend.

I add, "I am here to ask a favor. A favor that will impact the preservation of the entire world."

"What makes you think I'd be interested in preserving the entire world?"

"Because we both have so much invested in this universe. Our interests are completely different, but we both require the world to remain in existence, if one of us is to succeed."

"We cannot play football if there is no field," says Townsend.

I am wishing he would spare me his corny, lame metaphors.

"That's one way of putting it," I say.

Then he flashes the tiniest of smiles and speaks.

"I know why you're here. You need help. Specifically, you need my help. More specifically, you need the help of the World Associated States to combat the Newbola disease and the massive ecological destruction."

In a split second I realize that Townsend knows as much as I do about these two horrid situations. He may actually know even more.

Finally he smiles, a full grin stretching from ear to ear.

Then he says, "Am I right, Mr. Cranston?"

"You are absolutely right, Mr. Townsend."

The new smile disappears.

"I will help you. But as I'm sure you suspected, we will first have to do a small bit of negotiation."

CHAPTER 89

TOWNSEND AND I despise each other. We have diametrically different views on how to bring peace and happiness to the world. But I must add, Townsend is anything but a fool. He no doubt believes that I am setting him up for some form of betrayal.

But I have no way out of my extraordinary dilemmas without Townsend's help.

He knows this, and he knows that I know that he knows. As a result, I must look like I am acting in good faith, and the fact is, I really will act that way. I will actually *be* that way. And if—or more likely, when—he betrays me, then, and only then, will I retaliate.

The deal he presents is simple: I get his assistance, and he gets anything else he asks for.

Yes, Townsend agrees to launch stealth rocket monitors to obliterate any rockets or rocket launchers that Ambrose is working on. Townsend's air team can "indubitably" (his word) locate and control Ambrose's designs and plans.

"Your Peruvian adventure was a fiasco," he tells me. "Too elaborate. Too human. A schoolboy's idea of combat."

I am furious with his condescending opinions, but I work hard to keep my anger from showing.

Townsend builds on his demands. He not only wants me to share the details of Dr. Laksa's involvement but also needs access to whatever computer messages we have from Ambrose.

"My government-trained people are not as skilled at extracting technological data as your little team of children," he adds.

Children? He calls them children? Jericho? Margo? Burbank? Tapper? Hawkeye? My friends? My colleagues? The best of the best?

"So, we're going to be sharing information?" I ask.

"Yes," says Townsend. "In a manner of speaking."

Then my frenemy says he wants to move on. "Let's discuss this nasty little flu bug that has everyone so upset."

I could jump up from my chair and strangle this devil, this monster, but I am tired and weak, and I really do need his help.

"Dr. DaSilva was anxious to work with you, even though I advised against it," he says.

Remembering her somewhat lukewarm reception in Australia, I can't help but wonder if Townsend put it into her head that I would try to take credit for any miraculous discoveries.

"I questioned her judgment at the time," Townsend continues. "I would only use her services if I had a sprained ankle or a bad case of the sniffles."

"The woman is a genius," I say, "and she is risking her life, under the most awful conditions, to get the Newbola under control."

I'm much more positively inclined toward Dr. DaSilva than I was earlier. After I confronted her with Jericho's evidence from the UNC meeting regarding how Newbola is spread, she retracted her suspicion of me and my team as the source. She even released a PSA relating to the public that there was no reason to believe that my team and I had any connection to the pandemic. Given her credentials, the public accepted her word, making it much easier for all of us to move about freely in public.

"Well, she'll have a better chance of success if we get her here in Washington, and she can assist my Swedish virologist team at the Johns Hopkins Research Center, where, by the way..."

He pauses for a moment, touches his computer; the screen fills with numbers and equations. He looks at it, then looks back at me and continues.

"...where, by the way, my team doesn't even think they are dealing with a virus. They suspect it is an airborne bacterial infection, probably just a dangerous one-cell rogue bandit."

My weakened power notwithstanding, I cannot bear to

listen to him any longer. I got what I came for. I'll deal with the government air force. Anna will deal with the Swedish virologists. I've got to get back on the trail of Maddy. My cell phone has been on nonstop vibration since I entered the Square Office. I stand up and speak to Townsend.

"Well, thank you, Mr. Townsend. I appreciate your cooperation."

"You are certainly welcome. I appreciate yours as well."

He tells me that his secretary of protocol will see me to my car. The protocol guy will be waiting outside on the front portico. I head for the office door to leave, but Townsend has one more question to ask.

"Haven't you forgotten to mention something, Mr. Cranston?"

"No, I've said everything I needed to say."

"Everything? What about the girl!" Townsend says. "Why did you not ask for assistance in finding the girl?"

Shit! Shit! Shit! He even knows about Maddy's vanishing.

I think I might lie and say I was afraid to overstep my boundaries on a family matter, but instead I create a new lie right on the spot. I say, "I think we have some fine leads on Maddy's disappearance. Maybe later I'll come back if I could use your help."

"Oh, I assure you. You will need my help on this one, getting Maddy back safely."

"I'll be back," I say.

The stupid phony smile appears on his face.

"Why wait when you are here right now? Why wait when time is of the essence?"

I walk back to Townsend's desk. I sit down in the visitors' chair. We begin to talk.

CHAPTER 90

NOTHING UNUSUAL OCCURS in the final moments of my meeting with Townsend. He promises to help me find Maddy, and, of course, I don't actually believe him. I promise to share espionage info with him and the American government, and I'm certain he doesn't believe me.

Our truce is based on the foundation for most mutual agreements in today's world—anger, deceit, and total mistrust. Yet, one immediate positive result does emerge from this meeting: Townsend offers to allow me and my team to travel to Dubai on a secret military transport jet.

I assume that Townsend realizes that I may be suspicious of his generous offer. So he quickly adds that this gift of safe travel will be "impeccably secure" (his words). Then he adds more assurance.

"Let me put you at ease," he tells me. "The national transport is equipped with a device that can detect and dissolve any airborne projectiles. It will automatically release, aim, and fire when any destructive geological material is within a two-hundred-mile radius."

I have a question.

"Doesn't that assume that a Terrageddon launch device will be tracking our flight to Dubai?" I ask. "What about another satellite attack exploding and destroying other places in the world?"

His eyes narrow as he looks at me and responds.

"You mean like the destruction that you allowed to happen in Peru?"

I have no defense for my ineptitude, which caused that tragedy. So Townsend fills the silence with more of his considerations.

"At least you and your team will be safe," he says. "And just remember. This is merely the beginning of our offensive."

Hmm. This sounds like an eminently reasonable assessment. But since it's coming from Townsend, I'm scared of such deep concern and cold logic.

He speaks again. "I will be following your flight, and I will see to it that even if this Ambrose monster launches an attack, he will be destroyed before he can do harm."

This confrontation could go on and on. Right now—whether Townsend is to be trusted or not—I must begin the search for Maddy.

"I think it's time for me to get started," I say. "I've got to first pick up my team and, of course, Margo."

He smiles and speaks.

"Ah, of course, the lovely Margo, your elegant paramour. I hope to spend some quality time with her one of these days."

My elegant paramour? That word, coming from Townsend, sounds vulgar and dirty. I am sure that's why he phrased it that way, purposely ignoring the fact that she's my wife. My blood is boiling.

Townsend presses a button on his computer, and within seconds, two armed security guards enter the room.

"These gentlemen will escort you to the aircraft," Townsend says. "I sincerely hope that you are pleased with this situation."

"I guess I don't have much choice," I say.

Townsend's smile cannot mask his pleasure at holding my fate in his hands.

"Good luck," he says.

Should I say "I'll need it"? Should I say "Thank you"?

I decide to say nothing. The security guards and I head out.

CHAPTER 91

I TRY VERY hard to convince myself that the flight to Dubai will be very safe, very fast, and completely uneventful. On the other hand, maybe I'm just a fool who's swallowed a bunch of lies and bullshit from Townsend.

Our escort to the vehicle explains what I already knew, that in government air transports these days, all control is accomplished by self-piloting, with monitoring and mechanical observation performed from the ground.

What about the inside of the vehicle? Margo describes it as "techno-luxurious," which, as you might guess, means that it is a flying big shot's office, glistening with steel and bronze, sofas and chairs of rich black leather. The rest of the interior? Panels of video screens with endless buttons and levers and handles and knobs.

Our official escorts head for the plane's exit door. They bid us safe travels and much success. We buckle ourselves in, and—I must be honest—upon hearing the access door shut and lock, I feel nothing but fear in my chest and stomach. My shoulders tremble slightly; my palms sweat. I am somewhat calmed by the takeoff and ascent—so smooth and quiet that I can barely perceive that we are moving.

So here we are. No Townsend. No Townsend emissary. No assistant. No escort. Not even a pilot. But, of course, we know that we're not really alone. We are aware that everything we do or say is being listened to and watched by Townsend and his subordinates. I can imagine the bevy of government agents scanning video screens while cross-referencing statistical information about us on additional computers. It is probably safe enough to discuss our plans for our search for Maddy when we actually arrive in Dubai.

But before we have that discussion, I speak...not to my colleagues but to the room, to the air.

"I know you are listening, Mr. Townsend. Of course you would be monitoring us and our flight. But I will try to keep my belief in our mutual trust. That trust, as we discussed, is not based on our mutual understanding on how the future of the world should be governed...oh, no. That trust is based on our mutual understanding that there must actually *be* a future world."

Then I stop talking. Perhaps there will be a voice response from the earth below.

Nothing. Just the barely perceptible hum from the air vehicle's engine.

"Let us begin," I say to my team. "We must assume that

they've heard us, and we must also assume that we are all on the same side. At least temporarily."

At precisely that moment, Burbank, to get our attention, waves his right arm and unbuckles his safety belt. He walks a few feet to one of the many wall panels. He points to something. There, amid an array of illuminated red and yellow buttons, he gently touches a specific button that stands out, a blue button at the very top of the panel.

Margo and I, along with Jericho, Hawkeye, and Tapper, unbuckle and join him. Suspecting that we might be under surveillance by a hidden camera, we feign a casual style, walking calmly about the cabin, taking unhurried turns reading the description next to the blue button. It says:

COUNTER CHEM ATTACK

We all remain perfectly silent. We don't even exchange glances.

Suddenly the blue button begins flashing, not quickly, not alarmingly. But it is the only one of the many illuminated buttons that is blinking.

Then, just as unexpectedly as it began, the flashing stops. Everything returns to normal, or, at least, everything seems normal.

"Let's get back to our planning," says Margo, who is now closely studying her handheld electronic device. Then she adds, "By my estimations of wind velocity and our destination latitude, I can calculate our arrival time. We are less than an hour from Dubai."

CHAPTER 92

WE DO OUR best to relax for the rest of the flight and discuss our plans for locating Maddy in Dubai. Tapper, Hawkeye, and Burbank individually have laid some significant groundwork. Burbank has been in touch with important French and Lebanese archaeological experts who have been excavating an ancient underground network of tunnels and caves that extend from about five meters from central Dubai to the Jumeirah Mosque. It is an access route that could provide shelter and a hiding place if necessary.

There is both great anxiety and some hope in our discussions for finding Maddy. You see, to put it simply, a world without our Maddy is no world at all. Of all the mysterious problems I've helped control, this one is, understandably, closest to my heart, closest to Margo's heart. As for Grandma Jessica's feelings? When we bid her farewell, her eyes filled with tears.

"Just get my girl home" is all she said. Those words echo through my mind as we await our arrival in Dubai.

And, although Tapper, Hawkeye, and Burbank have, with their hard work and keen intelligence, set up some assistance for us, the fact is we will be running more scared than we usually do.

Suddenly, we hear a loud beeping sound. Loud? It grows even louder. Almost earache-inducing levels of loud. We all stand up fast, and Tapper points to the panel of lights and knobs. The blue button that we observed earlier is once again flashing brightly and quickly. The beeping noise is in sync with the flashing light.

I rush to the video screen nearest the light panel and randomly slam and push as many buttons as I can. To no avail. Yet when I stop my haphazard assault on the panel, the video screen below the panel comes to life. I've accidentally done something right. Now I can see, on the screen, a gray boxlike object with neat blue stripes. Since it is in isolation against a black background, I have no way to know how small or large the thing is. It could almost be a birthday present, a beautiful gift box floating through a nighttime sky.

But something tells me this is a present no one would want to receive.

Margo, Tapper, Hawkeye, and Burbank all begin talking at once. Whatever force weakened my powers before, I have been feeling better since we took off. I try to channel my anxiety into strength, into focus, but I am overwhelmed by emotion, and emotion is not a wise way to aid my powers.

The video screen suddenly flashes a message.

MALICIOUS ORGANIC/NONORGANIC MATERIAL APPROACHING

"It's a chemical attack missile," I yell.

"How do you know?" asks Tapper.

I have no time to answer. The video screen displays another message.

ACCESS B-19 COUNTER

"Over here," shouts Burbank, who is standing a few feet away from the video screen and flashing blue light.

Sure enough. The moment we join him we see what he sees: a small dial, the size of a child's hand. The dial, marked B-19, is pulsating. Clearly this is the device to launch some action against the blue-striped box, which is hurtling toward our aircraft.

Damn you, Townsend, you lying bastard!

Burbank tries turning the dial.

"It's loose," he announces. "I can't turn the damn thing."

Tapper steps in and pushes Burbank's hand away.

It is then that I decide that I absolutely must call on whatever power I can conjure up. I dig deep. I wish for every power I've ever had, wished for, or even daydreamed about. I ask inside myself for the peace of Dache, the joy of helping the good, destroying the evil.

Then suddenly the hideous beeping noise stops. Yet the aircraft we are riding in begins to shake and then tips violently from side to side. It now looks like every light on every panel in the aircraft is flashing.

I keep trying to adjust myself to a state of mental control, to physical strength.

"Do something, sir!" Hawkeye shouts.

I am trying. I am trying. This is no exaggeration: I think I might actually burst.

I watch as Margo reaches in and grabs hold of the dial.

She does not struggle. She does not strain. She does not cry out. The dial turns under her hand as easily as if she were drawing bathwater.

The lights come back on. The aircraft begins to straighten out and calm down. As do I.

What did Margo do that the rest of us failed to do? The four men look at her in shock and joy and total puzzlement. She sees how astonished we are.

"It's a good thing I'm the one who gives Bando his medications," Margo says, lifting an eyebrow.

I'm too tired to understand. Hawkeye, Burbank, and Tapper continue to stare at her. She sighs at how slow we are.

"Ever heard of 'push down and turn'?" she asks. "This dial performs a very important task; they don't want just anyone accidentally bumping into it."

"It's childproof!" Hawkeye shouts.

"Well, it *is* installed on a government aircraft," Margo adds.

We have avoided a catastrophe of enormous consequence, thanks to Margo.

And, of course, I realize now that Townsend betrayed us utterly. He must have alerted Ambrose to our flight, leaving us at the mercy of a madman.

We are all still anxious and shaking, but we are safe, at least temporarily.

I am hating myself for allowing myself to be so smoothly deceived by Townsend. If I had any more tears inside me, I would weep. But I'm tired of crying. First for Jericho, and then for Maddy. I'm tired of being one step behind and blundering ahead.

I scream what I feel, "That bastard. That evil devil. That filth. That monster."

But it is only after this outburst, as I sense a personal power and force from within me, that I realize our salvation comes with another reward.

Glenn Ambrose just suffered his first failure.

CHAPTER 93

WE ROAM THE streets of Dubai searching for Maddy. I have no words of inspiration for Margo, for my team, for myself. Anything I might say would be empty, useless. We wander the city, learning it as we go.

The place itself is a mass of contrasts. Emirati men in dark kanduras. Emirati women in colorful abayas. Others, presumably tourists or those on business, are in Ralph Lauren and Armani. While the streets are bustling, they are not nearly as full as I had expected for such a large city.

Around every corner, we look, we search, we call her name. Maddy? Maddy? People sidestep us, annoyed as they try to move about their daily lives with us in their way.

Both Margo and I try to use our powers to look through walls, to transform ourselves into flying creatures, to jump from street to building to park to restaurant. Anyplace. Anywhere.

The rest of the team check in with their contacts in the

area, meet with people who might know something, and, of course, walk the streets themselves.

With a touch of hope, we visit the vast Dubai Mall, full of luxury retail stores, movie theaters, and high-end restaurants. The day grows darker, but the weather remains stiflingly hot.

"A little bit of food would help," says Margo. "It's been quite a while since we've eaten."

"Energy," Hawkeye says. "We need food for energy."

Like all of us, he does not want to put his needs above the focus on our mission. But he and Margo are correct. We need sustenance if we are to succeed.

When we do agree to fuel up, we find, ironically, ridiculously, that we are standing outside a restaurant called Somewhere.

Yes, of course Maddy is somewhere. The thought is both comforting and infuriating.

We order, and dishes with unexpected combinations of ingredients arrive. Chinese-style dumplings with Mexican flavors. Barbecued Greek-style grilled chicken breasts with a Canadian maple-flavored sauce. Lovely though the food might be, and hungry as we all are, we are mostly interested in hydrating ourselves with seltzer water and chai tea.

Our waiter, a sweet-looking young woman who wears a burgundy hijab covering her hair, her neck, and much of her chin, delivers a second pot of tea along with a third bottle of sparkling water.

The young woman finishes her delivery and walks away.

Tapper tells us that she has dropped a small piece of paper on his lap. The paper is folded into a neat triangle.

"The check?" asks Margo.

Tapper hands me the paper and I unfold it. A short handwritten message, in pencil.

SOUK AL BAHAR. ASAP. STORE OF CARPETS.

I pass the note around to the others.

I consult my handheld device. In fact, we all do. The location of Souk Al Bahar is a short distance across the nearby river. Our devices will guide us there.

"Do you think...?" Margo asks. Then she adds, "I'm afraid to even say her name."

On this day of awful luck, I understand Margo's superstition and fear.

I tell the others that they should stay at the restaurant while Margo and I follow the directive to visit the carpet vendor.

I try to find words of hope and help.

"Restore your strength. Conquer your thirst. Monitor us on your devices. Join us if you sense trouble."

Then Margo and I are on our way.

CHAPTER 94

THE BIG RED sign on the carpet store gets to the point quickly.

The name translates to VERY GOOD RUGS. Okay. And why not?

Margo and I enter through thick glass doors into one huge room where people are wandering quietly among stacks of beautiful, colorful rugs. We are inside for only a few moments when a young man approaches and greets us. The young man is dressed in white pants and a white linen shirt. He cannot be much older than twenty-five, and he is remarkably handsome, with dark hair and sharp features.

"My name is Abdul Aziz, and I shall be of assistance to you," he says. "Your future and your joy will be in my hands, and I will transfer that joy to you."

Huh?

What should Margo and I do next? Why didn't Maddy—or whoever it was who wrote the message—give us a few more details?

Margo and I are not frightened. We're simply confused. Does Abdul really want to sell us a carpet? Or is there more to him than that?

We follow Abdul Aziz to the center of the huge store. He pauses beside a two-foot-tall pile of rugs. All the rugs are very large, living-room-size large. Our salesman bends down and begins folding the rugs back to reveal that most of them have interesting floral geometric designs. In the case of each and every rug, the artful designs are set against a bright, silky red background.

"Tell me when you see something you like," he says, as he energetically flips more and more rugs. We say nothing. He begins flipping the rugs faster. But Margo and I only stand there, not knowing what to do. Except we know we're not buying a rug.

"Fine. Fine," he says. He sounds disappointed, almost embarrassed, as he continues to speak. "That is fine and good. I understand. You do not like the selection."

"No, that's not it," I say.

"You must come now with me," he says, and he begins to walk toward the rear of this big showroom. My instinct is to follow him, but it also tells me to be careful.

"I shall show you the room where—" he begins.

Margo now interrupts.

"No, thank you," she says, clearly having come to the conclusion that Abdul really is just a rug salesman.

But Abdul Aziz's only reaction is to keep talking.

"Yes. I shall now show you the room where we keep our

most treasured objects, our most exquisite pieces," he says. He keeps walking. We nervously follow.

Within seconds, the three of us are standing in front of a large gray steel door with a barcode lock. Abdul Aziz punches in the code, then pushes the now-unlocked door open and speaks dramatically.

"Behold the treasures for which you are searching!"

CHAPTER 95

IT'S HER.

It's Maddy.

It's so far beyond a miracle that Margo cries, and we both tremble with joy.

We hug and kiss and touch Maddy, who quickly introduces us to her friend Belinda. We welcome the girl into our arms, then turn back to Maddy and hold her again, in the way people do when they doubt the very reality of the flesh and blood right in front of them.

We finally separate and study one another, as if we were observing a sculpture in a great museum. Margo and I take in all the details of Maddy and Belinda.

They have identical haircuts, chopped off sloppily near their ears. Their lips look dry, but their eyes sparkle. They could easily pass for Emiratis. They wear long blue cotton robes and white scarves. I suppose that the modest face and hair coverings lying on a nearby table go on when they are out on the street.

"I'm so glad my messages got through to you," Maddy says.

"Because of this guy," Belinda says as she gestures toward the handsome young man. "Abdul Aziz is our angel of mercy."

Margo cannot contain her own questions. "Are you both healthy? Have you been hurt? Where have you been? Who took you from us?"

Maddy jumps in, and with happiness in her voice she says, "Margo, please stop. We'll tell you everything. We're fine now. It's been pretty much a living hell, but we're okay."

"Again," says Belinda. "Thanks to this amazing man." Abdul Aziz looks shyly toward the ground.

As the young man pours coffee into glasses filled with ice, we learn how Belinda and Maddy made it from their terrifying nightmare in the luxury hotel on the ocean to the secret showroom of a rug merchant's store.

There are parts of the tale that bring me personal satisfaction and great joy. As the bits and pieces of the story unfold, I learn how Dache's shape-shifting lessons for Maddy paid off royally after they escaped Burj Al Arab. She tells us how, after regaining her strength, she transformed into an extremely strong swan, able to ferry Belinda to shore. She managed to recharge an abandoned, rusted cell phone with her own energy. She managed to nab loaves of bread when she and Belinda were hungry and to start a small fire on a cold night, rare but not unheard of during summer in Dubai.

Maddy's abilities and Belinda's street smarts kept them

alive, but they were still extremely lucky to accidentally run into Abdul Aziz, who had intuited that the girls had fallen on hard times. For further luck, their handsome young protector had a wealthy father who had a well-protected building where they could stay.

Margo and I shake our heads in amazement at the story the girls tell.

Yes, we still have to find a safe place to shelter.

Yes, we have the horrors of an environmental nightmare and a worldwide plague, and now, of course, I have to be aware of the fact that President Townsend can be counted as not only an irritant but also an enemy.

And, damnit, why do I refuse to completely trust Abdul Aziz, the handsome young man who saved both the girls?

Messages—that's why. Maddy said she was relieved that I received her messages sent via Abdul... but I only got one.

Yes, I'll need to keep an eye on him.

CHAPTER 96

WE HAVE MADE it back to New York. Maddy, Margo, Belinda, and I, along with our other team members, have arrived at the family mansion. Grandma Jessica weeps with joy, but before we even greet and embrace one another, Margo does a patch test on all of us to see if we are carrying the Newbola virus. News organizations around the world are reporting different ideas about how the virus is spread, so we must be extra cautious.

Every one of us tests negative—even Margo.

"Clearly, Dr. DaSilva's vaccine worked," Margo says. "We should let her know so that it can go into mass manufacturing immediately."

"Hold on a second," I say. "You weren't vaccinated, remember? And neither were Maddy and Belinda. We can't know that it was the vaccine that kept the rest of us safe, since those who *weren't* vaccinated also tested negative."

"True, Lamont," Margo concedes. "But we've traveled across the world and were shoulder to shoulder with a large population in Dubai. If the virus isn't *only* spreading through injection, transfusion or sexual contact anymore, the possibility of contagion was overwhelming."

"Yes, but is that convincing enough for you to advise that the entire human race should be injected with this otherwise untried vaccine?"

"No," she agrees. "Maybe our bad luck is actually changing. Why don't we just accept it and enjoy these good results?"

Even if I'm not convinced the vaccine is what kept us safe in Dubai, I decide to get in touch with Dr. Anna DaSilva and let her know that it may have been effective for my team...

Dr. DaSilva begins the conversation.

"I prayed for your safety," she says.

"The prayers worked," I say.

"You know the old saying," says Anna. "The prayers of great sinners can work miracles."

Clever banter. Witty dialogue. Neither one of us is good at it. But more than that, I need an update on the status of Newbola. Has the vaccine she tried on us been tested more widely? Has good progress been made? Could our optimistic test results be incorrect?

"I have some important questions for you, Doctor," I say.

"I'm sure you do," she says. Her voice is calm, pleasant, confident. "Ask away. I'm sure I'll have some helpful answers. Dealing with—and destroying—Newbola is now the most important thing in my life."

"Me, too, Doctor," I say, and then I begin.

"I need to let you know something. Margo administered the vaccine—"

It is at this precise moment that Margo madly waves her arms at me and then makes the football referee signal calling for a time out.

"Hold on a minute, Doctor," I say to Anna DaSilva.

"President Townsend is calling," says Margo. "I think you should talk to him."

I begin my angry response. "Why would you say that, after everything that has—"

Margo interrupts loudly. "He said it was urgent."

It's then that I deliver to Dr. Anna DaSilva one of the most annoying phrases in the English language.

"I've got to take this call," I say.

I click off Dr. DaSilva. I click on President Townsend.

CHAPTER 97

I KNOW I'VE made this very clear, but let me state it one more time—I believe that President Townsend is the most reprehensible world leader alive today. But at this moment I force myself to take Townsend's call, mostly because I am bursting to confront him about his massive treachery.

My first words to him? I immediately explode. "You betrayed me, Townsend! You are a liar and a devil."

"Control yourself, Cranston," he says, his own voice relaxed, pleasant.

"Damn control! Damn you! Damn your lies!" I reply. Yes, I am absolutely off the rails with no intention of getting back on. "You promised protection. You promised help. Support."

"And that's what I delivered," Townsend says.

I angrily but briefly recap the missile attack for him. I detail our horrendous, frightening near-death experience aboard an aircraft that he provided to us.

Townsend puts forth his point of view.

"You've been misinformed and misled, Cranston. Or maybe you're simply a damned fool. As promised, my people destroyed the Ambrose missile as soon as we saw it advancing toward your airship," he says.

"You're lying, Townsend. It was because of the quick response of Margo that we were able to disengage and destroy the attacking missile. You aided and abetted the enemy."

"Believe what you want to believe," he says. "I am certain that we destroyed the weapon when it was launched, with your team as the target."

All my anger spent, I find that I have to consider the situation at hand, not dismiss alternatives simply because of my personal beliefs concerning Townsend's character.

What if Townsend is actually telling the truth? What if Ambrose has circumvented the plan both Townsend and I put into place? Yes, that might have happened.

Dache often says, *Always remember that it is possible that nothing is actually impossible.*

What if, even with Townsend on our side, there is no way that we will ever end the power Ambrose wields, the power of Terrageddon?

As I consider the possibility, I stop talking.

Eventually Townsend speaks. "Are you still there, Cranston?"

"Yes, I'm still here."

"When all your ranting and raving stopped I thought that perhaps you had simply disconnected," Townsend says.

"No," I say. "I have not disconnected."

"Good, because—" Townsend continues.

"But I am now," I say, and hang up.

CHAPTER 98

ONCE I'M OFF the phone with Townsend, everyone on my team looks at me expectantly. They all know the question:

What's next?

I turn and face the roomful of family and friends who will help me hatch big ideas, help me create peace and joy for the future. But at this moment they need to help me formulate a plan. Now that Maddy is safely back home, we need to decide what to do with the information that Ambrose is somewhere in Africa—and how we can possibly disarm a man who controls a machine with the power to destroy the entire planet.

"Here is the oldest advice in business," I tell the group. "When in doubt, when all looks lost, when solutions are scarce, when morale is low, when the enemy is strong, there is just one thing to do... have a meeting."

Then I add, "So, let us gather here again in fifteen minutes, and somehow, someway, we will build a plan."

The small crowd quickly disperses, all of them thankful for the break.

Maddy has her own plans. She tells me, "I've got to take Belinda back to her place. She needs the comfort of her own bed, but she's too scared to go home alone."

"I understand," I say. "Do what you have to do."

Ten minutes later Belinda and Maddy are standing in front of Belinda's recently replaced apartment door—or at least, what's left of it. It's been ripped off its hinges, shards of wood still hanging in the doorframe.

As soon as they walk inside, Maddy and Belinda are overwhelmed by the condition of the filthy room. They cover the bottom half of their faces, speaking through splayed fingers to avoid the smell.

"God," says Belinda. "I thought it couldn't be worse than it was when I lived here."

As if to prove Belinda's point, three very fat rats scurry across the floor, scattering trash as they go. Belinda yelps and jumps onto the coffee table, which collapses under her weight, dumping her onto the floor. The rats race toward the girl, curious, but Maddy jumps in front of her friend, waving her arms and yelling. The vermin dash away, disappearing into the ripped side of the couch.

Maddy points out that the ceiling above is stained with big brown blotches.

"I don't even want to think what that might be," she says.

"No, you don't," Belinda agrees. "I think that's where my neighbor's bathroom is."

Maddy moves into the kitchen and flips on the light. Immediately, thousands of cockroaches scramble for cover. There are so many that it seems as if the entire floor is moving.

"You can't stay here," says Maddy. "This isn't sanitary, to say the least. You don't even have a door, Belinda. Anyone can walk in and out of here."

"Gosh," Belinda says. "Who'd have thought there'd ever be a break-in in a classy building like this?"

"At the very least we'll need to get you a new door," Maddy says, eyeing the empty frame. "And definitely a new lock, plus a dead bolt."

"Yeah, sure, that way no one can come in and steal the rats and the roaches," says Belinda.

Maddy smiles as she taps quickly at her phone, trying to find an emergency contractor. Then she suggests that they both do their best to clean up the place.

"Maybe we should just put everything in the middle of the room and set it all on fire," says Belinda.

"Then I'll have to defend you against an arson count," Maddy says. "And at this point, I've missed so much work I don't even know if I have a job anymore."

They begin by clearing the mattress of moldy sandwich crusts, old cigarette butts, and empty plastic bags that still hold traces of what Maddy suspects is cocaine.

When the mattress is finally cleared, Belinda pulls off the filthy sheets.

"The time has come to wash these rags," Belinda says.

"The time has come to *replace* these rags," Maddy says. Then she adds, "I'll go out and buy some new ones for you. Think of it as a birthday gift."

"My birthday isn't until February," Belinda says. "And I don't take charity."

"February?" Maddy asks, pulling out her phone to mark her calendar. "What day?"

"The fourteenth," Belinda says, touched that Maddy is adding it to her calendar.

"Not a birthday present, then," Maddy says. "But how about I be your early Valentine?"

"Ha," Belinda says, her eyes suddenly going dreamy. "Somebody beat you to it."

Maddy goes still, a suspicion that had taken hold in Dubai resurfacing. "Is it Abdul?"

Their handsome protector had been a miracle for sure, but Maddy had noticed right away that he paid a little too much attention to the overly young Belinda. To Maddy he had always been polite, but to her companion he was friendly—even affectionate.

His behavior had been a red flag for Maddy, but she'd kept it to herself, knowing they had much bigger problems at the time, and no way to survive in Dubai without Abdul's help. Even so, she'd been sure to keep Belinda by her side at all times to make sure that Abdul never got her alone.

Now she looks at her friend with concern. It's time to have a hard conversation.

"Belinda," she says quietly. "I know that you liked Abdul. I know that it was all very romantic, how he swooped in and saved us. But—"

"But he's too old for me?" Belinda finishes Maddy's sentence.

"Well, yes," Maddy says. "That's one thing."

"He's twenty-one," Belinda argues. "I'm fifteen. It's only six years. If he were thirty and I were twenty-four, you wouldn't say a damn thing about it!"

"Except you're *not* twenty-four," Maddy bites back. "And I bet once you are, he won't be interested anymore."

"That's a horrible thing to say," Belinda says, crossing her arms. "Is it so hard to believe that he likes me for me?"

"No," Maddy says carefully. "After all, *I* like you for you. You're a wonderful person, Belinda. You're caring and smart, you're tough, and you've got the determination of a pit bull."

Belinda's face softens at the compliments.

"But you are still a minor," Maddy says sternly. "And Abdul has no business being around you."

"He's a wonderful person, too!" Belinda insists. "He's caring and—"

"Okay, listen," Maddy says sharply. "I'm going to tell you who Abdul actually is, and it's not who you think."

"What?" Belinda asks, her eyes narrowing.

Maddy sighs. Her suspicions about Abdul had kept her on alert at all times, and unable to sleep, even though she and Belinda had a pile of expensive rugs as their bed.

"I saw Abdul in his father's office one night when I got up to use the bathroom," Maddy explains. "It was way after hours and the shop was closed up."

"He works hard," Belinda says. "He has to—"

"He had a second phone," Maddy goes on. "One we didn't know about. And here's the other thing—Lamont only received our first message. None of the others got through to him."

"What?" Belinda asks. "What are you talking about?"

"Think about it," Maddy continues. "Abdul miraculously crossed paths with us in the massive city of Dubai. He offered to let us use his phone in order to gain our trust, but when I saw that the keyboard was Arabic, I couldn't send the message—just as he planned. I gave him Lamont's number, and he *had* to send that first message, because I was watching him. But I never knew what he typed."

"But he did sent it," Belinda says.

"He did, but it was vague, at best," Maddy says. "All it said was that I was in a large city. It was Burbank's ability to trace the signal that made it possible for Lamont to narrow it down to Dubai so quickly. My grandma Jessica's grasp of Arabic helped, though it would have taken longer for them to find us with only Abdul's message."

"But he sent the other messages in English! You watched him!" Belinda insists.

"And none of those messages went through," Maddy says. "It was a dummy phone that looked exactly like his real one. Whenever I tried to use it to dial Lamont's phone, the signal was lost. I chalked it up to trying to make an international call, but after I spotted Abdul's second phone, I figured out what really happened.

"Once Lamont was spotted in the city, Abdul knew he didn't have much time—we'd be found eventually. So he plotted to have the waitress drop that note in the restaurant. That way he could look like our hero and not a villain."

Belinda sags, her head hanging as tears brim. "I can't trust anybody," she says.

"That's not true," Maddy says, coming to her side. "You can trust me."

CHAPTER 99

I USE MY fifteen-minute waiting time to reconnect with Dr. DaSilva over video-conference.

"Sorry about hanging up on you," I say.

She responds, "Did Townsend have any useful information?"

"No," I say. "Just the usual. Lies. Arrogance. Stupidity. Narcissism."

Anna shakes her head. "I manage to have a positive working relationship with him, Lamont. I don't understand why you can't."

"Because I don't want to be on the same team as that—" I stop short. I cannot find a word strong enough without resorting to schoolyard vulgarity.

"Let me ask you something, Lamont," Dr. DaSilva continues. "Did Townsend bring you up to date on the Newbola situation?"

"No, not at all," I say. "We had a different issue to discuss. I was going to tell you before, Margo, Maddy, her friend

Belinda, myself, everyone on my team tested negative for the virus."

"Listen to me, Lamont. The tests that you took are no longer valid. The virus has mutated. Do you know what that means?"

I immediately become annoyed. She is speaking to me as if I were a child, or an untutored bystander. My knowledge of medicinal research is as strong as my knowledge of science and general humanity.

I wrestle with my anger. I try to get it under control. I need a meeting with *myself. Damnit, Lamont. Calm down. Erase your ego. Be part of the team, part of the solution. Listen to Dr. DaSilva. Ask the right questions.*

"You said the virus has mutated?" I ask.

Dr. DaSilva nods. "Everyone who works here with me is now calling the new strain Newbola Strong. We have calculated it to be almost 200 percent more deadly than its original form."

CHAPTER 100

I INHALE DEEPLY. *Stay calm. Don't be foolish, Lamont,* I think. *Get informed. Get to work.*

Dr. DaSilva says that she is now sending me all the information she and her staff have accumulated on Newbola Strong. "We've been working around the clock," she adds.

They have identified and relocated two hundred patients who have tested positive for Newbola Strong to a secure, guarded army barracks outside Sacramento. Three hematologists from three different medical universities are working 24-7 to isolate the chemical structure of the new virus.

As for me, I am working hard to remain focused on this new and awful information. I listen as Dr. DaSilva explains the chemical discovery routes that she and her team are pursuing. I try to think how I can aid and abet their progress. Intruding on my thinking, however, are my suspicions regarding Townsend.

"Are you getting all this, Lamont?" Dr. DaSilva asks. Her own voice is filled with anxiety.

"Yes, I'm getting it," I say.

"The material I've just sent you will clarify a great deal," she says. Then she adds, "Prepare yourself for the descriptions of the symptoms. The effects of this mutated virus are horrible beyond anything we've seen."

We wind down our conversation. Before I accuse Townsend, before I download the info from Dr. DaSilva, before anything else, I must share this awful news with my team.

The fifteen-minute wait is up.

The small, smart, brave group assembles in front of me. I'm about to start talking when I realize that not everyone is present.

"Where's Maddy?" I ask. "Where's Burbank?"

Margo speaks first. "Maddy called. Belinda's apartment was broken into. The girl doesn't want to intrude on our family anymore, so Maddy's taking her to a hotel for the night."

"And Burbank is lying down," Hawkeye supplies.

"*Lying down?*" I repeat, shocked that my teammate would take a nap with so much at stake.

"Yes," Margo says, clearly worried. "He said he has a really terrible sore throat."

CHAPTER 101

HOW STUPID OF me. How ridiculously, blindly stupid of me. When we arrived back in New York, I had actually convinced myself that our extraordinary amount of bad luck had come to an end. How much horror could the world bring down upon us?

As you have most likely realized... I was wrong. Horribly wrong.

Burbank's sore throat only worsens, giving us no doubt that Newbola Strong is present among us, bringing with it exceptional pain and suffering. It takes only thirty minutes for the horrid disease to explode and infect every person in the house.

Large red and yellow pus-filled sores begin to spread across our necks, backs, and legs. Elbows and knees seem particularly vulnerable. It is in those vital joints that Newbola Strong not only disfigures the skin but penetrates to the bones themselves, causing excruciating pain.

I am not spared. Along with the same throbbing pain

and mutilated skin that are cursing my family and friends, I am flushed with an alarmingly high fever and a headache so severe that I think I can hear the pulsing of the veins that surround my brain.

I am trying to figure out what, if anything, I can do to help all of us.

Then, unexpectedly, Grandma Jessica—her own voice raspy with pain—announces that Dr. DaSilva is calling on the video screen.

Sure enough, Dr. DaSilva looks calmly—even happily—out at me. It's understandable that she is calm. She does not yet know that the new plague has exploded in my specific world.

"Did you get the documentation and analysis I sent you, Lamont? I'm anxious to hear your thoughts."

I sputter and stammer.

"Is something wrong on your end?" she asks. "I'm having trouble hearing you."

"Anna, it's here!" I say. "It's in my home! It's inside my family and my friends!"

The woman on the screen looks confused.

"What do you mean?" she asks.

I realize that my voice is soft and weak. I try again.

"Newbola Strong. The new strain. We all have it," I say, my throat on fire. My lips and tongue are quivering.

"I warned you that it was spreading," Dr. DaSilva says. But there is no "I told you so" tone to her voice. She is clearly as alarmed as I am.

"Hold on a moment," she says.

I watch the video screen as Dr. DaSilva taps some keys on a nearby computer. In the few seconds it takes her to perform that task, Margo slowly walks toward me and shows me a message on her handheld device. It's from Maddy:

Me Belinda sick. Skin pain. Sores. Bad heads.

In my sick, confused state it takes me longer than it should to understand that both Maddy and Belinda also have been struck by Newbola Strong.

Then Dr. DaSilva begins talking excitedly.

"Lamont, you can try taking an experimental formula that my team has created. It's not been thoroughly tested, of course," she says.

"Then give me an *un*tested antidote," I say. "Anything. Send me that or send me a gun so I can shoot everyone. This is horrible."

Anna closes her eyes for a few seconds. When she opens them she says, "We know nothing about its effectiveness. We know nothing about side effects. It is not ready to even risk testing on the severely suffering patients being held in the army barracks."

"Just give it to us," I say. "I think every one of us would agree that any side effect cannot possibly be as bad as the symptoms."

She speaks.

"There is a model of the capsule being formulated at the confidential pharma creation lab on 124th Street. If you could send someone up to 350 East Twen—"

"I can't send someone," I tell her. "We're all too sick. Way too sick. We can barely move. Tell the lab to set the medication next to an open windowsill on the south side of their building."

I am, of course, hoping that I have enough remaining mental power to get the medication to us.

Dr. DaSilva says, "Will do."

I break the connection with her and then bow my head. I try desperately to make my way through the pain and fever that have invaded my brain. *Focus, Lamont. Unleash the power. Focus, Lamont. Harness the power and let it move forward. Harness and work. Work. Just work.*

I keep trying. I stay focused

I squint hard. I think. I work. I focus.

I open my eyes. Then I look down at my hands.

I am now holding a small bottle of tiny green pills.

I distribute them quickly to my team. Then I invoke my recently dormant atomic dissolve-and-rebuild power to mind-messenger two pills to Maddy and Belinda.

CHAPTER 102

WE ALL GET better. Quickly. Easily. Our extraordinary muscle aches disappear. The raspy, burning soreness in our throats disappears as well.

But, as has been consistent in our lives lately—the best news is almost always followed by the worst news.

When I contact Dr. DaSilva to let her know about our almost miraculous recovery results, a different person appears on the screen, a young man I've never seen or heard of before.

He cannot be more than twenty-five years old. He wears a black T-shirt along with large glasses in thick black frames. He is a no-nonsense, very self-important sort. He waits for no explanation or introduction.

"Dr. DaSilva is unavailable to take this call. Therefore, I have been tasked with responding."

The terse voice? The formal manner? The enormous seriousness of this young man is confusing to me. What's going on?

"Who are you?" I ask, but I have already formed an opinion. I believe this young man is likely an AI creation. So many people these days are living in a world of bots. Dr. DaSilva must have generated an assistant to help with her workload.

"My name is David Preston Klehr, and I am—"

Suddenly the man claiming to be David Preston Klehr disappears from the screen and is immediately replaced by Dr. DaSilva herself. At least, I think it is Dr. DaSilva herself.

"My apologies, Lamont," she says in a nervous voice filled with anxiety. "I am sorry, but David is my finest subordinate. I task him with taking my calls when I am unavailable."

I continue to be confused. I am especially confused by the title of "subordinate," but I want to engage immediately with Dr. DaSilva.

"I wanted to let you know that the medication you sent me is, in a word, wondrous."

She reacts with neither joy nor satisfaction, which makes no sense.

"I am thrilled to hear this, Lamont. However, we have a related problem. One that I fear may be unsolvable."

"Go on," I say.

"There is an extraordinary infestation of Newbola Strong in West Africa. Check your geo-monitor."

Margo, who has been monitoring this conversation, adjusts an adjacent screen to reveal a map from DaSilva's team of the affected area.

"The areas shaded in burgundy are the major areas of the viral horror. The areas in green are predicted to be hours away from the same medical crisis. We are talking about thousands of victims, perhaps hundreds of thousands, who will—as you yourself have now experienced—suffer incredibly, perhaps even die."

I take in the map quickly. Both Niger and Nigeria are completely painted in the color burgundy. The color extends through all of neighboring Mali and begins to slacken off—but only slightly—as it encroaches on Mauritania. The rest of the map's western corner consists of blotches of green.

"How fast can we get your remarkable medicine to these people?" I ask.

"That's the problem. This is the worst viral invasion the world has ever known. So many people are stricken. We have absolutely no manufacturing capabilities available," she says.

"But, Doctor," I say. "Only minutes ago, not more than a half hour, we received these miracle capsules from your Upper Manhattan pharma manufacturer."

"Have you not seen the news?" Dr. DaSilva asks.

"No, I was busy dying," I snap back.

"Lamont," she continues. "The world has changed in that half hour. The building that housed the capsule maker was struck by multiple explosions. They leveled the building. Even worse, they killed all seven of the people who were working on production."

"Surely, there's someplace else—"

"Certainly there's someplace else. We have sent our analysis and formulae to our partners in Bloomington, Indiana, and Casper, Wyoming. But they won't be able to supply us with anything for at least three days. Part of the difficulty of creating—"

I interrupt.

"Save the explanation about what we can't do," I say. "I need to focus on what we can do.

"And what is that, Lamont?" Dr. DaSilva asks. I know the answer, and I give it to her.

"I've got to go there."

CHAPTER 103

I TELL MY colleagues of my decision to go directly to Nigeria. Their response? A combination of extreme apprehension *and* extreme understanding. I am personally highly gratified that all of them, without exception, volunteer to accompany me on this enormously challenging journey.

I tell them (and I mean it) that the plan is far too dangerous to risk the lives of anyone else. Since my Dache-taught superpowers are almost completely restored, I remind them that I have manipulative skills such as shape-changing, mind control, internal speed, and energy mechanisms that they do not share.

"Indeed," I say to them, "even though Margo and Maddy have gradations of powers similar to my own, I will not permit them to confront such a dangerous situation."

Then I share with everyone my plan. As of right now, all signs are pointing toward Africa. We know that's where Ambrose is, and the fact that the largest outbreak of

Newbola Strong is located there proves to me that he is responsible for the virus as well as the natural disasters.

If I can find Ambrose, there's a chance I can destroy Terrageddon and end the plague at the same time, as he certainly has an antidote on hand, if only to keep himself safe.

I have to throw caution to the wind. Plan or no plan, I have to go to Africa.

Right after I end the meeting with my team, I connect with an old friend. Gutta Linderson is a former colleague of mine now teaching science at a private university in Helsinki, Finland.

Gutta is way beyond delighted to help. He is ecstatic.

"Anything I can do, small or large, to restore some peace and order to this awful universe is a great privilege."

I explain to Gutta the intricacies of my planned, somewhat crazy rampage. I further caution him that it is only my personal instinct that the Terrageddon satellite attacks are supported by President Townsend, though executed by Glenn Ambrose.

"This is based partly on my intuition," I tell Gutta. "I have been wrong before. You don't have to help if you don't want to."

Gutta laughs, then speaks. "Don't want to? Don't want to? Listen, Lamont. You are my hero, and there's no way I'm backing out on a chance to help you save the world."

After that burst of hope and praise, I tell Gutta that he

must immediately arrange to have a ship fortified with advanced antiaircraft artillery and superior technocommunication capabilities.

"I'm on it. You know that you can depend on me," he says.

"Yes, I know that." At least, I think I know that. There is always a tiny bit of doubt that I carry with anyone, everyone. I see potential betrayal everywhere, except within my own family and team.

Even a man who has powers beyond belief cannot work alone. I must trust that Gutta will do as he says.

But my trust extends no further than that.

CHAPTER 104

I AM ALONE. Alone in the middle of the Atlantic Ocean, somewhere miles away from the west coast of Africa.

I am alone, standing on the top deck of a Bandon Sapphire 220 battleship, a small, tough, nimble ship that last saw action fifteen years ago, during an unsuccessful Russian invasion of Poland and Germany.

No other crew members, certainly no other passengers.

My battleship is operating by remote navigation. Although Gutta Linderson is thousands of miles away, the multiple onboard cameras, along with my voice commands, help guide his manipulation of the vessel.

The ocean is not gentle. The mid-Atlantic is never a safe location. But my luck, recently astonishingly bad, has changed, at least momentarily. The waves are no higher than a few feet, relatively gentle for this time and place. Gutta has transmitted his evaluation that the winds are significant but not treacherous. There is no other natural force at the moment to interfere with the radar tracking and satellite identification of the battleship's location. In other words, my ship and I can easily be traced by Gutta and by his monitoring allies from among the European coast guards. And most importantly...by the insane and vigilant Glenn Ambrose.

And that is precisely what I want.

CHAPTER 105

OH, DAMN, HOW painfully I feel the wicked wind. I watch the thick, charcoal-gray clouds above. The ocean spray bombards my face and hands like sharp bullets. And yet my power and determination overwhelm whatever fearfulness I might once have had.

It is my chance to confront my enemy. It is my chance to protect the world. Am I exaggerating? I wish I were.

No human voice is strong enough to guarantee that the enemy will hear my message. So I call upon the power inside me to change my physical body.

I must begin. I concentrate. Yes!

My very neck expands. From a twenty-inch circumference it grows into a fifty-inch circumference. I grind my teeth and force my vocal cords to grow and swell and spread. More and more and more, so much that they can barely be contained by the super-huge neck that holds them.

My chest begins to ache. I know my lungs are increasing to match the size of my vocal cords. I recall that Dache always taught me that a charge of new power almost always causes more power to erupt.

I watch the dark and gloomy sky. I watch and a thought erupts in my mind.

Is it merely Glenn Ambrose whom I am bursting to confront? This insignificant little nobody of a clever, well-educated science student. A boy. A child. A brat.

What if Glenn Ambrose is the tiniest cog in a gigantic wheel of evildoers? What if there are a thousand other devils in league with him? What if he is merely a servant to the greatest horrible genius of them all? Could my nemesis, Shiwan Khan, have returned? What if Ambrose is in the control of Satan himself?

I clear my throat. The rumble in my chest is my new and gigantic larynx. It clicks into place with my new vocal cords, my new lungs, my new strength.

It is time to shout to the heavens.

But first a test run.

"I am here!" I scream.

The volume of my voice booms out louder than thunder. My overpowering sound moves the clouds, churns the ocean waves. Rain descends. Then all is calm until the echo of my booming, rolling, roaring words stops.

I scan the sky for a sign of something, anything. A drone? A missile? Terrageddon itself?

But there is nothing but the dark sky and the fat clouds and the yellow of the moon, a moon that looks as if it is watching me with disdainful amusement.

Are you ready, young Ambrose? I hope so. Because what happens next should banish every trace of your existence.

CHAPTER 106

I TILT MY head back. Way back, farther back than a man's neck was ever designed to tilt. The rear of my neck could probably touch the tops of my shoulders.

Then, gazing hard at the sky, I raise my trumpet voice, my violent, angry, incredibly loud new voice.

This world does not belong to you!

Again I say: this world does not belong to you!

Nay. And nay. And nay again.

The world belongs to the good and noble who inhabit it.

You can dare to destroy it. But you will fail.

I will see to that!

I wait. The *slap-slap-slap* of the waves, the spatter of sea spray and the drumming of rain on the top deck, squawking sea hawks, their sounds all suddenly seem to disappear. For the first time ever I understand the phrase *the silence was deafening.*

Is this insane silence a fantasy inside my head? Or is this the response of the madman I want to lure into battle? If this is his response, it is insulting. I deserve more. I deserve an opponent who will face me.

I bring my head back up to its upright position. My next action is an attempt to confirm that Ambrose or Khan or Satan or whoever is behind the scourge of the world has received my challenge.

Only the just will command the world.

Control will live only with the good.

And then I flatly and loudly and threateningly announce:

Destroy me if you dare.

Destroy me if you can.

It is then that all sound and fury return. The ocean begins to roil. The clouds dissolve and then re-form, new clouds following the same pattern. They, too, dissolve, then they, too, reappear.

But this is merely the beginning.

I have predicted that the enemy might retaliate against my furious threats by causing the oceans to suck me into a churning vortex. In my mind, the skies will turn black with adversarial action, the floor of the sea will crack open, much as they did during the attacks on Kyoto and Copenhagen.

But Dache has warned me in the past, *Rarely trust your instincts. Always trust your brain.* This, the worst challenge of my life, will prove that my wise teacher is always wise.

The dark sky begins to brighten. Each and every cloud dissipates, and a dazzling yellow light bathes the battleship, the water, the sky itself. The comforting sounds of nature—birdsong and gentle winds—replace the eerie quiet.

None of this new environment calms me.

This understanding does not come from an instinct. Rather, it comes from my brain, and from so many lifetimes of battling evil.

I have been allowed a few seconds of reprieve, but I know it only means that my enemy is preparing to attack. Yet again, it is nothing I might have predicted.

The yellow sky begins to fade, but not to a lighter hue. It seems the enemy has flipped a switch that infuses the heavens to explode with an intense orange. The orange seems to join with the ever-fading yellow, and to my amazement the firmament changes from orange to a deep bloodred. The red turns scarlet, and the scarlet becomes burgundy, and then... the water, the water, the water.

The small, safe waves grow into swells that expand higher and wider. I have no control over them. They climb above me, an enormous weight of water gathered together. How high are the new waves? My estimate is three hundred feet. And climbing.

The battleship lurches wildly from the unbridled power of the ocean. My battleship turns and tilts beneath my feet. With growing fear, I watch the wave reach its zenith—and then fall back toward the earth... toward me. Yes, then it happens—this war-tested twelve-thousand-ton pile of strength capsizes completely.

I am now underwater. And I am now fighting for my life.

CHAPTER 107

HERE IS WHAT I discover about drowning.

There is no top nor bottom to the depth of the water. It is *not* like being in a huge fish tank. Not at all. Instead, I am wildly, absurdly, insanely suspended in an infinite amount of water.

The water grabs me, chews me, tosses, and hurts me. I fall in and out of consciousness, and, of course, I try, in my conscious moments, to find a solution, a personal solution, a powerful solution, frankly, the kind of very special solution that might belong only to me, Lamont Cranston, the Shadow.

An eel. That's it. Lean and skinny and leathery. A transformation, but a foolish one. As an eel I am overpowered by the strength of the waves. I feel as if I am swimming on my own, but I quickly realize that I am the aquatic equivalent of a feather in a storm.

A swordfish. Not an easy order to fill. So many pieces, the body strength to fight the currents, and then the sword.

But what good is the sword? Why force the effort to transform into a swordfish, when there are no predators to combat, no twisted trees and branches to cut through?

"Sloppy thinking," Grandma Jessica might gently warn.

"Slothful consideration," Dache would angrily charge.

Meanwhile this useless swordfish feels himself rising. I cannot discern in which direction the surface lies, but my shakily controlled fish body feels the surge upward. Perhaps I'll become a shark, so I can be covered with denticles, small V-shaped attachments to my skin that should create a smoother swim, a faster speed, a salvation. But no, I realize that the shark is another stupid choice. Even creatures of the sea are at its mercy when it rages with unnatural strength.

I flail. I fail. I return to my human shape. Perhaps an even more reckless decision than becoming a shark.

My first event as a returned and once strong man is to pass out. It happens within seconds. My shoulders and legs begin to ache, then burn. My lungs sting with every gulp of salty water. I push mightily forward one last time, gulping for air, and my hands find purchase on a piece of the battleship. Thankful for a moment's rest, I close my eyes.

I understand that I am nearly dead, half-drowned, an only partially alive thing. It seems, at first, that everything is unchanged: I am still immersed in a horrible churning ocean that pitches me wherever and whenever it cares to.

I become aware that I will not last much longer. I have forced my lungs to supersize, which gained me precious seconds when I was forced beneath the water, but even so, my body is exhausted. I have forced my arms and legs to push way beyond their natural strength, but I am, very simply, prepared for the end.

A whale? A catfish? An octopus? A nautical magical horse? A swimming dinosaur? *Do something, you fool, Lamont.*

Ambrose or Khan or Townsend or a consortium of all three are literally destroying the world at this very moment, and—*oh, useless powers, return, save me!*—I am a flailing, fading piece of nothing in an ocean's hell.

I am about to fall once again into an unconscious state. If I lose my grip on the floating piece of the battleship, I will surely sink beneath the waves and die.

Suddenly, the amazing electrodes that are stored in all human brains—yours and mine—make a last, great effort to remain alive. The survival instinct is so great in every single one of us that in this moment, the great accumulation of useless or useful knowledge inside my brain is accessed, and it comes to me.

The *Pakicetus.* I suddenly remember the *Pakicetus.*

Yes, the *Pakicetus,* the wolf-sized, four-legged, prehistoric ancestor of the whale.

When did I ever hear of this incredible nimble monster? What book did I read? Who taught me about this extraordinary animal?

I struggle to re-create the image in my mind, then shape-shift into this ancient phenomenon. If I am creating a goofy hybrid in my brain, the transformation will fail, but a significant quiver through my limp human body teases me into believing I might be on my way. The legs, the snout, the strength, they invade me. It is happening.

I am the *Pakicetus.*

CHAPTER 108

"IT'S JUST LIKE a horror film," says Margo.

"It's worse than a horror film," says Maddy, as she quickly turns her head away from the giant computer screen.

The team has set up a satellite monitoring system to track the movements and progress of Lamont's treacherous adventure in the middle of the Atlantic Ocean. They see it all, and they see it with a clarity that is both a blessing and a curse.

When the destructive powers from the skies explode into the sea below, the assembled group instinctively reach out and hold one another tightly. Margo looks down to the floor and shakes with fear. Bando cowers between her legs. Even Jericho is cursing and gasping. Burbank, Tapper, and Hawkeye stare, transfixed. Maddy steels herself and stays fixed on the terror she's watching.

"The ship is turning upside down!" shouts Maddy, reporting on what they all can see for themselves. They watch as

Lamont is dumped mercilessly into the raging water, and they wait breathlessly for him to appear above the ocean. They wait. They watch. But of course, it does not happen. Lamont does not appear. As the seconds turn into minutes, they all watch the gigantic swells, the extraordinary churning of the ocean, the disappearance of the remnants of the battleship, and they each tremble with fear.

They see what the lost Lamont cannot see. Terrible drones hovering near the ocean's surface send explosions of power slamming into the water. They see the tons of dirt and sand and plant life spewing up from the Atlantic floor like volcanoes into the dark air.

Maddy breaks out from her tough composure and yells.

"Can we do something? Can we do anything?" she asks. Then she begins a kind of incessant babbling. "Anything? Something! We have to help. We have to do something!"

Grandma Jessica speaks. "There is nothing *we* can do. Any salvation that arrives must come from Lamont himself."

But without discussing the matter, it seems they all know that there is little that even Lamont can do.

As they watch the unrelenting assault from the sky above into the water below, their monitoring system shifts away from its current focus. For just a second, they see the bow of the ship appear above the water once more. But there is no time for hope. The ship disappears back into the water.

Everyone watches with baited breath, waiting for a figure to resurface.

It doesn't.

"Oh, no, oh, no," Margo says, her head dropping into her hands.

Jessica jumps in, not giving up hope just yet. "Wait a second. Just wait a second. Do you see that wake? There's something very large swimming. It's making its way toward land."

Burbank touches two icons, zooming in.

"Is that... is that?" Hawkeye asks, his nose almost touching the screen.

"For God's sake, man!" Burbank sputters. "Back up so the rest of us can see!"

When Hawkeye does, the team can make out a large animal crawling out of the tide and onto the shore.

"He's a *Pakicetus*!" Maddy yells.

"A pack-a-what's-is?" Tapper asks.

Burbank twists three dials on the control panel. Then he moves two screen icons to the right side. These actions make the scene a bit clearer, as the animal collapses onto the shore.

But the ocean isn't done with Lamont yet. Suddenly, the tide begins to rise, overwhelming the beached animal.

"Wake up! Wake up!" Margo yells.

As if he can hear her, the animal begins crawling once again, although it's form is better suited to swimming. It moves slowly, the tide licking at it.

"Oh, no," Hawkeye says, pointing to a large wave that is forming farther out in the ocean.

"Run!" Maddy yells. "Or change into something else! Something better on land."

The thought must occur to Lamont at the same time, as the animal suddenly blurs, shifts, and becomes a tree.

They all watch the screen as if they're hypnotized. They watch the tree grow larger, the roots digging into the earth for sustenance and strength. It gains purchase and stands against the wave as it batters the shore. Strong and healthy, it withstands the sea, and the waters recede. And then, just as the tree is blossoming with new life and restored energy, the screen goes blank again. Burbank does anything he can to restore visual power. He twists dials, pushes buttons; he even bangs the screen with his fists.

"Something's happened. The connection is gone. It could be a result of the explosive condition of the oceanic attack, or it could simply be the evil work of the person or persons manipulating the attack," he says.

It is two o'clock in the morning. Tapper announces that all they can do is wait for a reconnection and hope for Lamont to reappear.

Margo says that she will remain on watch in the communications lab to see what happens. "The rest of you go rest the best you can."

Grandma Jessica says she will relieve Margo in one hour.

Jericho says that he must catch a nap in order to be of use later. Burbank, Tapper, and Hawkeye second this.

Maddy says, "There's someplace I've got to be. It won't take long."

Before anyone can question Maddy, she leaves the room.

CHAPTER 109

BELINDA THOUGHT THE idea was hers.

Maddy thought the idea was hers.

In any case, they both agreed that it was a very good idea. They also agreed that it was a very dangerous idea.

They planned on abducting Detective Robert McCarthy, the mastermind and instigator of their abduction and abuse, which had nearly led to their deaths in Dubai. Yes, they were rescued through their own wisdom and bravery, but the horrors of the experience have stayed with them.

At this moment Maddy is focused on Lamont's terrible trip to Africa, but she also believes that putting in some face time with the despicable McCarthy could be a very prudent way to use her time—and perhaps lead to whoever is stealing the young drug dealers off the street.

Together the two women head to the underbelly of the 59th Street Bridge, a location that both Maddy and Belinda know all too well.

Nothing has changed.

Slender, pretty, solemn-faced girls walk slowly, breaking into forced smiles when a vehicle approaches.

The drivers are there also, circling the girls, ready to pick up or drop off according to whatever directive they get from Carla Spector. The average street junkies are there, two or three sleazy-looking men in cheap clothing and worn sneakers. The upper crust is present as well, cruising by in expensive vehicles, good-looking men in high-end suits and Gucci loafers.

This is yet another alternate world inside New York City.

Road and sanitation department equipment are not just resting under the bridge overnight but serving as cover for illicit drug deals.

An occasional police cruiser drives by, always stopping for just a moment, most likely picking up a payoff.

"Seems like old times," Maddy says. A shrug from Belinda.

They walk. They watch. They talk.

"You scared?" Maddy asks.

"Nope, this is my world. Anyway, I know you've got my back."

"I'll do what I can," says Maddy. Then she adds, "I think that some of my powers are returning."

That news is greeted with one of Belinda's rare smiles.

Maddy continues. "I've been testing my limits, judging the depth of my recovery. I tried some jump-up kick defenses. I practiced some very strong strength exercises. I worked on some core concentration exercises for shape-shifting. I think we'll be safe."

"Just in case your crazy special powers let us down, I brought another special little friend along," says Belinda, reaching inside her jacket to reveal a small pistol.

"What are you doing?" Maddy cries, pushing the gun back down, out of sight.

"One bad turn deserves another," says Belinda. "Anyway, it's just an itty-bitty baby gun."

"That can still fire an itty-bitty ball of metal at top speed and shatter human bodies," says Maddy.

"You've been taking all the risks," says Belinda. "I've had all the benefits. It's time I contributed to this relationship."

Maddy considers for a moment. "All right, but this is only in a worst-case-scenario situation. You don't draw your weapon unless you're willing to use it."

"Oh, I'm willing," Belinda says, a little too eagerly for Maddy's taste.

Suddenly, a strange, high-pitched singsong voice comes from behind them.

"Well, well, well, look who's come home."

A cop? A driver? A customer?

The two of them turn around quickly.

"Mama-Girl!" Maddy yells, surprised at how glad she is to see the older woman. And Belinda, she just bursts into tears.

Mama-Girl steps forward and puts her arms around Belinda.

"Let me hold you and make certain I really got you standing here," says Mama-Girl. Then she adds quietly, sadly, solemnly, "We heard that you two were gone. Very, very, very gone. Gone like Chloe. Gone like Travis."

Maddy nods, then says, "They tried to send us off to some hell, but they couldn't do it."

Belinda rubs her eyes, sniffles, then gets back to business.

"We came by to visit our old friend Detective McCarthy," she says.

"He doesn't work this road anymore," Mama-Girl informs them. "Someone said he was afraid one of the rare decent cops would squeal on him and his whole operation. But he ain't dead. That's for sure."

"I'm sorry to hear that," says Maddy.

"Don't worry about old Bobby-boy," Mama-Girl says, taking a drag on a cigarette. "He's not here at the bridge, but he's around. You can find him on the commuter car strip going uptown on Third Avenue."

"Thanks, Mama-Girl. Appreciate the info," Belinda says.

"God bless you. Good luck, ladies," Mama-Girl says.

She hugs Belinda, then Maddy. Then she says, "Y'all come back when you don't have to run off to beat the shit out of someone."

CHAPTER 110

MADDY HAILS A cab and tells the driver, "Just take us to the general neighborhood of Third Avenue."

Belinda immediately interrupts and revises the order.

"Make that Second Avenue and 30th Street," Belinda says. Then she adds, "You forget. I'm something of an expert in these things. I'm certain that's where the other dealers are, and I'm certain that means McCarthy is there, too, doing whatever Carla says."

Sure enough, they find McCarthy in a cheap blue suit with a shirt unbuttoned to mid-chest standing outside a 7-Eleven, sucking on a straw that's connected to a giant-sized Slurpee.

The two young women walk closer to McCarthy. When he sees them he loses interest in his Slurpee, throwing it to the ground in surprise.

He instinctively backs up a few inches.

"How the hell? You two assholes are... are supposed to... supposed to be..."

"Yeah, I get it," says Belinda, sounding bored. "We're supposed to be dealing drugs in Dubai."

"I've got some questions for—" Maddy begins, but she doesn't get the chance to finish.

Belinda whips out her pistol, aims it at McCarthy's head, and pulls the trigger. But . . . nothing happens.

"What?" Belinda asks, looking at the gun in confusion.

"Safety, dumbass," McCarthy sneers—and then pulls his own gun.

Maddy tightens her shoulders and spine. She concentrates with an intensity so overwhelming that her heart races and her head aches.

McCarthy points his weapon at Belinda, finger curled over the trigger. Suddenly, he goes flying backward, thrown by some invisible force. McCarthy falls hard to the cement ground. The detective goes completely still. Blood oozes from the back of his head.

Belinda, now standing, looks down at the bloody McCarthy. Then she swiftly and firmly kicks the side of his head.

"Superpowers, dumbass, " she says.

CHAPTER 111

MADDY AND BELINDA have shared incredibly uncertain times—in New York, at Harriman, in Dubai. Their friendship has been laced with terror and occasional joy. Their experiences together have afforded them both the opportunity to really get to know each other. Closely. Carefully.

Maddy learned early on that Belinda is very complicated—sad, funny, anxious, and a little bit crazy. But now, in the pursuit and capture of Detective McCarthy, Maddy is suddenly discovering a cold, hard-hearted part of her friend. Maddy knows Belinda to be brave and resilient, but now she is seeing a side of her friend that runs entirely on anger and revenge.

Now fully aware of Maddy's abilities—and having accidentally taught Belinda about the safety on her pistol—McCarthy must do whatever his captors tell him to do.

First they drive to Belinda's grubby apartment. There's

even an additional bit of satisfaction for Maddy. She gets to drive McCarthy's unmarked police car.

The scene remains tense once they enter the apartment. The angry, squirming detective is pushed to the floor and held in place by Maddy's mental powers while the two young women sit on the side of the mattress. They secure his hands behind his back using the handcuffs they found in his car.

Then yet another additional pleasure. As soon as McCarthy manages to sit up, a foul-smelling fat rat and a few large roaches scuttle across the floor where McCarthy sits. He seems as fearful of the vermin and insects as he is of the girls he previously enjoyed terrorizing.

"Get these disgusting fucking creatures away from me! This sucks. We can go to a place where we can have a drink and discuss what's happening. That's how deals are made, girls. Not like this."

"What are you? Insane? Really and truly insane? Are you too stupid to see that we are not interested in making a *deal*?" sneers Belinda, truly angry.

Eyes wide, fists clenched, she jumps to her feet and slaps McCarthy—hard. McCarthy cowers. Belinda hits him again.

"Calm down, Belinda," Maddy says. "We need to hit this guy with questions, not the backs of our hands."

"How about I ask the questions?" McCarthy says, still searching for a semblance of control. "Like, exactly how crazy are you? I'm just a cop doing his job. Yeah, I take a payoff now and then. But nothing more."

"Bullshit," says Belinda.

"Nothing more?" asks Maddy, her own anger rising. "Not kidnapping? Not assault? Not transporting an underage girl halfway across the world for nefarious means?"

"Oh, *that,*" McCarthy says dismissively. "Your new boss would've taken good care of you, and besides Dubai is beautiful. You're the dumb bitches who chose to come back. I was trying to do you a favor."

That statement seems to set off an explosion inside Maddy. It's as if the hate and anger inside Belinda have invaded her friend twice as much, three times as much, a million times as much.

Maddy leans in close to McCarthy, almost nose to nose. "You fool. You sick, hideous fool," yells Maddy. "You allow these girls to become drug mules. You provide them as cheap labor to Carla Spector."

Perhaps Maddy has absorbed all the anger in the room. Belinda has become uncharacteristically calm, almost hypnotically quiet. It looks as if Maddy and Belinda have traded emotional places. Maddy is a case of fury unleashed. Belinda is a vessel of peace.

But maybe not.

"Let me handle this, Maddy," says Belinda. Then she gently pushes Maddy away from in front of McCarthy. Belinda grabs McCarthy's hair and pushes his head backward. She pinches his Adam's apple using her thumb and index finger. McCarthy begins to spit out a gurgling series of hoarse and horrible shrieks, as Belinda's face twists with a sick kind of joy. Maddy has to wonder where she learned this torture technique and if it has ever been used on her friend.

"I can keep doing this for the next ten hours," Belinda says.

McCarthy's eyes roll insanely around in their sockets, finally landing on Maddy. There are no more shrieks, no more gasps for air. Soon there could be no more McCarthy.

"Stop, Belinda. Stop," Maddy says firmly. So Belinda stops. But McCarthy falls to the side, no longer breathing.

"Is he dead?" Belinda asks.

"Faking it," says Maddy, her arms crossed. "And not very well."

When McCarthy doesn't react, she gingerly picks up a rat by its tail and drops it onto his upturned face.

With a shriek, McCarthy opens his eyes and lets out a long wave of harsh, hacking coughs. Finally, he speaks again.

"I don't know shit. You've gotta believe me," he says.

"I'll take it from here," says Maddy, who pushes back her shoulders, eyes on the rat that scurried into the corner, taking a few pieces of McCarthy's hair with it.

Suddenly, the rat changes direction. It crawls across McCarthy's thigh, rushes up his chest, claws at his face, then stops, draws back its head to display short, vicious teeth, and takes a significant bite out of the detective's right cheek. Blood spurts out, then turns into a steady dribble.

The detective flinches, then turns to the side and spits. "That all you got?"

The rat immediately moves closer to McCarthy's right eye. When he instinctively shuts it, the rat delicately takes hold of his eyelid, pulling it out, then snapping it back against his eye. Again, blood drips. The rat crosses the bridge of McCarthy's nose. The rat takes another chomp out of the other cheek. Matching rivers of blood flow down both sides of his face.

It is then that McCarthy finally starts to tell the two young women what they want to know.

CHAPTER 112

MADDY PSYCHICALLY COMMANDS the hungry rat to stop torturing McCarthy. But the rat doesn't go far. It simply leaps to McCarthy's shoulder and rests there, awaiting further instructions.

"Get him off of me," McCarthy says.

Maddy quietly answers. "Yeah, eventually. But for now—tell us everything you know about what's been going on. Tell us about Chloe. Tell us about Travis."

"You know a lot of this shit already," McCarthy says, cautiously eyeing the rat.

"Just make believe that we don't know anything," Maddy says. "You seem pretty convinced that we're stupid, so why don't you start at the beginning. But I wouldn't go slow—brother rat will get hungry again."

"Okay," says McCarthy. "Okay. This might not come as a big surprise, but Carla Spector has a list of clients that have very specific tastes. They want a certain kind of drug, and they want a certain type of young girl—or boy—to bring it to them."

"I see," says Maddy, though she wishes she didn't.

"Wait a minute," says Belinda. "Do you mean like what happened to Joanna?"

"What?" Maddy asks, almost losing her control of the rat. "What happened to Joanna?"

"She's fine," Belinda says quickly. "But one time she said that instead of doing a drop, her driver took her straight to Carla. There was some big-deal guy on the other end of a video call. Joanna and a bunch of other girls had to walk in front of the camera, and he, uh . . . he picked one."

"Picked one?" Maddy asks, her gaze going to McCarthy, who shrugs.

"Yeah," Belinda goes on. "She said she was real bummed, because Carla said whoever the guy picked was going to have it made. Money. Travel. Clothes. Whatever they wanted."

"Sure," Maddy says skeptically, still looking at McCarthy. "I'm sure that's exactly how that played out."

"Yeah, sure," says McCarthy meekly. "I'm sure they're all together on a beach somewhere sipping daiquiris, or some stupid girl drink with a toy in it."

"What does that sound like to you?" Maddy asks Belinda.

"Bullshit," Belinda says.

Maddy closes her eyes and clasps her hands together.

When she opens her eyes a few seconds later, three

cockroaches are crawling up McCarthy's arms. They make their way to his neck, then his jawline. He squeezes his mouth shut, but the lead cockroach pries his lips open. Its legs are just entering his mouth when McCarthy folds. He starts talking. In fact, it seems that McCarthy won't shut up.

It's a bizarre, astonishing, repulsive tale that he tells.

The chosen kids—about thirty of them over the past two years—are provided to special clients with special tastes. This means wealthy, important types. The lowest of scum sitting in the highest of income brackets.

"Chloe?" Maddy asks. "Travis?"

McCarthy nods but doesn't add anything.

"What happened to my friends?" Belinda yells.

The cockroaches spring back to life. One of them is halfway up McCarthy's nostril before he relents.

"They can't exactly go back home," McCarthy says. "Not after the things they've seen. When the people who hired them are finished, they're sent to a confidential research lab outside of Sacramento."

He begins to explain. He tells Maddy and Belinda that there is a medical research lab in a town named Rancho Cordova. There the abducted victims are injected with a very specific dose of Newbola. Then they are reassigned to foreign dignitaries and global celebrities—from CEOs in Japan to university professors in South America, sheiks in the Mideast and presidents in Africa—so they can spread the horrendous disease around the known world.

"Do you know the specific locations?" asks Maddy.

"I heard that some were sent to Japan, some to Denmark. And, like you already know, we were working to get some girls to Dubai."

"That's what you injected us with, isn't it?" Maddy asks, horrified.

"Yes," McCarthy admits. "But don't get all freaked out about it. The strain that the abductees are injected with is a special, dormant kind. The carriers can't drop dead; they wouldn't be very useful, then, would they?"

Maddy and Belinda are, of course, horrified by the revelation. Maddy wonders if the injection of Newbola affected her differently than Belinda because of her innate powers.

"These places you mention were struck by Terrageddon," says Maddy. "That means there's a connection between the kidnapped kids, the spread of Newbola, and the natural disasters that are destroying the world."

Belinda nods in agreement.

They both look at McCarthy. The sneer on his face has disappeared. His shoulders have slumped forward. His eyed are partially closed.

"Is that what's going on, McCarthy? Is Glenn Ambrose working with Carla Spector to disperse Newbola far and wide?"

"Wait. I think he passed out," says Belinda.

"As soon as he comes to I have a lot more questions that need answering," says Maddy. "If the Newbola strain that the carriers are injected with isn't meant to kill them, it's possible we could still find kids like Chloe and Travis alive."

The only problem is that Detective McCarthy can't answer their questions.

He's dead.

CHAPTER 113

THE LIFE-GIVING POWERS of the earth nurtured me through the close shave in Africa. Now recovered, I sit and listen at home while Maddy updates us about her extraordinary confrontation with the late Detective McCarthy, who had ultimately made use of a cyanide capsule under his tongue. At one point, he knew he'd said too much and would never be forgiven by Carla Spector.

Margo is shocked and furious at Maddy's revelations. I am shocked and furious and—I must also admit—proud of Maddy.

With the vital information that Maddy gives, I believe, more than ever, that another expedition—this time to East Africa—is the only way to combat Newbola Strong, and possibly advance some sort of solution or defense to the Terrageddon crisis. The sooner the better. And by "sooner" I mean immediately.

I was unprepared on my first attempt, and possibly still in a weakened state. Quite simply I believe that the return journey I will soon undertake is the most important mission I have ever had and will ever have. I also realize without a doubt that it could be my final mission.

There is a group of evildoers at the root of these exceptional tragedies. From Carla Spector to Glenn Ambrose, but who knows how much further their circle extends? It could be anyone from Townsend to Khan. One of them? All of them? It is my job to find out. Then it is my job to do something about it.

I organize my thoughts. Then I gather my colleagues and inform them of my plans. I begin my remarks with an honest note of reality and humility.

"I realize that I am the person in this group who is fortunate enough to have special powers. The ability to shape-shift, the ability to exert control over the minds of others, the ability to defy the structure of time and space. But these powers can weaken and disappear without warning. Thus, I need strong and smart and faithful colleagues on this mission. It will be a tough, smart, and small group."

Everyone is standing very still. I now say what they all want to know.

"Margo will accompany me. If I am the power in this project, she is the brains."

My wife's face remains placid. She knows that this is not idle flattery on my part. I really mean it, and, deep inside herself, I sense Margo knows that this is true.

"Maddy and Grandma Jessica will remain here in New York."

I can easily tell that Maddy is disappointed...no, not just disappointed, angry. But she knows that this is not the time for protest.

"We'll keep everything in top form," says Jessica. Then she turns to Maddy and says, "Won't we, Maddy?"

Maddy says, "Of course." I believe she's frustrated by being excluded, but I hope she will come to see the wisdom of my decisions.

"For the sake of expediency and efficacy, I can designate only two more people to accompany me. This is a difficult decision, for all the people I work with are the absolute best. As such, I am offering no rationale for my choices."

I look around the room. While I sense anxiety in the air, I see nothing but stoic expressions on each and every face. Then I continue speaking.

"Burbank and Jericho, please prepare for the expedition. Margo, same for you. We'll be leaving in the next five minutes."

There will be no exchanges of "safe travels" or "good luck." That's not the way we operate. What's more, everyone understands the gravity of the situation.

Before I end this meeting, I have one more piece of information to impart.

"I am about to contact Dr. Anna DaSilva. I'm asking her to join us in East Africa. You all know that Dr. DaSilva is the world's leading expert on the Newbola virus. She understands the complexities of the new strain called

Newbola Strong and has created the antidote as well, although it hasn't moved into mass production as yet."

There are nods of agreement in the room. I know I have everyone's support. Then I say something I have never said before to my family and friends.

"Please say a prayer."

CHAPTER 114

OUR PLAN IS to start in Nairobi, Kenya, then travel together to Zanzibar in Tanzania.

My good and able associate from Finland, Gutta, was able to supply us with a self-powered hypersonic aircraft. So my four colleagues—Margo, Dr. Anna DaSilva, Burbank, and Jericho—make the journey to Kenya in fewer than four hours.

I, being uniquely self-powered, was able to make the journey in less than a minute by manipulating space and time.

Every second is vital to our success. We share no warm greetings. Instead, we take a jet-powered open safari vehicle. Gutta explained to me before the trip that it is on loan from a covert engineering unit in Russia. When I asked him how he managed to obtain use of this extraordinary transport, he responded in direct and simple Finnish.

"Lamont, esität liikaa kysymyksiä."

The translation is equally simple: "Lamont, you ask too many questions."

Because I was close to Ambrose's location when I engineered our face-off on the Atlantic Ocean, Tapper was able to triangulate the satellite signal that was used to deploy Terrageddon, narrowing down the area where Ambrose could be.

Now we are standing halfway up a twelve-hundred-foot mountain only miles outside the city of Zanzibar. I would not even call the location "rugged." Overgrown, with a great deal of orange flowers and scraggly green bushes; there are no sounds of animals or birds. The air is humid, but not unbearably so. That's it. That's the location. Not pretty, but not ugly or scary, and certainly not rugged.

Burbank, Margo, Dr. DaSilva, and Jericho set up a very primitive camp under what I identify as a huge rubber tree but what Jericho informs us is specifically called a *Ficus elastica*.

Then Dr. DaSilva speaks. Her voice is uncommonly harsh and impatient.

"If I might have your attention, lady and gentlemen," she says. "The four of you are so focused on finding the master of Terrageddon that you seem to have lost interest in the equally important, perhaps even more important, reason we are in East Africa. The scourge of Newbola Strong."

"Of course," I say. "We—"

But Dr. DaSilva interrupts. She has a speech she is bursting to unleash, and there will be no stopping her.

"Am I the only one who saw the dead camels and water

buffalo on the side streets of Zanzibar? Am I the only one who saw the infected children and their parents resting on piles of dirt and garbage? We were only in the city for a few minutes and it was a lesson in devastation."

"Of course," I say once again. Silence follows. Then Dr. DaSilva continues, but this time her voice is sad, soft.

"By all means, find Ambrose. But, please, find him quickly. Always remember, there is more than one way the world can end."

CHAPTER 115

AS ALWAYS, OUR plan is designed to be as efficient as possible. We break into two teams: Margo and Burbank are one team, Jericho and I the other. Dr. DaSilva will remain to guard the vital vaccine bundle and to stay in constant touch with both her laboratory in California and Maddy, Hawkeye, Jessica, and Tapper in New York.

As a simple first step, Jericho and I will walk south; Margo and Burbank will head north. So we split up.

Our mountain, as explained, is not much of a mountain, but it is slippery with patches of mud and wet greenery. A thick mist begins to fill the air, and the temperature feels like it's climbing. Jericho and I remain comfortable and enthusiastic. Are we afraid? Of course we are. Or, better put, I know that I am anxious. That being reported, I believe we all feel more secure because of the fortification from Dr. DaSilva's vaccine.

Jericho and I have very helpful devices at our disposal. Our handheld equipment supplies us with notifications of any human presence, change in soil type, or variations in oxygen and carbon dioxide levels. Our device also keeps us connected to Margo and Burbank on their exploration, as well as Dr. DaSilva back at the camp.

As Jericho and I walk quietly but quickly around the jungle passages, thick with vegetation, I tell him that, at any time, I am ready to shape-change when it serves our purposes. I can become and will become a wildebeest, an electric drill, a falling rubber tree, a drop of acid rain.

"Good to know," he says with a trace of a smile. I am assuming that his comment is meant to be amusing, not sarcastic. But I am so anxious about our mutual adventure that I can't be completely sure. *Stay calm, Lamont.*

Still no sign of animal life. I mention this to Jericho. And he agrees. It is perplexing.

We have been exploring for a little more than an hour when we notice a small stretch of land—not more than four feet long—that is . . . completely barren. All we see is a combination of mud and gray pebbles.

I try to imagine that this is a path, a clue, a direction. But as we carefully investigate the area around the empty barren land, we find nothing helpful. So we walk some more. A quarter mile. A half mile. A mile.

I receive a message from Margo.

Nothing so far. You guys?

I reply.

Same as you. Nothing.

Then a sound. Both Jericho and I hear it—a strange,

weak bleat. Yes, *bleat* is the proper word. Perhaps a large injured bird. An ostrich? An ibis?

"Over there," Jericho says.

He points to his right, and there, standing still and bleating, is a goat.

The goat walks slowly and calmly away from us, completely disinterested. We follow the animal for five or ten yards. Then it suddenly stops in front of a crude, jagged entrance carved into the side of the mountain.

The opening is large enough for a person to pass in and out of. And that is exactly what happens.

As Jericho and I approach the cave opening, we hear human sounds: a cough, a throat clearing, the scratch of shoes against the dry ground.

And then . . . a skinny young man emerges.

The young man can be no older than twenty. He wears black-framed eyeglasses. He wears tan Bermuda shorts and a white T-shirt.

We see him. He sees us. We are surprised. He is not.

He speaks. His voice is soft, almost a whisper.

"I'm Glenn Ambrose," he says. Then he adds, "I think you may be looking for me."

CHAPTER 116

I HAD NEVER considered what the mysterious Glenn Ambrose looked like. If I had been told to guess at his appearance, I would most likely have imagined tall and evil, maybe even with a comic handlebar mustache and an exaggerated sneer on his face, wearing a white lab coat.

But here, in the flesh, Glenn Ambrose can be described easily with one classic, very old-fashioned schoolyard taunt—*NERD*. He looks like a lonely teenager who spends too much time trolling online message boards.

It is difficult for me to believe that this is the person with the goal and the power to destroy the world. Still, we must remain cautious. I order Jericho to frisk Ambrose for weapons. Then Jericho secures him, tying the scientist up with steel-reinforced wire we have brought. Ambrose offers no resistance.

"How did you find out that we were trying to locate you?" I ask our now completely immobile prisoner.

Suddenly, his face seems to change. Ambrose's eyes

widen. His mouth opens, and he begins speaking with a new voice, a voice that is painfully loud. It is booming. It creates an echo. No, he is not changing into a superhero, but he certainly is not the nerd he seemed just a few minutes ago.

"*There will be no answer! You will find in me no information!*"

The new voice is so angry, so loud, that Jericho reflexively moves back a step. I force myself to stay stony and stand still. I must be ready for a fight.

While Jericho watches Ambrose, I walk a few feet to the jagged entrance of the cave. I look in and see a surprisingly small steel-paneled room. I hear the soft, easy whirring and whistling of machinery. Yet I can see only a few computer monitors, plus a modest-sized video screen attached to the wall. The entire setup looks shockingly basic. It looks like any one out of a billion very unimportant offices.

Wait a second. Ambrose is going to destroy the world with a few souped-up computers? I'm clearly missing something.

"I'm going inside to examine this room," I tell Jericho. "It looks like you've got Ambrose under control."

Without taking his eyes off the tied-up Ambrose, Jericho nods and says he'll yell if he needs me.

Then I step into the cave.

The room is just as simple and modest inside as it appeared to be when I glanced in.

Two large computer screens. Two large keyboards, one

with the English alphabet, the other with the Russian alphabet. Two large closets. The first closet that I open holds nothing but three white shirts on three wooden hangers, as well as a small refrigerator. The refrigerator is empty. I open the second closet. It, too, is empty but for another small refrigerator, the twin of the refrigerator next door. I open this refrigerator. This appliance is holding a metal case about the size of a shoebox. The metal case has an ordinary-looking plastic light switch on its top. Next to it is the word IGNITE.

This must be the mighty Terrageddon.

This is, of course, not the time to test the switch.

I lift the box. It's deceptively heavy, certainly at least ten pounds. I am still holding and examining the box when I hear Jericho's voice coming from outside the room.

"Lamont, come out here," he shouts.

And so I go quickly outside and see that Ambrose is squirming and struggling against his wire confinement. Somewhat foolishly, he is trying to break free. But given the strength of the steel wires encasing him, I know that Ambrose is waging a losing battle.

It turns out that I am very wrong. The wiring around his chest begins to break. Then the wiring around his stomach bursts open. How is this possible? Has young Ambrose managed to harness radioactivity inside his own body? Has he transferred some of the power of Terrageddon into his own flesh?

Somehow his very struggles and actions seem to have

created other reactions within the cave, as if the machines inside are reacting to the movements of their maker. He must have created some kind of electrical connection between himself and the technology he has spawned.

As Glenn Ambrose begins to break free, the natural world around us immediately begins to turn violent. I don't know how, but clearly the man himself has become Terrageddon.

The sky turns dark, very dark, almost too dark to see clearly beyond a few feet.

Thunder. Lightning. And then a terrible shaking earth beneath us.

As fast as our world turned dark and ominous, so does it instantaneously return to enormous brightness. Exquisite quiet. Complete stillness.

Jericho and I look back at Glenn Ambrose. He is standing. He looks at the two of us. He is free of his bonds, but he makes no attempt to move. Tendrils of electricity run across his skin, illuminating it in a blue glow.

"It worked!" he cries, raising his hands in victory.

The lovely quiet is pierced by an ear-splitting thunderclap, and a bolt of lightning tears through the sky.

Then we watch as Glenn Ambrose bursts into flames.

CHAPTER 117

I STAND TREMBLING in this splendid new atmosphere of clear skies and brilliant brightness. What does that matter? I have just witnessed a human being become a pile of ash in seconds.

I look down at the ground where Ambrose was just standing. All that is left of him is a small pile of gray ashes and a few charred bones, some of which are still on fire.

"What the hell is going on, Lamont?" Jericho asks. It is more of a sad plea than an actual question. But I have no answer, and even if I did have an answer, I feel so weak from shock that I can barely speak.

"Lamont, answer me, please," Jericho pleads.

I manage, with great effort, to get out the words "I think he managed to transfer some of the power of Terrageddon into his own body. But he did not account for the frailty of human flesh."

The steel box that I carried from inside the cave drops from my hands. It lands very close to Ambrose's remains. I wonder if the box itself—the original Terrageddon—still holds any power, or if it's all evaporated along with Ambrose.

Jericho suddenly bends at the waist, grabbing his midsection.

"Lamont, I can't...I can't..." He falls to the ground next to the fiery remains of Ambrose, which is when I notice a sliver of rock protruding from his belly. It must have been blown into his body from the force of the lightning strike, but shock kept him free of pain until this moment.

I give my full attention now to Jericho, touching the side of his neck with two of my fingers. Yes, there is a pulse.

I need to concentrate. I need to shape-shift myself into a vehicle or an animal or anything that can help get Jericho back to the camp for help.

Please help me, memory. Please help me, instincts. Please help me find inside myself the teachings and training that Dache once gave me. Just a bit of power from some hidden spot inside me. If not to change physical shape, then to be able to make psychic contact with Margo or Burbank or Dr. DaSilva, since my handheld device seems to have been fried by the nearby lightning strike.

But before I can, I hear a voice, a comforting, familiar voice, a woman's voice.

"On your knees, Lamont? Are you praying?"

My God. It is Dr. DaSilva. If I had been praying, the wise and kind Dr. DaSilva would indeed be the perfect answer to my prayer.

She stands looking down on me, on Jericho, on the smoldering fire that was once Glenn Ambrose. Her hands are on her hips. She makes no effort to assist me and Jericho.

"Please," I say. "Jericho needs help. He's—"

Dr. DaSilva finishes my sentence. She shouts, "Dead! Yes, he's dead and gone and over. Unlike the last time, he will not be coming back. But who cares about a wretch like Jericho? Let us consider the new leader of the universe. Let us consider the great Khan!"

What the hell?

I am, all at once, frightened and confused. Am I hearing correctly?

"This is what I've always wanted, Lamont. This is the dream come true. You have stopped me so many times before. But now, with impeccable planning, with exquisite precision, now I am ready."

What in hell is she talking about? Who the hell is this new and terrifying woman?

I try to stand, but, weakened by shock and grief, I cannot hold myself up. I lie on the ground between the sad pile of Ambrose's ashes and the metal box.

My eyes, tired and burning and aching, remain the best they can on the good doctor.

Then Dr. DaSilva's body begins to vibrate.

The wind picks up, causing the flames to spread onto Jericho's unmoving form.

The vibration grows faster, and then faster, and then

faster. She becomes a vibrating blur, a jumble of pulsating color. She is unrecognizable, but this cyclonic storm of color does not disappear, does not speak, does nothing but...

Unbelievably, Dr. DaSilva turns into a whole other person.

Unbelievably, Dr. DaSilva turns into Shiwan Khan.

CHAPTER 118

THIS NEW PRESENCE, this new person, this Shiwan Khan, a man of unparalleled greed and evil, begins shouting and babbling. Complete insanity is unraveling all around me.

"You have ruined everything," my longtime nemesis yells. He then continues yelling. No pause. No relief. Nothing but madness.

"Don't you see, you incompetent, ignorant fool? I am the genius. I am the power. I created the Newbola virus. Through my carefully built network it was poised to infect the entire world, passing from person to person. From Australia to Europe to the Americans, to Asia... to everyone. Billions of people, almost everyone, would be wiped out. Only a few select colleagues of mine would be spared. Then together we would breed a whole new universe, a universe where I would once again be in supreme control."

Khan pauses. He almost seems exhausted from his rant and rave, from the recollection and communication of his original vile plan.

I tap into my small amount of remaining energy and speak.

"But then... but then..." I try to say more. But I am horribly weak.

"But then someone who foolishly thought he was stronger and smarter than I created Terrageddon. The world could now be destroyed, literally destroyed, wiping out all forms of life. *There would be no world because of Terrageddon. And... how could I rule the Earth if there was no Earth left to rule?*"

What is the state beyond unbridled anger? Unbridled insanity.

As for me right now, watching Khan and learning the true details of the situation, discovering that throughout the entire execution of Khan's fantasy of world domination, he was posing as Dr. Anna DaSilva, I begin to understand how I came to experience the horror I find myself in right now.

As Khan admitted, he was the creator of the Newbola virus, and, as Dr. DaSilva, he enlisted my assistance, not to advance the cure for Newbola but to find the creator of Terrageddon. And that is exactly what happened. I led Khan directly to Glenn Ambrose and his mysteriously powerful Earth-destroying machinery. And with our finding Ambrose, Khan will be rewarded with the success of his plan to rule the Earth.

Khan's plan required genius and patience, and—damnit—his plan worked.

CHAPTER 119

KHAN SEEMS DELIGHTED to have captured me. He parades around me like a winning fighter in the ring after a knockout. What's more, there is nothing I can do about it—the parading, the strutting, the happy hatred that is spewing from his eyes.

Khan extends his right index finger. The very tip of that finger suddenly shoots out a long tapered weapon, a sleek bullet-shooter of some sort. He aims it frequently, carelessly, happily, at the quaking helpless heap that was once known as the Shadow.

Khan now speaks to me with contempt and strength.

"So, I have decided to extend an incomparable act of kindness to you. I will offer you a choice of destruction. You may choose to die by my hand *or* you can choose to die alongside all of your family and friends."

"My family? My friends?" I ask. "But how?"

"Because you were stupid enough to inject yourself with the syringes I sent directly to your doorstep!" Khan crows.

"That was a special delivery, to be sure. It wasn't a vaccine, you fool. It was an injection of nanobots. They are present even now in your bloodstream—and those of your loved ones."

From his pocket Khan produces a slim device with a single red button.

"All I have to do is press this button, and they will explode inside your veins. But... slowly. They will expand, but it will take minutes. Minutes that will feel like hours, days, years, as your body is ripped apart from the inside out. As will the bodies of everyone who injected themselves."

God, how could I have been so stupid? When everyone else had no reaction to their injections, I assumed Dr. DaSilva's gift was safe, not lying dormant waiting for a command. No wonder I became so weak right after Margo injected me. The nanobots must have interacted with my powers in some way, disarming and sickening me, although my immune system was eventually able to produce a response.

So, the choice is really no choice at all. I can die on my knees in front of Khan, executed by his own hand. Or I can allow those who were also injected to die along with me.

"I'll die the way a hero does," I tell Khan, lifting my chin. "Defending others. Kill me yourself, you coward."

Khan only smiles and takes a step toward me, finger extended.

I close my eyes and dig deep, willing any semblance of strength I've ever had to rise to the surface. But the shock of Jericho's death, the revelation of Khan's involvement, and the fact that I myself participated in his success have zapped me of any powers. I have no faith in myself. I have no faith in my abilities.

My hands fall to my sides. I am defeated.

But...wait.

My fingers brush the top of the metal box, of Ambrose's hideous creation, Terrageddon. He may have transferred its powers into his own body, but is it possible that some of its horrible capabilities remain? And do I dare use the weapon of one villain to destroy another?

The answer comes quickly, easily. Yes.

I said that I would die the way a hero does, by defending others. I can save my team who were injected by choosing to allow Khan to execute me by his own hand. If there is any chance that I can save everyone else from Newbola Strong by activating Terrageddon, so be it.

I choose to take the risk.

I choose be the hero.

I choose to save the world.

I open Terrageddon and press the Ignite button.

CHAPTER 120

THE EXPLOSION IS so powerful, so deafening, that the earth vibrates and trees fall around us.

Jagged fractures split the ground. The fissures look like riverbeds gone dry. They grow deeper and deeper, wider and wider. Then the cracked earth begins spitting out fire. The trembling of the land beneath us is relentless.

Shiwan Khan falls to the ground just as the fierce flames from the fire begin shooting increasingly upward. More trees fall. More crevices appear and crack open.

Yes. Like Kyoto. Yes. Like Harvard. The bad memories grab and dazzle my brain, my mind, my life.

Then... amid all the unbelievable chaos, something even more unbelievable happens.

I witness a sight that should be totally satisfying. It is, however, so frightening that it actually stuns me.

A fissure widens precisely next to where Khan has fallen. He tries to rise but loses his balance. For a millisecond, he pinwheels his arms, trying to regain his balance, but to no avail. He free-falls into the horrid fire below.

If there really is a hell, I hope Khan's final breath will be like living in it.

I, of course, realize that the end of my own life is probably just moments away. Because I am already on the ground and no fissures have opened near me, my own destruction has been only momentarily postponed. But my safety cannot last much longer. I, too, am destined to fall into the fire. I consider this the worst possibility—to die alongside Khan.

The flames rage, growing higher and higher above the ground.

Then the sky quickly turns gray, then black.

And then, quite suddenly, the earth ceases its wicked vibration. There comes a stillness in the land, a stillness in the air.

Then rain. More rain. Torrents of rain.

I stretch out. I am on my back. The rain washes over me.

The rain stops.

Beside me Terrageddon lies, cracked and smoking, devoid of power.

Finally, it's over.

CHAPTER 121

THE LAND AROUND me is silent and looks essentially barren. The fallen trees have been battered and split, with branches that look like hastily chopped firewood. The entrance to the cave has been demolished, blocked by boulders. The crevices in the mountainside that only a moment ago were spitting flames that seemed to reach to the sky are still wide open. But they are dry and cold and look as if they have been there since the beginning of time, dormant.

I feel a certain sense of relief. But there is nothing but devastation in my field of vision. The harsh rains have, of course, completely eliminated the burned remains of both Ambrose and Jericho. This time I do not expect to be surprised by my friend's return.

I attempt to move. I manage to lift a hand, lift a foot. I am in shock.

I hear a voice, a woman's voice. The voice bombards me with questions.

I easily identify the voice. It is Margo.

"Oh, my God. What happened here? What have you done? Are you hurt? Are you alive?"

She is standing over me. Then she is kneeling beside me.

With Margo's help, I manage to sit up in a kind of cross-legged yoga position.

We slowly begin to exchange narratives of the past few hours of our lives. I am shocked to discover that she and Burbank experienced not even the smallest disturbance—no eruptions, no earthquakes, no storms. I am apparently resting on the only patch of land that was attacked so viciously, most of Terrageddon's power having been eliminated when Ambrose was struck by lightning.

I tell Margo and Burbank my horrific tale. It is so startling—the death of Jericho, the astonishing uncovering of Dr. DaSilva as Khan, and my own encounter with fear and imminent death—that their eyes fill with tears, as do mine.

I use Margo's handheld device to contact Gutta in Helsinki, arranging for him to get us the hell out of here. I contact Hawkeye and Tapper, relaying to them the information about nanobots being present in their blood, along with the rest of us who were injected. They immediately begin conversations with medical experts who will find a way to remove them.

On our flight home on a military aircraft provided by Gutta, I bite the bullet and video President Townsend, letting him know the actual identity of Dr. Anna DaSilva—all the while dissecting his reaction. His face and tone betray nothing to me. It seems that he might have been ignorant of what was occurring right beneath his very nose.

That, I can believe.

But it still doesn't mean I trust him.

With a few hours left in the flight, Margo takes my hand in hers and gives me a small smile.

"Sleep," she advises.

I glance around me to see that Burbank has already dropped off and that Margo is almost there herself. She's been valiantly ignoring her own needs in order to stay with me while I work. I tell myself as I drift off into a deep sleep that I'm doing it for her sake, not my own.

Not to escape the world.

One that—once again—no longer holds Jericho Druke.

CHAPTER 122

THE FUNERAL IS a small affair, with no casket.

In fact, it's not even in a cemetery. With no body, no ashes, and nothing to remember Jericho by except our words, we decide to honor him by gathering around the table in our meeting room, inside the family home.

Grandma Jessica, Burbank, Tapper, and Hawkeye are pale, and I have to admit that my own energy stores are low. Removing the nanobots from our bodily systems rather paradoxically required that we first be injected with *more* bots—these programmed to find the first invaders and destroy them, then self-destruct once their mission was accomplished. The process caused our immune systems to activate, draining our energy.

As a result, Jericho's memorial service is a quiet one. We share stories of our past victories, sadly recall a handful of failures, but in all of them, we honor our fallen friend. Bando rests under the table, and I swear his tail thumps against the floor every time Jericho's name is spoken, remembering his friend in his own special way.

Maddy and Belinda are present as well, both of them trying to match our somber moods, even though their own mission has ended quite successfully. Detective McCarthy's admission that kids like Chloe and Travis were used as disease vectors to spread Newbola brought with it a silver lining—Carla Spector was paid well by Khan to ensure that they remained alive.

Though they suffered untold abuses, most of them were recovered once Carla Spector's drug ring came crashing down. Her cowardly associates—including the nefarious Abdul Aziz, who had been tasked with locating Maddy and Belinda when they escaped the hotel in Dubai—had been more than happy to talk once they were in custody. Chloe and Travis were back in the Americas and housed with foster families within a week. Belinda, meanwhile, had found a work-study program that would help lift her out of her life on the street—along with Maddy's help and newfound friendship.

An even greater revelation was that Carla herself—as payment for her services to Khan—had been injected with the only known, truly effective vaccine against Newbola Strong. In exchange for a reduction in her sentence, she allowed some of her blood to be drawn, and the antibodies found within one of the most horrible people on earth became the salvation of the human race.

Some endings are happy, some bittersweet.

But ultimately, good has triumphed over evil.

And so the Shadow can rest.

Until next time.

ABOUT THE AUTHORS

JAMES PATTERSON is the most popular storyteller of our time. He is the creator of unforgettable characters and series, including Alex Cross, the Women's Murder Club, Jane Smith, and Maximum Ride, and of breathtaking true stories about the Kennedys, John Lennon, and Tiger Woods, as well as our military heroes, police officers, and ER nurses. Patterson has coauthored #1 bestselling novels with Bill Clinton and Dolly Parton and collaborated most recently with Michael Crichton on the blockbuster *Eruption.* He has told the story of his own life in *James Patterson by James Patterson* and received an Edgar Award, ten Emmy Awards, the Literarian Award from the National Book Foundation, and the National Humanities Medal.

RICHARD DiLALLO is a former advertising executive. He lives in Manhattan with his wife.

For a complete list of books by

JAMES PATTERSON

VISIT

JamesPatterson.com

Follow James Patterson on Facebook
JamesPatterson

Follow James Patterson on X
@JP_Books

Follow James Patterson on Instagram
@jamespattersonbooks

Follow James Patterson on Substack
jamespatterson.substack.com

Scan here to visit JamesPatterson.com and learn about giveaways, sneak peeks, new releases, and more.